When art student Melissa Hopkins finally unpacks the two boxes her Aunt Phoebe left for her and sees Phoebe's black and white photos, it's like opening Pandora's Box. A simple quest to find a new job morphs into an about face—not just in her art, but in her career and personal life. Short on funds now that her graduate stipend is ending, she applies to work where Aunt Phoebe once worked: a center for sexuality and sex studies.

Sworn off women after a disastrous relationship, Center Director Harry Gage ignores the danger signals and hires the striking young woman who reminds him of his former lover. Her air of innocence will captivate center viewers, so he's sure she'll be a hit on camera. What he's not prepared for is how she pierces his heart.

When the sparks flare up, is it love or just sex—and what must each of them risk to find out?

This book was previously published.

Smoldering Passion

ISBN: 978-1-4874-3816-6
Cover art by Martine Jardin

Published by eXtasy Books Inc

Look for us online at:
www.eXtasybooks.com

Smoldering Passion
Passion 1

By

Adriana Kraft

Dedication

The Passion series is dedicated to a favorite aunt, free spirit and early pioneer in research on human sexuality.

Chapter One

New York, New York 2004

"You're not a virgin, right?" The dark-haired man asked the question with a straight face. His square jaw gave no suggestion of discomfort, though he did raise an eyebrow slightly.

Melissa Hopkins flipped her hair over her shoulder and tried to hide her annoyance. She wanted this job. She *needed* this job. And she understood why Harry Gage had asked the question.

Who would want to hire a virgin to work developing instructional sex videos and DVDs? She frowned slightly. She probably wouldn't have found the courage to be sitting in his office if not for her aunt, who had worked for the Center for Sexuality and Sex Practices for decades before her death.

And Melissa wasn't the only aspiring artist in New York City willing to take extreme measures to support her dream.

She nodded at the unsmiling Gage. A sociologist, he'd said he'd been with the Center his entire career. He appeared to be in his late thirties, or at most, early forties. That meant he must've known her aunt, but she wasn't ready to acknowledge that relationship. If she did get this job, she wanted to land it on her own. "That's correct. I'm not a virgin," she said, shrugging as if she were accustomed to conversing with strange men about her sexual status. "Haven't been for years."

The man smiled smugly. "Figured you weren't. We don't get many virgins applying for our jobs, but it's not uncommon for women and men to come here expecting to work through their own sexual hang-ups."

"I can assure you I'm not one of them."

He eyed her thoughtfully. His appraisal, while guarded, took in her whole being. She could see his mind rehashing her personal and professional data. He was trying to determine whether she was stable enough to be a part-time research associate at the Center. The bulk of her work would probably focus on interviewing individuals about their sexuality and sex lives. She'd be expected to help with editing brochures and catalogs, as well as organizing the Center's extensive archival collection. And she'd be part of a production team making instructional videos. She sat primly waiting for his next question, then thought better of it and slouched a little.

He probably didn't want his research associate to look too prim and proper.

"So tell me, Ms. Hopkins." He paused to scan the questionnaire she'd filled out about herself. "There is no current boyfriend or girlfriend?"

She shook her head. "No."

"Good. We often like to hire couples. They're more reliable."

Melissa sat straighter.

"But the Center is definitely attracting more single viewers, and they don't want to always be watching married couples. So we're mixing things up as much as we can."

"I see." Well, she didn't exactly see, but neither was she eager to risk asking—but then Mr. Gage didn't seem bothered by her reticence.

Again, he looked over her questionnaire. "So let's see, you seem familiar with most of the basic sex positions." His dark brown eyes focused on hers.

She made sure she wasn't blushing under his close scrutiny.

"It says here you haven't had sex with a woman."

Melissa nodded.

"But you're willing to give it a try—to advance science and help besotted lovers out there looking for help?"

"You sound rather skeptical, Mr. Gage."

"Sorry," he said, not looking at all sorry. "It's my nature." He stared at her. "You didn't answer my question." He cocked his head to the side. "Having sex with a woman?"

She shrugged. "Shouldn't be too difficult."

He laughed, but his eyes held a surprising sparkle. "I didn't ask how onerous the task might be. I asked if you were willing."

Blinking, Melissa tried not to glance away from his steady gaze. "Yes, I'm willing."

"Good. I'd rather have you experienced, but I can't expect everything I want to find in one woman. Now, what is this little question mark doing by anal sex?"

She gasped. "I thought I erased that."

He squinted at the sheet. "You tried." He looked back up at her. "Have you, or haven't you?"

She squared her shoulders and forged ahead. "If you must know, I'm not exactly sure what that entails."

"Entails . . . entails . . . oh, that is a good one." He laughed, then sobered. "But you're willing to give it a try?"

"If I must."

"You must, if you want this job."

"Then I will."

"Good. You do have spunk, Ms. Hopkins."

Melissa relaxed a little.

"Your naïveté in that area may actually appeal to viewers for whom this is a new if not slightly taboo area. So . . . why don't you stand and take off your clothes so I can see what you've got?"

"What?" Melissa's hand flew to her throat before she could stop it. She was used to posing in studios for other artists, but in a job interview? "Here? Right now?"

"Melissa . . ." he began.

She wanted to throttle his condescending tone.

"How do you expect to have sex in front of cameras if you can't disrobe in front of me? Our actors and actresses seldom wear clothes."

"Oh," she sputtered.

Again, he tilted his head to the side. "I'm not going to hire you without seeing what I'm hiring."

"Oh, very well." Melissa rose to her feet, slipped out of her blouse, then unsnapped her black skirt and stepped out of it. She hoped he realized she wasn't doing anything to try to titillate him. She wasn't a stripper. Without any fanfare, she removed her bra and panties and stood before him with her shoulders slightly back and her hands relaxed at her sides.

If anything, he seemed surprised by her now calm demeanor. He probably hadn't read her resume carefully. If he had, he'd have known she'd modeled nude for fellow artists in her art department. She prided herself on being comfortable with her nudity—though Harry Gage's experienced eyes roving over her did kick into gear a goose-bump or two. He was not evaluating her with an artist's eye.

Gage stood.

Melissa used every ounce of willpower not to step back from him. How far would this interview go? Did he have to sample everything she had to offer before making his decision?

But he was hiring her to have sex. Well, not with himself, but . . . He was more intimidating standing than when he'd been sitting. He had to be over six feet. His shoulders were square and thick, more characteristic of men who worked outside than those bent over a desk all day.

He had large hands. Not shrinking a bit, she watched one of those large hands cup her breast.

"Nice," he said, matter-of-factly. "Sizeable, firm. But not too sizeable or too firm."

"What?" The man was talking in code.

"You're attractive, Melissa. Curvy." He walked behind her and patted her rump. "Very nice ass." Standing in front of her he said, "We want our performers to be attractive, but not too attractive."

"Thanks." Unable to stop herself, she added, "I'm glad I'm not too gorgeous for this job."

"Don't get huffy with me—you're a beautiful woman in your own right, but you're not so stacked that the average viewer, particularly a woman, can't identify with you. And you're all natural." He scowled at her. "Why else did you think I squeezed your breast? All of our women are natural."

She believed him. No doctor had examined her more clinically than this man was doing. If her nakedness turned him on in the slightest, he wasn't showing any effects. But then, how many naked women had he been around?

Gage stepped back and gave her a last once-over. "You'll do."

Melissa exhaled.

"Except for that thick pelt you've got between your legs."

She followed his gaze. Reflexively, she dropped her hands to her loins, then raised her chin. "What?"

Gage retreated to his chair and sat back down before answering.

She remained frozen in place.

"You're going to need a much neater pussy than that before we put you in front of a camera."

"But . . ."

"Your choice." He scowled. "You've got the job if that

beaver pelt becomes history. Good God, that must chafe like hell in the summer. So do you still want the job?"

She nodded, trying to find her voice. "Does it have to be bare?"

"Nah, just neat and trim. We don't go out of our way to turn our viewers on, but we don't want to turn them off, either."

"I see," she said, retrieving her clothes. "Can I ask you a question?"

"Shoot."

"Why are you willing to hire me?"

He smiled. "I wondered if you'd ask. As I said, you're not unattractive. Your inexperience may actually be a bonus at times. You've got guts to try some things beyond the usual, and I like that. You have the capacity to work flexible hours, which is a must here. And," he eyed her carefully, "you project a dispassionate persona."

Melissa scowled and redid the last button on her blouse before sitting down across from him. "What in the world do you mean by that?"

He chuckled. "I want a woman who can keep herself in check."

"Oh."

"You don't come every five minutes, do you, Ms. Hopkins?"

She shook her head.

"But you do come."

"When I want to."

"Exactly. When we're shooting, having a woman come every five minutes is a distraction and makes for too much downtime. That translates into lost dollars. You are self-possessed. I like your air of self-control. A little aloof. A little innocent. You should photograph quite nicely. Yet I expect you're quite coachable. You are quite coachable, aren't you,

Melissa?"

Melissa swallowed hard. "Yes, I believe I am."

"One more thing," he said, grabbing a contract from the corner of his messy desk and handing it to her. "What happens here at the Center stays here."

"Of course," she replied, reading over the rather straightforward contract. "I've never been into telling stories about work."

Gage nodded. "That, too. What I really meant is that this Center is about sex. It has been for decades. We have an excellent reputation in the academic and the therapeutic world."

"I know that, or I wouldn't have applied here."

"We aim to keep that reputation intact. There will be no outside liaisons with partners from the Center."

"That won't be a problem," Melissa said, reaching for the pen he offered. "I can assure you of that."

"Very good." Gage stood and retrieved the signed contract and his pen. "I expect to see you next Monday at eight-thirty. Our shooting schedule changes often and quickly for lots of reasons. You may do library work for several days before having an opportunity to help us with a shoot." He gave her a crooked smile. "But I do expect you to be trimmed and ready by Monday."

"Do I report to your office, raise my skirt, and drop my panties first?"

His laughter surprised her. It started deep in his diaphragm. "That won't be necessary. I trust you'll be ready, but do come to my office. I'll introduce you around and show you the ropes." He winked at her. "Actually, we don't use real ropes."

Her eyes shot wide, and he laughed again. "Run along now, Melissa. Till Monday."

As soon as his office door closed, Harry Gage rummaged through the bottom drawer of his desk until he snagged a sheaf of photos. He leaned back in his chair and studied them. "Uncanny," he mumbled. The resemblance was definitely there—rich dark hair dropping well below her shoulders, similar puffy lips, and eyes that could peer into his soul.

Melissa Hopkins could pass as Phoebe's daughter. He shook his head. He knew that wasn't possible; Phoebe had never had kids. Still, what he found most eerie was the way both women carried themselves—a bit aloof, subtly innocent, and definitely mysterious.

He grimaced and tucked the photos back in the drawer. There'd never been anything truly innocent about Phoebe. He owed her a lot. She'd been the older woman in his life who guided him along a bombastic sexual odyssey. He'd fallen in love. She hadn't. She adhered to the Center's no fraternization rule. He was the one who'd wanted to break that rule, if not erase it.

They'd never made love outside the Center. He smiled sadly. But inside the Center, they'd done it every which way, in every corner of the damn building. There had been weekends when they'd never left and ordered in food.

Why had Phoebe had to be so damn stubborn? That was another quality he'd observed in his newest employee. He'd bet Melissa Hopkins could dig in her heels just as firmly as Phoebe about things that mattered to her.

So what would matter—he peeked at Melissa's fact sheet—to the twenty-five year old mirror image of his past? That uncanny resemblance had made it nearly impossible for him not to hire her. Her willingness to move beyond her sexual experience intrigued him. So why was it so important to her that she have this particular job?

There had to be more than resemblance that led him to say *yes,* to give her a try. Had she shown up as some delayed penance? Phoebe had left him and the Center six years ago. He'd never found another woman to fulfill his image of her.

He winced. He'd only recently learned of her death from breast cancer. He squeezed his eyes shut. Nothing good would come from going there.

He blinked and stared at the door. Phoebe was a woman with deep smoldering passion. It seemed highly unlikely that the full-bodied young woman who'd just left his office had such a reservoir of passion.

Was that it? Was that why he'd hired her? He had to find out, but he'd keep his distance. He knew from experience how badly he could be scorched by a woman's passion.

Taking short breaths, Melissa stared at the black-and-white photos she'd spread across her bed. It was the discovery of these photographs that had drawn her to the Center in the first place. They were pictures of her aunt engaged in various sexual acts—some with men and others with women.

She'd been surprised by the exquisite magnetism of each photo. None were tawdry. Individually and collectively, they celebrated the act of lovemaking. Initially, she'd been shocked to recognize her aunt, and then she'd been jealous. The delight and pleasure on her aunt's face spoke so loudly and clearly.

Was that why she'd resolved to apply for the Center's job opening? She'd convinced herself it was only because she needed the money. And she did need to pay her bills. Yet the photos had infused her with a yearning she couldn't name.

She peered at them again, and then it struck her—one of the men in three of the photos looked like Harry Gage. A younger Harry Gage—but it had to be him.

She picked up a photo of a man and woman in doggie position and examined it closely. She shook her head. It was

Harry, all right. He was buried to the hilt in her aunt.

"Holy crap!" Did that change anything? If she'd thought things through thoroughly, finding Harry Gage in the picture with her aunt shouldn't have surprised her. Aunt Phoebe had probably been at the Center long before Harry. Melissa smiled thinly. Perhaps *he'd* been learning all the ropes.

He was a handsome young man—quite muscled, and apparently, quite taken with her aunt. Pictures of other partners with her didn't display the depth of emotion so evident on Harry's face. Melissa scowled. He'd been in love with her aunt! Sometimes she wished she didn't have the artist's eye.

She leaned back against the pillows. She'd had the distinct impression during her interview that Harry no longer performed on camera in any of the video productions. It was clear he was responsible for directing and supervising the process.

So how did it feel to think about screwing in front of a man who'd known her aunt that well in his younger days? She shrugged and decided it didn't bother her. Why should it?

What would Harry Gage think if he knew his most recent employee was the niece of a woman he'd loved?

Why hadn't her aunt told her about this guy? And how old was he?

Her aunt had been fifty-five when she died. Melissa peeked back at the photos. The man in the photos couldn't be much out of college, if that—so her earlier guess was about right. She chuckled softly. He shouldn't be over the hill yet.

Still, she hadn't turned him on in the least. *Thank God.* Melissa sighed, tucked the photographs in their folder and returned them to the drawer near her bed. Seeing the pink vibrator brought a smile to her lips. She hadn't used her phantom lover for some time, and she wasn't about to tonight.

She parted her robe and stared at her pimpled labia. Had Harry Gage ever waxed his pubic area? Probably not, or he would've warned her how painful that process could be.

She shivered. There was no way she'd be ready for anything sexual by Monday. Hopefully, she'd have a day or two of reprieve with library work before getting involved in video production.

She pursed her lips. What should she wear for her first day at work? For that matter, what did one ever wear to the Center if they never knew how long they'd keep it on?

Standing outside the modest Greenwich Village brownstone that housed the Center for Sexuality and Sex Practices, Melissa smoothed out her skirt and ran her fingers through her hair. She'd settled on an outfit she considered neither too frumpy nor too sexy. The pink blouse had been purchased at a middle-of-the-line chain store, and the black skirt fell well below the knees. She'd shied away from anything that might be construed as form-fitting and provocative.

She entered the reception area and was greeted with a warm smile by the kindly older woman who'd welcomed her the previous week. But it was the other woman, stepping toward her with hand extended, who caught her attention.

The olive-skinned woman had an infectious smile that put Melissa immediately at ease. They must be about the same age and were very similar in height and build. The woman wore a colorful peasant dress gathered at the waist and flowing freely at her ankles.

"Welcome," she said, "I'm Inez Ramirez. Harry asked me to show you around."

Melissa shook the woman's hand, not at all surprised by the warmth of her touch. She exuded warmth. "Hi, I guess you know I'm Melissa. Melissa Hopkins."

Inez nodded. "Did Harry give you much of a tour when you were interviewed?"

"Not really. I saw his office, and that's about it."

"We'll start on this floor. Follow me."

"How long have you worked for the Center?"

"Eighteen months." Inez led the way into a large room with wall-to-wall bookcases and files. Three computers, printers, and techie things beyond Melissa's knowledge sat on several desks and tables. "This is our library," Inez said with obvious pride. "We're also hooked up with three university libraries. We have access to just about anything that's been done in the area of sexology."

Melissa looked around curiously. "This is rather daunting. So are you a research associate, too?"

Inez smiled. "Yes. And much of our work takes place in this library. Of course, in addition to standard books, journals and papers, we have photo collections, film, video, and DVD collections."

"Of course," Melissa muttered. So how many references included her aunt?

"One of our major ongoing tasks is taking archival data and transferring it to the latest storage options. You are familiar with the computer and storage systems?"

"Some. I'm computer literate, but I don't know much beyond basic word processing." She frowned. "Funny, Mr. Gage hardly mentioned the library at all. He didn't provide much detail."

Inez laughed. "That doesn't surprise me. Harry—and we do call him Harry, not Mr. Gage—is the idea man. He's extremely committed to the Center's vision of educating and helping individuals own and honor their sexuality, but he's hardly a detail guy. That's more Claire's bailiwick."

"Claire?"

"Claire Johnson. Our co-director."

"Co-director?"

"He *really* didn't give you much detail. Claire Johnson and Harry co-direct the Center. Claire's in charge of marketing and development—kind of the pragmatic anchor for the vision man. Come on. I'll show you the main production room."

When they stepped into the next room, Melissa had to work at breathing. The room was mammoth. It had probably been two or three rooms in a previous era.

"There are at least two stages set in here at any one time. Depending on what we're working on, there may be more. Watch where you're walking. We don't want you tripping over cables your first day on the job."

"Thanks." Melissa chuckled. The floor was littered with cords running every which way. Much of the lighting system was in view, and there was a sound system and all the props of any stage.

"The bedroom set is quite standard," Inez's eyes twinkled, "though the bed is king-size. Over here is a fake fireplace, a plush carpet, and a couple easy chairs."

Melissa tried not to focus too much on what actually transpired on the bed, the carpet, and the chairs. She needed to take this entire situation one baby step at a time. "So are all the productions done here?"

"Goodness, no." Inez sounded surprised. "That'd get pretty boring for the actors as well as the viewers. These sets can be replaced, but the Center also has several rich benefactors who periodically provide access to their homes. And of course, there are outdoor shoots."

"Outdoors," she squeaked.

"Of course. Come on, I'll show you our offices."

She led the way upstairs. They walked past Harry's office. He didn't seem to be in. Another door had the label *Claire Johnson, Co-Director* on it. Interesting that Melissa hadn't met the other co-director—but maybe there was a sharp division of labor between the two directors.

At the end of the hall, Inez turned into a medium-sized cozy office area. There were two desks facing each other.

Behind one desk were colorful pictures of sun and surf. Clearly, that was Inez's work area. The wall behind the other desk was bare.

"That'll be your workspace," Inez said. "Our computers are networked with those in the library. I hope you don't mind sharing. Did you expect your own office?"

Melissa shook her head. "I didn't know what to expect. Maybe a cubbyhole. Harry never said. But this should be fine. It's quite spacious."

"We each have a desk, but we share the worktable and the couch."

"How many people work at the Center?"

"On a daily basis there are only eight of us. Much of the work is done by independent contractors. On days when there's a shoot, we might have a dozen or more people running around here."

"So most actors are what you call independent contractors?"

She saw a look of puzzlement flash across Inez's face. "Yes, most are couples. Most are married, actually."

"But not all."

"Right."

"So how many singles are there?"

"Two women and two guys." Inez looked like she was about to swallow her tongue.

Melissa blinked and gasped. "You?"

Inez nodded.

"And me?"

Again, Inez nodded.

"Harry expects us . . ."

"Yes." Inez's tone hardened. "That is part of what you signed on for, but if I don't live up to your expectations, I . . ."

"No," Melissa interrupted. "I'm sorry. I don't want to offend you. It's just that I've been trying to adjust to this whole thing in the abstract." She squinted at Inez. "But you're hardly an abstraction."

Inez giggled. "I hope not." She smirked. "So I will be your first woman?"

Melissa managed a faint nod.

"Terrific." Inez flashed a wide smile, then sobered quickly. "Don't worry, I'm not about to seduce you. Harry has a plan, or he wouldn't have hired you."

"You think I'll do okay?"

"You'll be fine. It's kind of neat to have sex without all the emotional entanglements. It can be fun, really."

"Fun?"

"It can be, but if nothing else, it's a job that pays well, and we *are* contributing to a good cause."

Melissa couldn't keep surprise from registering on her face.

Inez laughed. "Helping people have good sex."

"Of course."

Inez grinned lightly. "Hey, enough of this. When it's time for us, we'll both be ready. I do trust Harry. I've got things to do. Why don't I let you settle in here? There are the standard annual reports, summaries, and so on sitting on your desk to help you get familiar with our work. Any more questions?"

Melissa shook her head and stepped toward her desk, then turned back to Inez. "Yes, I do have one more. It sounds like Harry is in charge of video production."

"Absolutely. Claire generally only gets involved if we're testing a new product the Center is deciding to endorse or not, or if she has a special idea she's pursuing."

"Product?"

"Sex toys, usually. The Center puts out a catalog of videos, DVDs, lubes, toys, and so on. That's what Claire's in charge of. But I'm not sure I answered your question."

"Does Harry always work behind the camera, or does he work in front also?" Melissa held her breath.

Inez thought a moment. "I can't remember him actually participating in a video. Oh, he gives plenty of direction, but that's about all. He was quite involved in front of the camera years ago—that's clear from the video archives."

"Maybe he thinks he's too old for that."

"I don't know. Haven't really given it any thought." She winked. "But he doesn't look too old to me. He's got my vote if he wants to come out of retirement. Is that it?"

Melissa nodded. "Yeah, thanks."

She sat down at her desk and stared at the stack of reports. She was in. She'd been hired. So why was she still tense? She leaned back and looked at Inez's space. Melissa shuddered. Could she match the woman's perkiness? Would she be expected to? And how soon?

She turned the first page of the Center's annual report. So Harry Gage no longer worked in front of the camera. At least she didn't have to worry about *him* anymore.

CHAPTER TWO

Harry sat at his office desk and grumbled to himself. His newest employee had been on the job for two days and he'd hardly seen her. Why was he avoiding her?

He'd given her a couple research assignments, leaving the day-to-day supervision of those projects to Inez. But he couldn't delay further video development much longer. It was crucial to always have products in the pipeline. With the resignation of Melissa's predecessor and then the time involved in making the new hire, they were behind schedule.

He looked up at the sound of the knock on his door to see Claire marching toward his desk. Why didn't the woman ever wait for him to respond? Someday he was going to lock the door, and Claire Johnson would knock herself out on his closed door. He smiled. Damn, that would be a sight. Too bad the woman was so competent. There must be a more cooperative colleague out there somewhere.

"Yes?" he said.

"I didn't know you were into masochism. If you wanted a spanking, you should've come to me."

"You know I'm not into that stuff." He scowled. "What are you talking about?"

"Not anymore," she corrected. "I met the new research associate. Where did you dredge her up from? The grave?"

"Claire!" Harry sprang to his feet.

Claire held up her hand. "Sorry, that was out of line, even for me. But how did you find Phoebe's clone?"

He sank back down in his chair. "She's hardly Phoebe's

clone."

"No, I suppose not—no one could be. But she's too damn close. What were you thinking?"

He shrugged.

"You must've been thinking with your cock."

He glowered but remained silent. Her accusation might be closer than he wanted to believe. He watched the tall, shapely blonde brush at her sleeve as if a piece of lint would have the nerve to sully it. For being in her late fifties or so, the woman still exhibited a strong sexual presence.

Claire continued, "She's here now, but I bet you'll regret that soon enough."

Harry groaned. He already had regrets, but he wasn't about to confess that to Claire.

"I've received some new vibrators to test. Can the girls test them this week?"

Harry came alert. *Perfect timing.* That could be a way of introducing Melissa to film production without getting her in over her head. With any luck, she might quit. He glanced down at his hand. When had his fingers begun to tremble? He didn't want Melissa to quit. "We can probably set up a time for tomorrow afternoon."

"Good. I'll drop the toys by in the morning."

"You don't want to be at the shoot?"

Claire gave him a crooked smile. "You never hire women who are my type. She's too soft. I wouldn't be surprised if she's out of here before you get her to turn the vibrator on. No, I'll leave you to your girls. I've got more important things to do." She shut the door firmly behind her.

Harry wished he had something to throw at it. That woman could be very vexing. But she could probably sell a car with four flat tires and no engine. He never would understand how such a frosty woman could be so successful at marketing and sales. Somehow, Phoebe had come to appreciate the woman from hell.

Ah hell, so had he. He didn't know the first thing about marketing, and Claire mostly stayed out of the creative end of things. She preferred her sex much more edgy than anything they portrayed on Center tapes and DVDs.

Chewing on her lower lip Thursday afternoon, Melissa fixed her focus on Inez. Thankfully, Harry had come up with this idea for her maiden voyage on camera for the Center. She and Inez were assigned to test a couple new vibrators. They sat across from each other in front of the fake fireplace in easy chairs. That proved easier than if they'd been on the bed. The distance provided a sense of security.

This was only one step—well, maybe several—beyond modeling in the nude. She knew Harry sensed her nervousness and was working with her and Inez to make this as smooth an experience as possible.

"Remember," Harry said, calmly, "focus on Inez—forget the cameras. Melissa, you are to be Inez's mirror image. Whatever she does, you do. Okay?"

She nodded her agreement, not wanting to risk uttering a word.

"Good," he replied. "Go ahead, Inez. Let's put these gadgets through their paces."

"No problem." Inez winked at Melissa and parted the thin pink robe that had provided very little cover. Her dark brown nipples were already hard nubbins. She separated her thighs, displaying a thin dark line of curly hairs leading to a semi-hidden crevice.

Melissa's breathing stopped. She tried not to gawk.

Inez smiled easily and waited.

"Melissa," Harry prompted softly.

"Of course," she mumbled. She parted her own wrapper

and seated herself securely on the chair. She appreciated the gleam in Inez's eyes.

"Splendid," Inez responded. "We're going to have so much fun together. I love your trim."

"Quiet, please," Harry said, "the tape is running. Speak with your eyes and bodies only."

Inez picked up the curved blue vibrator sitting on a stand next to her chair. Melissa reached for the red one at her side.

Once the vibrators were humming, Inez slowly slid hers across her cheek and then down the side of her throat. Melissa locked her focus on Inez and let the red vibrator energize her cheek and throat. She'd never used a vibrator with anyone watching. This was indeed different. She couldn't tell what was vibrating most—the vibrator, or her loins in anticipation.

Inez teased a dark nipple with the tip of the blue vibrator. Melissa held her vibrator between two fingers and brought its tip to bear on her pink nipple. She gasped and saw Inez smiling knowingly. She watched Inez slide the full length of the blue hummer across her flat belly. Without hesitating, Melissa did the same. Her hips flinched. A movement out of the corner of her eye caught her attention. She flicked a glance to her left, where Harry was holding a camera. Claire Johnson had come to stand by his side.

"Thought you didn't want to be here," Harry muttered, without lowering the camera.

"I changed my mind," Claire said. "Wanted to see how your protégé was coming along. I see I'm not too late."

"Whatever. Just be quiet and don't get in the way."

"Carry on, ladies," Claire said, more loudly. "We shouldn't keep Harry waiting."

The older woman's presence made her uneasy, but she could hardly tell the co-director of the Center to leave. Melissa peered at Inez.

"It's just us," Inez whispered before moving the vibrator to rest at the apex of her loins.

Melissa sank deeper into her chair and let the red vibrator slip downward. She closed her eyes, reveling in the tingles rushing through her body. Then she remembered her instructions and opened her eyes quickly.

Inez nodded. She used the vibrator to trace the edges of her vulva. Melissa did the same. Her pussy was catching fire. Her fingers trembled with desire. How could Inez be so calm? Especially with people watching?

Melissa's eyes widened as she watched Inez's labia opening. Moisture glistened in the soft light. Melissa was certain her own were doing the same.

Inez lifted the vibrator to her mouth and wet it. Melissa did likewise.

Inez mouthed one word: *Ready?*

Melissa nodded.

Inez placed the tip of the blue vibrator at her entrance and eased it in.

Gasping, Melissa felt the red vibrator easily sliding into her own vagina.

Inez twisted her vibrator and pushed it in and out.

Melissa's eyebrows arched when she saw the blue vibrator nearly disappear, and then she lunged forward as her own vibrator probed her depths. "Jesus."

Inez giggled. "Okay, let's come together, girl. No more waiting."

The blue vibrator moved quickly in and out while Inez clawed at her clitoris, which stood visibly seeking its own pleasure.

Melissa shook her head and lost track of being Inez's mirror. Her focus was on one thing and one thing only—her orgasm.

She closed her eyes and concentrated. Inez's scream of joy filled her ears. And there it was—her orgasm rested on the boundary. She encircled it and hugged it close. It filled her and then flowed out of her. She groaned over her fullness and then for her loss.

As an afterthought, she withdrew the vibrator and peeked over at Inez, who smiled broadly back at her.

She jerked her head toward the sound of light applause, then pulled the wrapper around her body under the frank assessment of Claire Johnson.

The woman clapped her hands. "Well done, ladies. You could have prolonged things longer, but that will do. Right, Harry?"

"It'll do." He stared at Melissa. "You okay?"

"Of course." Luckily, her bravado hadn't evaporated. She really wanted to crawl back to her office and sort out her feelings.

"I trust, from what I saw, that these vibrators are keepers?" Claire smiled and arched an eyebrow, first at Inez and then at Melissa.

"Mine was quite fine," Inez said.

"Mine, too," Melissa echoed.

"Good. I wouldn't want the Center endorsing anything that isn't genuine."

Melissa watched the tall blonde leave, then glanced at Harry. He seemed rooted in place. "Is that all?" she asked.

"Huh? Yeah, that's all. You can clean up if you want to."

She nodded and stood, not bothering to hold the wrapper shut. That hardly seemed to matter at this point. She stretched, feigning more nonchalance than she felt.

Harry scrutinized every movement she made.

She brushed her fingers across her pussy. "I trust this trim meets with your approval."

Inez coughed, and Harry jerked a step backward. "What? Oh. Fine. You're doing just fine. I've got other things to do. Go ahead and clean up. You two can go home early. Good work, both of you."

Setting the paintbrush down late on a Saturday morning, Melissa stood and stared at her canvas. She'd been at the Center for two full weeks, but hadn't returned to her art until now. She'd begun the painting without knowing where it would take her. That in itself was a very unusual step for her. She'd picked up a canvass she'd already painted black weeks earlier, then begun dabbing small dots of red randomly across the background. She seldom worked with primary colors, and usually chose pastels over her acrylics.

She made a face at the canvas. Was this the beginning of unlocking her passion? Maybe the change in medium would be good for her. She laughed aloud. How many times had mentors, instructors, and judges told her she displayed considerable promise? She was quite skilled at composition, yet there was some important quality lacking in her work.

In a word—passion. Those critics who knew her well were quick to point out that they didn't doubt she possessed passion. Were they simply being kind? But they didn't believe she was in touch with that passion.

Her pulse slowed. Was this the real reason she wanted to work at the Center? Had the discovery of the photos of her aunt drawn her to try to find the key to unlock her own passion? Clearly, her aunt had found such a key.

Melissa flushed. Was Inez the missing key? She couldn't remember ever being so turned on as she was the day the two them had tried out the new vibrators. Even though she and Inez had never touched, she'd given complete control over to Inez, replicating every move she made. She scowled. Or had she given complete control over to Harry? He was the one who'd devised that little erotic game.

No matter. She and Inez had worked on the same set a few more times over the past couple weeks, but they'd still never touched each other. Melissa's partner, Brad Jefferson, had been quite fine. Although he had more experience than she did, she was pleased to discover that her skills were on a par with his. They hadn't tried anything outside her range. She supposed she had Harry to thank for that, too.

They had done the basic man on top and woman on top positions. The most challenging aspect of demonstrating sex techniques was the constant stopping and starting. She thought of her interview with Harry and chuckled. It wasn't all that difficult to maintain control of her orgasms when she felt so out of sync most of the time.

Harry always wanted to try a different angle, change cameras, or take a phone call. Why couldn't the guy at least turn off his cell when they were recording? It wasn't as if he didn't know what it felt like being in front of the camera.

She studied her painting closely. There was no hidden pattern in the red dots that she could discern. Did she really believe Inez could help her find the source of her passion?

How was she going to find out if they never touched? Maybe she should talk to Harry. Was he holding back because she was inexperienced? But he'd said her innocence might prove valuable.

Melissa removed her smock, left the large bedroom she'd converted to a studio office, and headed toward her kitchen.

Standing at the kitchen counter, she poured another cup of coffee, rotated her tight shoulders, and walked into her favorite room—the living room. Its one window looked out onto a busy Brooklyn street. She spent a lot of time there watching people pass by beneath her. She lived in what some would call a polyglot neighborhood, with people of every shade of color. Often she'd stroll the sidewalk and not have a clue what people behind her were saying. The lilt of a foreign language intrigued her, but never enough to seriously study one.

Her apartment over a laundromat was seldom cold in the

winter, but could be pure hell in the summer when the air conditioning was on the fritz, which was too often. She loved her little place in the big city. But how long could she keep it?

Even with her new part-time job, holding onto her apartment was iffy now that her graduate stipend had run out. How much longer would her savings last? An involuntary shiver ran up her spine. Those funds had come from her parents' life insurance, after their death in an auto accident five years earlier, while she was still in college. She swiped at an unbidden tear.

She really didn't want to advertise for a roommate. That would mean giving up her home studio—worse yet, her privacy. She valued both too much to do that. Could she hang on with her current resources for another few months? She'd do her best. By then, hopefully she'd have finished her degree and be ready to find full-time work.

Harry found Melissa in the library Friday morning. He knew he would. She spent more time in the library and the small screening room than anywhere else. He'd kept track of her fairly closely. That was his job—he always monitored new hires, though maybe not quite as closely as this one.

She looked up from the table where she was working.

He nodded. "How are things going?"

"Fine." She patted the materials in front of her. "I never thought about how much is known about sexual practices in ancient cultures."

He smiled and walked further into the room. "Guess there's been a healthy amount of curiosity about sex for a long time. At least in recorded history."

"Apparently. I've been particularly intrigued by how sex was depicted in art."

"Yes, that's right." He drew up a chair and sat down.

"You're an artist, aren't you? I forgot."

Melissa shrugged. "Sometimes I forget, too."

"So what is your medium?"

"I work in pastel and acrylics, mostly. I also do charcoal. I'm not sure I've actually found my ideal medium."

Harry nodded. "Suppose that takes time. Guess I'm still searching, too."

"Oh, not at all," Melissa said quickly. "You're an artist with a camera. By now I've seen hundreds of your still photos. I especially like how you do black and white. Even the videos display an artist's care for not explaining away mystery."

He frowned.

"You take a highly charged subject—sex—and treat it with sensitivity and honor. There must be a ton of videos out there that treat sex as simply connecting the dots."

"You're right about that." He chuckled. "Yeah, there's a lot more to sex than connecting the dots." He gave her a long stare, and she blushed. "What now? I'm not talking about love."

"I didn't think you were."

"Love, at least as it's understood in popular culture, enhances sex, but it's not absolutely necessary for sharing profound sex."

"I'm discovering that—to my surprise. It's almost as if sex, in itself, can be an art form."

Suddenly feeling very warm, Harry rose to leave. "I believe you're quite right about that, Ms. Hopkins. The human body makes a terrific canvass in the hands of an able artist." He smiled down at her as she shuffled the papers in front of her. "I'm pleased to know this job is stretching you, and that you've brought this artistic perspective to the Center. Remember, we've got a shoot this afternoon at two o'clock."

She nodded, and he left her to her work.

Melissa propped herself back on the pillows on the king-sized bed in front of the cameras. Her robe lay on the floor nearby. Brad Jefferson knelt beside her. His semi-hard cock was an indication of how slow and meticulous Harry was being.

"Okay," Harry announced. "Spread your thighs wider, Melissa. That's right. Now, Brad, it's your turn. We're trying to demonstrate to our viewers how a guy can help his woman by focusing on her G-spot."

Brad nodded—did he understand that?

"So go ahead. Locate her G-spot and help her find ecstasy."

Melissa ignored the hint of a smile on Harry's lips and concentrated on Brad's finger, which had already entered her. She shoved down against it.

Pausing, Brad looked up at her with an expression she couldn't read.

"What's wrong?" Harry didn't wait long. "Can't you find it?"

Brad shook his head.

"It should be between eleven and one o'clock."

She felt Brad's finger slide back and forth, searching. Since when had she become a clock? She closed her eyes and waited for her partner to locate what he was seeking. *Good luck.* She'd never come across the famed G-spot. She'd begun to think it was a fable. Or maybe she was some sort of cuckoo clock.

"Dammit," Harry snapped. "Inez, you find it for him. Mr. Studly seems to require a GPS indicator."

Melissa smiled as Inez took Brad's place. There was little question in her mind that Inez would find the elusive spot of pleasure.

"Hi," Inez whispered.

Melissa arched against Inez's finger as she probed gently. Keeping her focus on Inez's face, Melissa shrank back when Inez looked up with a quizzical expression. Inez, too, had come up empty. Did that mean *she* was empty?

Inez turned and shook her head at Harry.

"Jesus," he snarled, "do I have to do everything around here?" He climbed onto the bed.

Melissa looked away from his glare. At least he wasn't removing his clothes. He was on a fact-finding mission. A little demonstration project, no doubt.

He licked his lips and breathed deeply.

She gave him credit for not barging in. Clearly, he was trying to rid himself of his frustration so he could focus on the task at hand.

"You okay?" he asked softly.

She nodded. What would he have done if she'd said *no?*

"Good. Relax."

"What if I don't have one?" she managed to whisper.

He gave her a quirky smile. "You've got one. We've just got to find it. Sometimes this little button can be very wary."

She stretched even more when she felt his finger pass through her entryway. She kept her eyes focused on his. He was concentrating on her interior, yet closely monitoring her response. She couldn't close her eyelids if she wanted to.

His finger roved back and forth across the apex of her interior. Like Brad and Inez, he found nothing. She felt him probing the entire entrance of her vagina. He never went deep, but stayed just inside. She settled back into the pillows. G-spot or not, this was starting to feel very nice.

She startled when his finger stopped at the seven o'clock position. It pressed firmly. Her pelvis leaped and her thighs squeezed, trapping his arm. "Cripes," she moaned.

"Damn," he said, staring at her in amazement. "You're one in a million."

His finger increased its pressure on what felt like a growing nodule. The finger softened. Momentary relief. And then it rubbed that spot until she feared she'd shake apart.

He smiled at her. "That's right. Come for me, girl. We didn't go through all of this effort to just wonder if you had a G-spot. This is the hot button of sex."

She forced her widening eyes to stay open. Her breathing became ragged. She drew her knees forward. Nothing stopped or even slowed Harry's finger. She tossed her head from side to side. She didn't want him to stop. It was way too late for that.

She flung her arms around him, and he guided her from one plateau to another until she was coming all over his fingers. She sobbed into his shirt. Where had the tears come from? She'd never experienced such an intense orgasm.

He held her without speaking or moving. She shuddered. They couldn't stay this way forever. She sighed and lay back on the pillows.

Gingerly, he removed his finger.

She'd never felt so bereft. She refused to cry again.

His eyes clouded over before she had a chance to read them. She knew he'd been moved by what he'd just done—she could feel that in his touch. Maybe that was because he'd been able to find her G-spot while two others had failed before him.

When she swung her head around, Brad was staring at her with a gaping mouth, and a broad smile split Inez's face. Claire was now operating the camera. Melissa cringed—when had that woman joined them? She was as stealthy as a cat.

"Should be a very helpful tape," Claire commented, turning off the camera.

Harry jerked around to face her. "I don't think so."

"Nonsense," Claire retorted. "You were always good in front of the camera. This tape will show the novice just how difficult it can be to find the G-spot. It should be affirming to those who are having difficulty. And it clearly shows how rewarding finding the precious spot can be." Claire looked at her with a curious smile. "And it was rewarding, wasn't it, Melissa?"

All she could do was nod in response.

"Good." Claire smirked. "Harry may be getting a little gray around the temples, but apparently he hasn't lost his erotic sensors."

Melissa closed her eyes and nestled into the pillows. Whatever was going on between Claire and Harry could happen without her. But Claire was right. Harry hadn't misplaced his erotic sensors. Cripes, no man had ever touched her that way. His finger had been like a lightning bolt, splintering her into a thousand pieces. Would she ever be able to put herself together again?

Chapter Three

Harry stalked to his office, slammed the door behind him, and poured some whiskey into a tumbler. With a trembling hand, he lifted the glass to his lips and drank deeply. He coughed and sputtered. The whiskey burned his throat, and her scent—so evident on his fingers—burned his nostrils.

He refilled the glass and sat at his desk. What had gotten into him? Was he like some teenager having to show off before a crowd? Damn!

He blinked. He lifted the whiskey glass and set it back down without sipping any. She'd been so damn hot. He sensed that her bombastic orgasm had briefly frightened her. It was crystal clear that Melissa Hopkins had passion. She might need someone to help her find it, but she sure had it.

He crumpled back into his chair, then bent forward and held his head. How many women had he been with over the years?

He raised his head and gulped in air. Only one other woman he'd ever known had her G-spot in the same place. Phoebe.

Laughing gruffly, he reached for the half-empty glass. Maybe Claire was right. Maybe Phoebe *had* come back from her grave to haunt him.

"You okay?"

Melissa glanced up from her desk and shook her head at Inez. "I'm not sure. I'm not sure of anything anymore."

"He really did a number on you, didn't he?"

"You were there. You know he did. Why did he do that?"

Inez shrugged. "Neither Brad nor I were successful at finding it."

"So how could he?"

"I don't know."

"And when he did, why didn't he back off and let one of you bring me to a climax?"

"I don't know that either, but did you really want him to turn you over to one of us?"

Melissa opened her mouth. She wanted to scream, but she didn't. She shook her head. "I might've died if he'd left me hanging."

Chuckling, Inez stepped around Melissa's desk and began massaging her shoulder muscles. "I doubt that you would've died," Inez murmured. "But you—all of us—would've missed out on something pretty damn special."

"What do you mean?"

"Harry was a virtuoso working you, with the care a violinist might give an ancient Stradivarius. Watching you and Harry work together was like watching art come to life."

"Um, that's good. It felt that way, too. Who would ever have thought Harry Gage could be such a skilled lover?"

"Any woman who watched the older tapes in which he performed."

"Oh. I haven't gotten around to viewing those yet."

"You should. It's not often we get to see Harry in action."

"How often?"

Inez laughed, then planted a wet kiss on Melissa's neck. "This was the first time I've seen him—live and in person, that is."

"He doesn't do this often."

"Never, that I know of. He must find you quite alluring."

"I don't think so," she huffed. "He must've really been

pissed that you and Brad couldn't find my G-spot."

Inez lifted Melissa's hair from her neck and worked her fingers down it. Her lips nestled against Melissa's ear. "He didn't look pissed at all when he was bringing you off. Everyone in that room was turned on."

"Including you," Melissa teased softly, covering Inez's hands with her own.

"Especially me. If I had found your G-spot and you'd responded that way for me, a team of wild horses wouldn't have been able to tear us apart. I would've taken you and given myself in every way I know how."

Melissa lowered Inez's hands until they settled over her breasts. "You would've done all of that even with the camera running?"

"Camera be damned."

Melissa gasped as Inez's tongue licked her earlobe and her hands fondled her breasts. "Do you suppose Harry was turned on?"

Inez chuckled softly. "You've got to be crazy to think he wasn't. I thought he might have to pole vault out of the production room. There was no way he could hide his erection."

"Inez," Melissa whispered, turning her head to look in her face.

"Yes?"

"When do you suppose Harry will let you and me make love together?"

Inez never closed her smiling eyes but slanted her lips across Melissa's. Melissa parted her lips in further invitation. She welcomed Inez's tongue seeking, searching, plundering her mouth.

Inez backed away, her mouth crinkling into a grin. "I can hardly wait."

"Do we have to?"

"You pout so seductively." Inez brushed hair from her

eyes. "If we don't wait, Harry will be furious, and we could lose our jobs."

"So?"

Inez's brow furrowed. "I need this job. I just found out I'm getting booted out of my apartment. I'll need to find another, and that means deposits, moving and so on." Inez sidled away from her.

Was she moving away from temptation? It was so new for Melissa to think of herself as tempting. "Why are you being kicked out? What did you do wrong?"

Folding her hands at her waist, Inez said, "Nothing. Some rich guy bought the building and is going to tear it down to build a parking lot."

"He can do that?"

"Do you think tenants can stop him? Not hardly."

"Why don't you move in with me? I need a roommate to help with expenses."

Inez scowled and stepped backward. "I couldn't do that. What would Harry say?"

"To hell with Harry. You need a room. And I have an extra."

"Nothing against you, Melissa, but I don't want to live with anyone." She glanced away. "Even if we were lovers, I wouldn't want that. I treasure my independence."

"Okay." Melissa brightened. "How about staying with me on a temporary basis while you save enough money to get set up in your own place?"

"I don't know." Inez shook her head, looking askance.

"What harm could come from two friends rooming together for a short time?"

Inez laughed. "Plenty. But okay. We can try it."

"Great!" Melissa leaped to her feet. "Let's run by my place now and I'll show you your new digs."

"My temporary digs," Inez cautioned. "Of course."

Harry watched the two women walking down the sidewalk holding hands. He restrained himself from smashing the window and yelling at them. What had they all unleashed earlier in the production room?

They looked so happy. He had difficulty remembering being that happy.

He shook his head. He should have brought the two of them together before now. He'd wanted to, but for some inexplicable reason he'd held back. Now they'd take the next steps on their own without his direction.

And what the hell was he going to do about that?

Leaning his head against the window, he sniffed the finger he'd used to find her G-spot. It was still caked with her dried juices. He watched Melissa's butt sashay down the sidewalk. Could he ever rein her in? Did he even want to try?

"I've yearned for this for some time," Melissa said softly, unsnapping the buttons down the front of Inez's dress.

"I know. I've seen the hunger in your eyes for me even when Brad was eating your pussy."

Melissa snickered and pushed the dress off of Inez's shoulders. It fell to the floor, revealing light olive skin. "I was imagining it was your tongue."

"Me, too." Inez grinned, unclasped her bra, and tossed it aside. She lifted a breast as an offering and Melissa covered it with her mouth. "Perfect," Inez breathed. "You knew we'd be doing this when we left the office, didn't you?"

Melissa pulled back and smiled. "You did, too."

Inez nodded and helped pull the shell over Melissa's head. Her bra quickly floated to the floor.

Giggling, Melissa and Inez rubbed breasts against breasts

and nipples against nipples. "I've never tried to seduce a woman before."

"You didn't have to try very hard with this woman," Inez said, skittering a finger across Melissa's panty line.

Melissa grabbed her hand and held it. "You're not worried about Harry?"

Inez shook her head. "I gave up worrying about him before we left the office. Harry is going to have to learn he can't control the lives of his staff on their own time away from the office."

"I agree." She smiled. She interlaced her fingers with Inez's and worked them inside her panties. She groaned when Inez dipped a finger in her already very moist chamber. "Thanks," she murmured.

"Thank *you,*" Inez moaned. "Harry was right about one thing."

"What?"

"You are hot."

Melissa laughed. "Now that we've established that fact, let me feel you, too." She slid her hand into Inez's panties until she found what she sought. "Wow," she murmured, easing her finger in. "You're pretty damn hot, too."

They stood exploring and playing for long moments. Inez groaned against Melissa's shoulder.

Melissa nibbled on her ear. "This is sweet, but I don't know what to do next."

Snickering, Inez stepped aside and dispensed with her panties, and Melissa did likewise. "Unlike working at the Center, we don't have a director, nor do we have a script. Do what comes naturally." She stepped into Melissa's arms. Their lips met. She planted several butterfly kisses before winking at Melissa and sliding down her body. Her tongue grazed Melissa's breasts and then her belly until Inez rested on her knees. "This is what I want to do next. Taste you."

"Please, be my guest," Melissa said softly. She wove her fingers through Inez's thick dark hair.

A moan escaped her lips as soon as Inez's tongue parted her labia. She tilted her hips forward.

Inez chuckled and lapped at Melissa's puffy lips. "Oh. So exquisite."

Melissa tensed when the curled tongue probed further. She frowned and clutched the back of Inez's head. Someone was lighting the fireworks she kept hidden inside. One by one, they caught flame and exploded. She rose to her toes and ground her pelvis against the delightful invader.

Inez drove her tongue in and out. There was only one end to this collision of forces. Melissa's loins popped and crackled like a hundred Fourth of Julys. She started to collapse. Inez wrapped her arms around her and kept her from falling.

Melissa flowed into her open mouth, then closed her eyes and gave into the demands of her body and of her lover. Where had Inez been all these years? Truly, she was the key to her passion. She hadn't lost the key! The key held her tight, protecting her from her own need to control.

Sliding lazily to her knees, Melissa smiled at Inez. "Wow. You're something else." She ducked her chin. "But now I want to taste you."

"I hoped you would." Inez chuckled softly, then lay back on the carpet and ran her fingers across her breasts and down her belly, pointing the way.

Melissa's breath caught when she saw Inez's fingers toying with her pussy lips and then separating them. Pink contrasted beautifully with dark olive.

"You like what you see?" Inez asked.

"Stunning."

Inez parted her glistening lips as far as she could. "My pussy's so full for you," she whispered. "Sip, taste, drink. But don't tarry. I'm not a painting to be caressed with eyes only."

"No, you're not," Melissa said, settling between her lover's legs. She dipped her tongue into Inez, who continued holding her lips apart. Melissa slid her tongue up and down the pink crevice.

She lifted her head and licked her lips. "Wow. You're delicious—incredible."

"I'm glad I please you." Inez stretched her arms above her head and arched her back, tilting her hips provocatively. "But you've only had a tiny taste."

"Not nearly enough." Melissa lowered her mouth to resume her feast.

She lapped at Inez and was spurred on by the woman's squeals.

"Mmmm," Inez whimpered. "I can't last much longer. Burrow your tongue in."

Melissa nodded, though she doubted her partner noticed. Inez's hips bucked wildly when Melissa drove her tongue into her partner's heat.

Inez clutched Melissa's head as if afraid she might leave.

Melissa squirmed, trying to sink deeper. There was no danger she was about to leave. She'd sipped. She'd tasted. It was time to drink.

Inez hoisted her hips off the carpet, nearly dislodging Melissa. And then she collapsed and howled softly, "You've got me. I'm overflowing—everywhere. What did you do to me?"

Melissa shook her head and gulped again and again. At last, her friend's flow ceased. She tapped Inez's beautiful pussy with her tongue in a farewell caress and sat back on her haunches.

Through half closed eyes, Inez nodded. "Hope you enjoyed that; I sure did."

"Tremendous." Melissa stood and extended a hand to Inez. "If you can move, why don't you join me in bed? We don't want to spend the night on the floor."

Inez rose to her feet and grinned curiously. "Who said I was spending the night?"

"I did."

"Oh." Inez stepped into Melissa's outstretched arms and whispered, "We've got the weekend. Why not?"

Monday morning, Melissa fought to keep her lower lip from trembling before Harry's blistering anger. He'd ordered her to come to his office as soon as he'd arrived. He'd been stomping around between her and his desk without actually saying why he was so upset. She figured she didn't have to spend very much energy guessing.

"What don't you understand about the English language, Melissa?"

"What do you mean?"

"Coy does not become you. You know what I mean. No outside involvement with Center employees."

"Oh." Could she bluff her way out of this?

"Oh. Is that all you have to say for yourself? Is Inez that good?"

She jutted out her chin. "That's none of your business." She paused. "I thought you meant guys."

He stopped pacing and stared hard at her. "Right. You're not very good at lying, either. Dammit, don't start blubbering on me."

Melissa slumped in her chair. "So what are you going to do?" She looked sharply up at Harry. "Please, don't fire Inez. It wasn't her fault. I seduced her. She needs this job."

"And you don't?"

"I do. You know I do. But . . ."

"But not enough to control your newly found libido?"

She shrugged her shoulders. She avoided looking at him. When was he going to say those awful words *You're fired*? She peeked at him through blurry eyes. "What do you want from me? I'm not going to apologize." She squared her jaw with renewed determination. "And I'm not giving her up."

Harry glowered. He began pacing again. He stopped. "I didn't expect you would." His voice was barely audible.

Why did he seem sad? She was going to be fired.

He pointed a trembling arm toward the door. "Get out!" he shouted.

She rose to leave. "I'll clean out my desk and be out of here within the hour."

"No! I didn't say you were fired. Just get out. I'm canceling this afternoon's shoot." He breathed heavily. "If I were you, I'd find some work to do that will keep you out of my sight."

"You're not firing me or Inez?" Melissa couldn't keep her body from quaking.

Harry ignored her question. "Go, before I change my mind."

An hour later Harry scowled at the intruder daring to enter his office without knocking. "What the hell are you doing here?"

"Why so happy, Harry?" Claire Johnson crossed her arms under her substantial breasts and waited.

He didn't see any reason to respond. Instead, he picked up a pamphlet from his desk and began leafing through it.

Undaunted, Claire laughed. "I thought for sure your young protégé would be out of here by now—or if not her, then Inez."

He gave Claire his fiercest scowl.

"You don't frighten me. We've been together too many years for that. Your growl always surpasses your bite. Cat got your tongue? So what are you going to do about them?"

He shrugged. "How did you know? Did one of them talk

to you?"

"Hardly," she scoffed. "They're not going to talk to me about their love life. Their newfound ecstasy was written all over their faces. The question remains, what are you going to do about them?"

He hated it when Claire sank her teeth into him. She wasn't about to let go. "We've got a policy on the books."

"Ah," Claire hooted. "And that takes care of it neatly and cleanly."

He scowled, wishing the solution could be so easy. He also wished he understood why it wasn't.

"You must be having second thoughts about the policy, or neither of the girls would still be here."

He glowered, shook his head, and looked toward the door.

Would Claire leave? Or maybe he should.

"Harry?"

The subtle shift in her tone surprised him, and he glanced up at her.

"Maybe it's time to revise or throw out the old policy."

His heart skipped a beat. "But . . ." he sputtered.

"It's nonsense that we should interfere with the lives our staff choose to live outside the Center."

"But . . ."

Claire held up her hand to stop further comment. "You, of all people, should understand the stupidity of such a policy."

"I didn't know it bothered you so much."

Claire grinned. "As I've said before, you don't hire women that would particularly interest me. Have you ever wondered what would've happened between you and Phoebe if there had been no policy?"

"Of course," he blurted out. He grew silent.

"Have you ever wondered where that policy came from?"

He gave Claire a quizzical look.

"You gave it birth."

"What the hell?"

Claire nodded. "I was in the meeting when Phoebe argued for it."

The air spilled from his lungs as if he'd been kicked in the solar plexus.

"That's right. You were still too junior to be included in management meetings. Mr. Howard was opposed to the idea on principle, but Phoebe insisted. And as was so often the case, Phoebe got what she wanted."

"I never knew." Harry curled his fingers into fists. *Why?* Why would she want such a policy?

"I'll answer the question you're not voicing. She wanted protection from you."

He shook his head, then stopped.

"That's right," Claire said, with more compassion than he thought she possessed. "She wanted your body, but she didn't want to be bothered with the rest of the trappings that come with commitment. And you were pushing her hard for something she didn't want to give. I'm sorry to be the bearer of bad news." She smiled at him. "I figured you should know before you do something irrevocable with our girls."

He nodded. He didn't doubt what Claire had told him. The puzzle pieces clicked into place—he'd never understood why Phoebe was unwilling to simply thumb her nose at the Center's policy.

Like Melissa was willing to do. He blinked and cleared his head.

Claire still stood waiting for some sort of response.

"I'm glad you told me," he said quietly. "I wish I'd known earlier. Thanks. I think I'd like to be alone now, if you don't mind."

"Of course. I'll come by later. We need to talk about a couple possible product additions to our catalogue."

"Sure. Later." He watched Claire leave, but never heard the

door shut.

Had Phoebe played a game with him all those years? Why? He'd wanted them to be together outside the Center. She hadn't. He'd wanted kids. Kids scared her. He wanted out of the Center. She didn't. The Center was her life—or at least that was what she'd said.

It turned out the Center had been her security blanket, protecting her from him. Why had she been so afraid of him?

Melissa's eyes burned. She had a hard time focusing on the screen in the darkened projection room. It wasn't that the tape was fuzzy—it was quite clear.

Her problem was the scene on the screen. Her aunt lay face down on a table with her feet on the floor, her face contorted with passion as the man behind her moved methodically in and out of her. The man was Harry. She could hear their bodies slapping together. Her aunt gave him a defiant look. "Fuck me," she snarled. "Fuck me as if this is our last time."

"You're not going to get me off that easy," Harry said, picking up his pace. He grabbed her hair. "Come for me. Now!"

Phoebe yelped and then let out a bellow. "That's it. Son of a bitch. I'm coming."

"Good," Harry snapped, relaxing.

Melissa knew he had not come with her aunt. She felt like she'd been watching some sort of competition between two sexual champions.

She never shifted her attention when the door to the projection room opened and closed. Inez often joined her to evaluate old tapes. They had to decide jointly which ones they wanted to suggest should be erased and which still contained educational merit for today's viewers. Knowing what they had available also fed into decisions about what kinds of videos to produce anew.

"Now that we've got that out of the way," Harry intoned on the screen, "maybe we can get down to some serious fucking." Melissa watched with keen interest as Harry again began to move in and out of her aunt.

She didn't even flinch when hands encircled her to fondle her breasts. Slowly, she realized those hands did not belong to Inez. They were too large—Harry! "What . . ."

"Shh."

Her breasts became alive under his expert touch. Her breathing turned haggard. "But . . ."

"Don't interrupt your work."

Interrupt. *Who was interrupting*? She wanted to scream the words, but she couldn't find her voice. He made short order of the clasp at the front of her bra. Cripes, his fingers were like burning embers against her nipples. His lips fluttered over her neck.

"Stand for me," he whispered.

She didn't hesitate. She stood and leaned over the table as her aunt was doing on the screen. He flipped her skirt up over her back and pushed her panties to one side. She fought for breath and groaned loudly as he pushed his cock into her.

"Ah," he mumbled, "you're as hot as she was."

"The woman in the tape, she . . ."

"Be quiet. She worked for the Center."

Melissa pushed back against his thrust. "I can tell that."

"Sh."

Melissa smiled thinly at the screen, at the images of Harry fucking her aunt. She'd tried. He'd have to find out later that they were watching him screw her aunt.

Right now, she didn't give a damn about Phoebe. She only cared about the long hard cock filling her. Harry shifted from side to side. He tilted to probe more deeply. Inez had called him a virtuoso. She wasn't about to debate that claim. But why now?

She shook her head. If not now, when?

His breathing became more labored.

The Harry on the screen hollered, ushering in his climax. His hips blurred. Her aunt emitted a triumphant smile.

The Harry behind her and in her began to churn with renewed purpose. *Come for me, Harry.* She feared saying the words aloud, but she welcomed his cock and did her best to help it unleash its payload deep inside her.

Harry quaked across her back. She sensed he was trying to hold something back. He bit her shoulder, and she exploded beneath him. It was as if he'd found her key. She could not have stopped if she wanted to. And she didn't want to. Not one nanosecond. She shut her eyes, waiting for him to finish pumping his seed.

Melissa blinked. Had she dozed? She heard the click of the door.

She was alone. She stood on rubbery legs and straightened her skirt. The screen had gone blank.

Melissa shook her head. If she didn't feel so full, so wet, and so exhausted, she might think her imagination had gotten away from her. She dipped her hand into her panties. She was sopping. *Nope, not my imagination.*

She removed the tape from the video player. Maybe she wasn't going to be fired right away. So where was Harry now? Did he plan on screwing Inez, too? Was this their punishment for transgressing Center policy?

Melissa smiled. If so, she might have to get out the rules and procedures manual and see how many other violations she could manage.

Chapter Four

The heavy drizzle hanging over Central Park late Sunday afternoon fit his mood. Harry leaned his forehead against the floor-to-ceiling window of his apartment looking down and across the park. Maybe Claire was right. Maybe he was a masochist.

Hiring Melissa Hopkins had been a huge mistake. He should fire her, but he couldn't. He still found it difficult to blot out Claire's revelation. The non-fraternization policy existed because of him. What was worse, it was Phoebe's idea.

He'd warped his brain trying to come up with a reasonable explanation for Phoebe's actions. He remained at a loss. She'd wanted his body, but not him. That was obvious, but why?

He stepped back from the window and retreated to his kitchen. The stainless-steel décor seemed stark, hardly comforting.

Comfort. He poured himself a little whiskey on the rocks. That was all the comfort he required. He'd done well, by most people's standards. And he had Phoebe to thank for helping get his career started. She'd taken him under her wing when he was still a graduate student and then offered him a full-time job heading up the research arm of the Center.

Their on-camera work had generated sparks between them—and apparently with viewers. They'd continued working together until she left. "Until she fled," he grumbled, picking up his drink and carrying it back into the living room. He plopped down on the love seat.

Yeah, he'd done quite well for himself. He'd invested well

in stocks and real estate. He sipped the whiskey. He'd been surprised by how much money there was to be made in healthy sex. Their market cut across aging baby boomers trying to maintain a spark in long-term relationships all the way to people in their twenties wanting to avoid getting into the ruts they thought their parents and friends were in.

Healthy sex. That was a joke. Nearly all his women had come to him through his work, and the one he'd fallen for had played games he'd only now begun to fully comprehend.

Healthy sex. Melissa Hopkins. Did she want him as badly as he wanted her? She hadn't balked in the dark. Would she in the light? Her puffy lips intrigued him. He'd yet to taste them. He would. Would she want him to? Would she offer her lips in the light, or only in the dark?

Neither one of them had exchanged a word about what transpired in the screening room last Monday afternoon. He shook his head. Nothing had happened. Not really.

He hardly knew anything about her. What was her favorite food?

Who was her favorite author, musician, artist? What was her favorite sexual position? What did she look for in a lover? Why hadn't she run from him Monday afternoon? How did she spend rainy Sunday afternoons?

Curling her body tighter around Inez, Melissa dozed off and on. Their lovemaking had been tender and warm. Making love with raindrops splattering against the bedroom window was mesmerizing.

She rubbed her nose through Inez's dark hair. She inhaled, filling her lungs with her lover's scent. Not bad.

For a person not keen on change, she'd proven to be quite adaptable. Her job at the Center was stretching her. She grinned. *In more ways than one.* She was making good money for the first time in her life.

She dropped a kiss on Inez's shoulder. She'd found a new lover. Oddly, she'd gained a greater sense of purpose in her life. She still wanted to flourish as an artist, but she'd already bought into the mission of the Center. What they were doing in their research and on the production sets was helping people live fuller, more enjoyable sex lives. She traced Inez's shoulder blade with a finger. And she was learning how important it was to have a full and enjoyable sex life.

What about Harry? Melissa's eyes widened. Where did that thought come from? She sighed. Did Harry make it a practice to only have sex with women in the dark?

And then treat them like strangers? The rest of the week, he'd given no indication whatsoever that he even recalled what had happened in the screening room.

She closed her eyes and again felt him ramming into her from behind. He'd been demanding, but she hadn't been withholding—not in the least. He'd surprised her with his size, with his passion, with his ferocity. She'd had bruises where her thighs had banged against the table. She wasn't complaining—not about that.

It wasn't like he was avoiding her. Not at all. They'd gone on about their business as if nothing had happened at all in the screening room. Apparently nothing had.

Inez stirred and cracked one eye open.

"Hi," Melissa whispered. "Did you have a nice nap?"

"I did."

"I thought it was guys who fell asleep after orgasm."

Inez rolled to her back and brushed a hand across Melissa's cheek. "It was your fault," she teased. "Your tongue led me up a high mountain where the air was so thin I had no choice but stay awhile and sleep."

"I'm glad. It's fun watching you sleep and seeing you come back to life."

Inez winced and propped herself up against the pillows. She started to speak and hesitated. "We have to talk."

Melissa pulled away and sobered. "The dreaded words. I've heard them before."

"It's not that. Not really. I love having sex with you. We're good together."

"But . . ."

"But I don't want to move in with you."

"Oh." Melissa steeled herself for more.

"I've agreed to move in with my cousin in Yonkers at the end of the month. She's a flight attendant, so won't be around all that much." Inez wrapped her fingers around her wrist. "I told you I treasure my independence. I'm not looking for commitment."

"I wasn't expecting commitment," Melissa protested.

"No, but you would. How would you feel if I brought home a guy or another woman?"

Melissa shrugged. "I don't know." She hadn't thought about that. There was probably a lot she hadn't thought about. What if she wanted to bring home a guy—or another woman?

"We can still be occasional lovers, if you wish. I'd like that a lot, but I'd understand if you don't."

Melissa shook her head. "No, I'm fine with that. I'm not ready to give you up entirely, now that I just found you . . . if you don't mind."

Inez's eyes sparkled. "I look forward to finding more ways for making love with you. But," she gave Melissa a hard glare, "at the first sign of clinging, I'm out of here. I've been in clingy relationships before. That's not what I'm looking for."

"Me either."

Inez chuckled. "Do you know what you're looking for?"

"No. Do you?"

"Probably not." She leaned over, planted a kiss on

Melissa's lips, then quickly separated. "Wouldn't it be something if we discover that what we're looking for all along is waking up in bed with a lovely woman on a rainy Sunday afternoon?"

Melissa stuck her tongue out. "Could happen, I guess. But we won't know until we're much further down the road."

"Thank you," Inez said. "Do you want to take another step down that road with me now, or should I leave?"

Shaking her head, Melissa reached across to tweak a dark nipple. "Don't leave. I'll try not to cling. Just love me as much as you can. That'll be enough for now."

"*For now* may be all we have." Inez winked. "Who knows, *for now* may be a lifetime. Is your rabbit handy?"

"Uh huh." Melissa pulled a drawer open and handed the pink and white rabbit to Inez. "Did you have something in mind?"

"Absolutely." Inez giggled. "I think we need a little mood change, don't you?"

Melissa nodded.

"Good. Let's have some fun. Open for me, please." Inez placed a palm on Melissa's inner thigh.

She complied and smiled as Inez ducked her head to trace a line from breast to breast with her tongue. Melissa tensed and relaxed. Inez turned on the rabbit vibrator until it was pulsating steadily.

"You have such a flat belly. I'm envious, you know."

Melissa shook her head.

"It's true."

Melissa leaned forward to watch Inez guide the rabbit to her belly button.

"Have you ever thought about getting a belly ring?"

Melissa shook her head.

"I think silver would look great on you. Oh, look who's coming to life already. I'll just help her along—a little. Watch me."

Inez stroked Melissa's clitoris between thumb and finger, making her gasp.

"Very nice," Inez said. "Erect. Alert. Looking for some loving. I'll try not to disappoint." Inez lowered her head and sipped.

Melissa tried not to screech. Her thighs bucked of their own volition.

"Patience," Inez cautioned. "But then I can see that might be more than either one of us should expect. Let me get the rabbit in place."

Inez ran the head of the vibrator up and down her slit, separating her folds.

"Jesus." Melissa groaned.

"I'll take that as an affirmative. The rabbit wants to check out your burrow."

Melissa curled her fingers into fists as Inez pushed the vibrator into her depths. "I'm right on the edge of the cliff, Inez. Help me."

Chuckling, Inez flipped on the butterfly attachment and brought it to bear on her clit.

"Holy shit!" Melissa pounded the mattress with her fists and thrashed her legs. Nothing she did dislodged the rabbit.

"Ecstasy has no mercy," Inez said softly.

Melissa tightened her abs and pushed against the rabbit. "I'm coming," she squealed, clutching a pillow to her chest. She was grateful when the rabbit pulled out of her. "Let me be," she whimpered. "Let me be."

Inez leaned over and nibbled on her ear. "Have a nice nap, lover. See you tomorrow."

Nodding, Melissa hugged the pillow tighter. Tomorrow was another day. She'd deal with that later. Now she had an orgasm to cherish. And she wasn't going to be denied that gift, even if Inez was not the permanent key to passion she'd thought.

Would Harry come to her tomorrow in the screening room at three o'clock? It would be a week to the hour from the last time. She'd be there. She squeezed the pillow tight. Her buttocks clenched against a tiny orgasmic aftershock. Was that appreciation for Inez's gift, or anticipation of what Harry might offer?

"Good afternoon, ladies."

Melissa glanced up from the video log she was creating at her desk. She heard Inez say, "Hi, Claire."

"Good afternoon," she said, wondering what would bring Claire Johnson to their office. She seldom simply popped in for a chat. She didn't think Claire was a chatty person.

Claire entered. "I want to give each of you a draft copy of our next catalogue." She handed a loose-leaf notebook to each of them. "This will be the first catalogue we've issued since you joined us, Melissa."

Melissa nodded and opened the notebook.

"I want any input you may have about how we represent the Center, our work, and products we're offering for sale." She eyed Melissa thoughtfully before continuing. "I'm sure I come off as a hard-ass to you." She shook her head. "Don't try to deny it. And I can be. I won't deny that either. But I do want your honest opinion. I won't bite off the head of the critic."

"Okay," Melissa said. "How soon do we have to get back to you?"

"By the end of the week will be fine. I feel like we need some new ideas around here. Harry and I have been at this for a long time now, maybe too long." She gave them a devilish smile and headed for the door. She turned around. "Oh, I nearly forgot. Did you two have a chance to try out that new rabbit this weekend?"

Melissa flushed and shot a glance at Inez. Neither of them could withhold a giggle.

Claire chuckled. "I see that you have. No complaints, I hope."

"None," Melissa said, shaking her head.

"It's a keeper," Inez chimed in.

"Good. Melissa, why don't you give me a sentence or two about the rabbit that I can play with for an ad?"

"Okay. I can do that." Melissa exhaled when she heard Claire's footsteps going down the hallway. She looked over at Inez, and they both burst out laughing. "Does that happen often? Does Claire really want our input? Or is she only nosy?"

Inez flipped open the catalogue workbook. "She's more human than you might think. She does seem to genuinely want our advice. That doesn't mean she'll take it, but you can tell her what you want to, and she won't hold it against you."

"Do you think she and Harry work well together?"

Inez shrugged. "They must. They've been doing it for over a decade."

"Do you think there's ever been anything between them?" She winced at Inez's scowl. "I mean sexually."

"I know what you mean. I don't know for sure, but I'd bet no. Maybe that explains how they've been able to work together for so long."

"You're probably right." She checked her watch. "I've done this long enough," she announced. "I'm going down to the projection room and review more of the older videos."

Inez nodded. "One of the things I like best about this job is the variety it offers."

Melissa tucked her panties in her purse as soon as she arrived in the screening room. Minutes later, she had the VCR running. She sat at the screening table and gawked at her aunt, who seemed to be scrutinizing her from the TV screen. Phoebe lay on her back on a couch, her legs raised and parted around Harry, who kept pace with her thrusting beneath him. As usual, he was a study in masculine sculpture. His hamstrings stood out. His butt was tight, and his shoulder muscles were tensed.

While Melissa watched the entire panorama of the couple copulating, it was her aunt's face that drew her practiced eye. First, there was the oddity that Phoebe looked directly at the camera rather than at her lover. She appeared vexed. Joyful one moment. Pained the next. And sad the next. Unlike the last tape, this one had music that made it impossible to hear what the two of them were saying. And of course, there were the irritating voiceovers with the hotshot sex therapist explaining technique, encouraging viewers to experiment, and holding out the promise of sexual joy if they but tried the techniques on this tape and others.

Melissa clenched her fingers around a pen. Her aunt didn't look overjoyed. Her lips moved. Melissa could see that her aunt and Harry were talking. Damn, she wished she could hear what was being said.

Melissa stopped the tape, backed it up and reran it in slow motion. She watched her aunt's lips moving. Melissa's hand flew to her throat. Had her aunt said what she thought she'd said? *Fuck me, don't let me die. Fuck me.*

A sudden draft announced the opening of the screening room door. Melissa pressed the play button and waited.

Once again he came to stand behind her chair. For what seemed like long moments, he did nothing. She assumed he, like her, was watching the action on the tape. Then he grabbed her hand and raised her from her chair.

She knew what he wanted. She wanted the same. Words were not necessary. She sat on the table and then lay back across it.

He grunted when she raised her skirt. He slid his two large hands up her thighs, then encountered her bare pussy. "Ah," he moaned.

She smiled when she heard his zipper. He cussed. She made no move to help him. At last, she felt his cock sliding along her thigh. *Come on home,* she wanted to scream, but she held her tongue.

He found her entrance. She raised her legs high in the air. She craned her neck so she could watch her aunt. His cock bulldozed its way in. She gasped. He waited, giving her body time to adjust.

She could hardly make out his frame in the pitch-dark room, but the flickering light of the screen told her what she already knew. He made no effort to cover her or hold her; he stood in place waiting for her.

"Now," she grunted.

He needed no further instruction. He pulled nearly all the way out and slammed forward, impaling her anew. She squealed. He didn't let up. Taking her lead from her aunt, she lowered her legs and used them to squeeze him tight against her. He roared. His intensity amazed her. Her own intensity nearly overpowered her.

This was different from the last time—this was better. She was making him hers just as much as he was making her his.

"Son of a bitch," he practically growled.

He stopped, but she continued thrusting, milking him, until she came, until she lost the capacity to push her muscles to move. The table suddenly became hard and uncomfortable. He pulled out of her none too gently. Again, she heard the rustle of clothes and the sound of his zipper.

The rush of air from the hallway chilled her flesh as he left. She flung her arm across her forehead; her breathing steadied. What in the world were they doing? What was *she* doing?

Days later, Melissa sat on the couch in the production room next to Inez. They had both slipped robes on after finishing with Brad and Doug on an advanced oral position video. Her jaw ached from all the stops and restarts.

Doing oral sex in the studio had actually proven more strenuous than most sex positions. Brad and Doug, also dressed in robes, sat in the straight-backed chairs. Harry and Claire sat in the easy chairs. She supposed that was appropriate, given their rank in the Center, but clearly the hard work was being done by the performers.

"Do you have a shooting schedule to share with us?" Claire asked Harry.

"Tentative." He nodded and smiled at all of them. "Isn't it always tentative?"

Wasn't that the truth? She never had a clue what Harry would be up to next.

"We have several opportunities with Melissa."

Melissa sat up straighter. He was talking about her. She'd better not daydream.

"As we all know by now, she comes to us innocent in some ways."

She scrunched her mouth.

"Don't be offended," Harry said. "You are what you are. You offer us some intriguing educational opportunities."

"What do you mean?" she squeaked.

"You two haven't gotten around to playing with a strap-on, have you?"

She shook her head. Inez grinned broadly and shook her head as well.

"Good. When you do, I want to get it on tape."

"Beautiful idea, Harry," Claire said. "Creative and sellable."

Claire caught Melissa's eye. "There are many women who might want to try it, but they think our performers are experienced or even professional. While most are experienced, we do not hire professionals."

"Plus," Harry said, "we need to begin getting Melissa involved in anal play."

She arched her eyebrows. It was bound to happen—apparently, it was about time.

"Just as Claire said, there are women and guys interested in exploring anal sex, but they don't feel confident in getting started. And given viewer feedback, we know our viewers assume our performers are already quite knowledgeable about and comfortable with anal sex."

"But I'm not," Melissa offered.

"Exactly. As with many of our videos, we'll do a segment here and there and piece them all together later. We'll want the viewer to know you are a novice."

"That shouldn't be difficult." She couldn't believe she was sitting there so calmly discussing this latest assignment as if it were part of her college education.

"I envision doing a video from start to finish on anal play. We'll work with you with butt plugs and vibrators first"—he glanced at Brad, then back at her—"before you'll be expected to take on a cock."

"Who will help her begin?" Claire asked with a mirthful look.

"I will," Harry said. His voice rose a notch.

"Okay. How will you do that and stay off-camera?"

"I've thought of that."

"I'm sure you have."

"I'll coach her. Any one of us can help her with the plugs. We can edit out voices and people if necessary. I want her ready before our young stud here gets involved."

"That should work," Claire agreed. "Are you okay with this, Melissa?"

She raised and lowered her shoulders and fixed her focus

on Harry. "Seems like he has a plan." She looked at Claire. "I'm okay with it as long as you keep signing my checks."

"Good." Harry seemed to relax a little. "Now that's settled, I have one more thing I need to ask of the women."

"You're on a roll, Harry," Inez quipped. "What else do you want?"

"You know we try to do several videos a year that appeal to an older audience."

"Of course we know that," Melissa said. "It's one of the things I like best about this place. We don't see sex as being the domain of the young."

Harry gave her a crooked grin. "I was hoping you'd say something like that. I have a Mr. Wilson coming in on Friday. He and his wife have been long time performers for us. That is, until his wife died a year and a half ago."

"I'm sorry," Melissa said immediately.

"He's still working through his loss, but Max remains committed to our mission. He's talked to me about continuing his work."

"Oh." Melissa frowned. She had an odd feeling she knew where this was going. "So are you going to find an older single woman for him to work with?"

Harry shook his head. "He doesn't want that. That would feel too much like deceiving his wife—though he knows his wife would be supportive of his plan. No, he wants to work with a younger woman for two reasons. First, he won't confuse her with his wife and all those emotions. Second, he wants our viewers to know sex isn't about age. As long as participants are of legal age and sound mind, there shouldn't be a problem."

Melissa held back a sigh. "And you want me to fuck this old codger."

"I think creating such a tape is a great idea." Harry scowled at her. "Hopefully, after meeting Max, you'll withdraw that *old codger* comment. Max has had a lot of years of pleasuring women. You won't be too disappointed. You should feel honored."

"Why not? You're the boss."

"Right. At least I sign the checks."

"But you're not my pimp."

Harry slammed his yellow pad to floor. "Where the hell did that come from? No one is pimping here. You knew the nature of the work when you signed on. If you want out, you know where the door is."

"I'm sorry," Melissa backpedaled. "That was out of line. You're right." She inhaled sharply. "But I'm not expected to fake orgasms, am I?"

Harry howled. Even Claire broke into laughter. Harry shook his head. "No, we don't expect you to do that. Let's just see how it goes. Who knows, you may be in for a surprise or two."

She nodded. Maybe she'd already had one or two surprises too many.

Chapter Five

Sitting at a small table and trying to not look too curious, Melissa glanced at the entrance to Jamie's Café. She was early, but she'd definitely wanted to be the first one to arrive for breakfast. She'd ordered coffee. Now she was trying to calm her nerves.

Why hadn't Harry come along? Because Max wanted to meet her one-on-one before their taping session.

Melissa stared at her coffee. She should've said *no.* It was one thing to agree to have sex with the guy on camera so they could send a helpful message to older viewers, but this getting to know each other first was quite different. She'd become accustomed to having sex with strangers in the rather rigid confines of the studio. This was much more demanding.

Was the guy checking her out? What if she failed to pass? And she didn't really want to listen to Max's story. It was enough that she'd agreed to work with him.

She studied the man entering the café and looking around as if he was meeting someone. She knew immediately when his eyes met hers. His face lit up in a broad smile ,and he walked directly to her table. Clearly, Harry had shared her picture with him and hadn't bothered to give her the same courtesy.

"You must be Melissa," the man said easily. "I'm Max. May I join you?"

She nodded and shook his hand. He didn't have to bother asking. She was here at his request. The twinkle in his eyes was quite infectious. She smiled softly. "Please, have a seat.

I've ordered coffee." She waved at the waiter.

"Let me take a moment to look at the menu," Max said. Melissa took the opportunity to consider him more carefully.

She gave him credit for staying in shape. While he wasn't buff, he wasn't flabby, either. He was mostly bald, with gray hair, including a mustache. What did they say about bald men? She couldn't remember, but she thought they were supposed to be more sexy.

She frowned. At least he didn't turn her off. He appeared healthy and seemed quite comfortable with their situation—more comfortable than she was. And there was that inexplicable sparkle about him. She sat back in her chair and relaxed a bit. Maybe this wasn't going to be as bad as she'd feared.

He sat the menu aside and smiled at her. "So do I pass?"

"What?"

"Figured you were sizing me up. Thought maybe you expected a dinosaur, or a dirty old man at the least."

"I . . ." She grinned at his broad smile. "I didn't know what to expect. You do seem quite civilized. And no, you don't strike me as a dirty old man. So what about me? Do I measure up for what you have in mind?"

Max leaned back and practically roared. "You're kidding!" He shook his head at her. "No, I see you're not. You're a very lovely young woman. Agnes would approve of you. She liked women with an air of mystery about them."

"Agnes?"

"My wife."

"Oh, I'm sorry."

"Don't be. She's been gone a year and half. Sometimes it feels like yesterday; other times it feels like forever." He shook his head and raised the coffee cup to his lips. After setting the cup down, he said, "Agnes was devoted to this work, you know."

"That's what Harry said."

"She was a zealot. She believed sex education in the schools should emphasize safe sex and ways of extending pleasure to both sexual partners. One of Agnes' favorite sayings was *Education is what separates humans from animals, so why does rutting like animals pass for sex, or for lovemaking?*"

Melissa nodded. "I think I would've liked Agnes."

"I know you would've. I do want to thank you for agreeing to work with me and for meeting with me this morning. I guess I've never quite gotten used to the idea that two people can hop into bed without at least knowing a little bit about each other. Perhaps that's old school."

"Perhaps," Melissa responded.

"Okay, I'll begin. I'm a retired English professor—so was Agnes."

"Really?" She didn't know why that should surprise her or even why it mattered. But it did. She knew professors. She knew how they thought. Not that all professors were alike, of course. But Max had become somewhat familiar. Maybe he did know what he was doing.

"Yes, I've written some." He shook his head at her quizzical look. "No, nothing you would've read. Very esoteric stuff that only a few English scholars would read. I live in Hastings-on-Hudson. Agnes and I have one child, a daughter." He tilted his head to the side. "She never did appreciate her mother's enthusiasm for educating folks about sex. I also have a granddaughter. Do you want children someday?"

"Yes," Melissa murmured. "I'm aware my biological clock is ticking."

Max chuckled. "I don't think that clock is pressing you much yet, but it can sneak up on you. So Agnes and I got involved with the Center a decade or so ago. It was her idea. I balked at it at first. But she kept wearing me down with all kinds of stories and facts about couples going awry because of not having a clue about sex. She was, of course, especially concerned about older couples giving up on sex as if they had outgrown the need or the desire."

Melissa shrugged her shoulders. She didn't know how else to respond. The few times she'd imagined her parents having sex, it creeped her out. It was better to assume they'd outgrown the urge. But with Max sitting across from her, it wasn't too difficult to put herself in his position. Would she ever want to outgrow sex or give it up because it didn't fit the image she'd had of older people when she was young? Not likely.

Max gave a reassuring smile. "I can see you're thinking with me on this. I appreciate that. I doubt many young women would seriously consider helping an old guy like me create a video for a bunch of old fogies."

"You," she protested, "don't look like an old fogy."

He chuckled. "I've never been quite certain what one of those looks like. They must be a generation or two ahead of me, no matter how old I am. Do you know Agnes and I firmly believed that an active sex life in the older years helped us stay limber and healthy?"

She tried to maintain a blank expression, but apparently she wasn't successful.

"Agnes died of cancer." His eyes misted. "Living active lives, eating well, doing all the right things doesn't necessarily prevent cancer."

Melissa nodded, fighting her own tears.

"But we managed." Max raised his chin. "And I know Agnes would want me to work on this video, and that you would make a fine partner. So are you still willing to work with me?"

"Yes, but I already told Harry that."

Max shook his head. "That's different. What he presented was an abstract concept. Here I am in the flesh—somewhat wrinkled, somewhat mature—but this is who I am. When we work together, if we do, I want you working with Max Wilson, not with an abstraction. I won't accept less than that."

Melissa reached across the table and squeezed Max's fingers. "Max, it will be an honor to work with you. And you're absolutely right, it was important to meet away from the Center. But I've haven't told you anything about me."

Max leaned back and grinned. "I won't pry, but if you think I'm not curious, you're quite mistaken."

"I'll give you the short version. I'm twenty-five years old, working on a master's degree in fine arts. I work in pastels and acrylics. I'm told I'm quite talented, but that my work is missing something."

Max nodded. "That little pizzazz that separates the excellent from the good."

"Something like that, I suppose. I work at the Center because they pay well."

Disappointment registered on Max's face.

Melissa flinched, then shook her head. "That's not exactly true. The money is better than I can make most places, but I've become quite committed, like you and Agnes, to the Center's mission." She scrunched her mouth—Max didn't need to know everything. "And I have other personal reasons."

"That's fine," Max said amiably. "I probably didn't tell you everything either." He grinned. "But we've shared enough to make this a human relationship before turning to sex. That's all I wanted."

"As you probably know, I wasn't too keen on this meeting, but I'm glad you insisted." She checked her watch and winked at him. "We better get going. Harry doesn't like to keep the movie crew waiting. They get paid whether we're ready or not."

"Well, let's be on our way, by all means." Max picked up the ticket and helped her up from her chair.

Melissa smiled. The day could get interesting. She was about to have sex not only with an older man, but with a gentleman. Maybe Max was a dinosaur.

Sitting next to Max, Melissa leaned back against the pillows on the king-sized bed. Harry was taking his time double-checking the cameras. They'd use two for this shoot.

She peeked out of the corner of her eye at Max and grinned a little—he might be trying to hide his excitement, but he wasn't succeeding. That pleased her. She was glad a man his age could still get excited. She withheld a snicker. Funny, he'd never told her his age. That certainly seemed irrelevant now.

They both still wore white robes. If she wasn't mistaken, she saw a small tent forming under Max's robe between his legs.

"Remember, you can say whatever comes to mind," Harry said. "We can make appropriate edits later. I don't want either one of you thinking about the finished product. Focus only on giving and receiving pleasure. We have no script. Do what feels right."

"In that case," Max said, meeting Melissa's gaze. "I'd like to begin by getting a good look at you. Is that okay with you, Melissa?"

"Of course. Let me get rid of this robe."

He lit up like a Christmas tree as she shrugged it off her shoulders. "You are so lovely!" He shook his head. "I am a lucky son of a gun."

"Nonsense," she protested. "I'm the lucky one." She took one of his hands and brought it to her breast.

He cupped it and gently lifted it, then rose to his knees and drew it into his mouth.

"Goodness," she murmured, running her hands over his bald head. Max knew how to pleasure a breast. He suckled tenderly as if he was seeking a life force. He used his teeth to bite her nipple—he soon had her teetering between joy and pain. "Already," she whimpered, questioning her own response.

Max chuckled looking up at her. "Why not? You aren't restricted to a limited number of orgasms, are you?"

She shook her head. He swallowed as much of her breast as he could and cupped his hands around her buttocks, kneading them, helping her unlock her first orgasm. "That's it," she wailed. "Wait."

Max didn't let her go, but he did wait.

Melissa tried to clear her brain. Max was proving to be a very patient lover.

She settled, and Max rested against the pillows, smiling broadly. "You look quite satisfied," she said, "and I haven't done a thing to pleasure you."

"That's not true at all. Giving you pleasure—having you respond to me spontaneously—that gives me a lot of pleasure."

"I'm glad. She reached for the folds of his robe and parted them. "But I expect there's a young fellow down here who'd like a little more direct attention."

Max chuckled. "Not so young, but you're right. What did you have in mind for him?"

"How about a little of this?" she said, leaning over and taking him in her mouth.

"Superb." Max groaned. "Your mouth is so hot."

She lifted her head and winked at him. "This is a treat, to have a cock grow hard in my mouth. I can deep throat him without gagging at all." She refocused on her task. Max's cock grew harder, thicker, longer, until it tickled her throat. "My, he was only resting. I adored him soft, but now he's wonderful. He does seem to have a mind of his own."

"Um," was the only response from Max, whose breathing quickened.

Melissa bobbed up and down, worrying more than a little about Max's heart. She peeked at him. His eyes were closed, his smile radiant. He looked like he'd found heaven, but he didn't seem at any great risk of dying. Harry would react if he thought anyone was in real danger.

Max cranked an eye open. "You're very good. Why don't you swing around here so I can do you, too?"

Without dropping him from her mouth, Melissa swiveled around until Max had his wish. She groaned when his tongue probed her pussy. She halted her movements and relished the way he caressed her, as if she were the most delicious morsel he'd ever tasted.

He tapped her rump with a palm, and she smiled, then renewed her pace along his length. If anything, he'd gotten longer. She knew immediately when he snaked a hand under her. He found her clitoris and went to work on it as if she had nothing better to do than to come again. What was he doing to her?

"Good God!" she screamed. She continued pumping him with her hand and pushed back against his masterful tongue. She was coming all over his mouth, and he hadn't shown the least indication of an approaching climax. She laid her cheek against his thigh and watched his cock weave about waiting for more.

She peaked at Harry, who beamed at her. She blinked. Yeah, maybe she was having a surprise or two. She closed her eyes. *Pleasant ones.* She liked pleasant surprises.

Languidly, she changed positions. She straddled Max, not wanting him to have to do more of the work than necessary. And it was time she brought him off. Holding his cock in one hand, she rose high above it, then lowered herself slowly until he filled her. She'd love to paint the picture of his smile as he watched himself disappear only to reappear. She started slowly, then rose and lowered at a faster pace.

"You're beautiful," he said. "I love the way your breasts bounce."

She nodded, acknowledging his praise, but not wanting to

be diverted from her ride.

"I've never known a woman's nipples to extend as far as yours."

She lifted her arms high above her head and slammed against his loins, driving him deeper and deeper.

"You are beyond hot. You're closing in on another orgasm. I can see it on your face."

She shook her head.

"Sure you are. I want to see you fondle your clit."

Her eyes widened.

"Do it for me, please. I want to watch you come."

"Oh shit," she mumbled, lowering her hand until she was clawing at her clit.

"That's right. Come for me, girl. Come for me. You are such a delight to watch. Pure abandonment."

Melissa closed her ears to his babble and concentrated on that huge ball growing in her loins. It expanded. She strained her hips. She rubbed her clit almost raw until she couldn't hold back a moment longer.

She crashed into Max's arms. His hands smoothed her back comforting her. "Incredible," he said, "absolutely incredible."

Moments later—she was unsure how much later—she became aware of where she was. She propped herself up on her hands and stared at Max, who continued to smile at her. She shook her head. "It's your turn, Max," she said with determination. "If we don't get you off soon, I may die at a very young age." And she'd been worrying about *him* living through their escapade.

Max chuckled and nodded. "Okay. Why don't we have you face away from me lying on your side? I'll enter from the rear. That's an easy position for me to get leverage without too much exertion."

"Fine with me," Melissa said, again switching positions. She reached between her legs and guided him into her channel. Thankfully, he hadn't gone soft on her. His lips nuzzled her back, and he began to move in and out of her. She twisted her head from side to side. She did like a man to pay attention to her back. His hot breath stirred her.

Max moaned and thrust harder. He reached around to caress her clit. She pushed his hand away. "Not this time, lover. You first. I may follow. But you first."

He grunted. He panted. Now she was seriously worrying. She bent over and cupped his balls. He groaned loudly. She slid her index finger lower until she could rim his asshole.

He stopped. She hoped she hadn't shocked him, but it was too late to worry about that. She shoved her finger in as far as she could and began massaging Max's prostate gland. She smiled when his hips slammed against her butt. She drove her finger in and out, matching him stroke for stroke.

"Jesus H. Christ, woman. What are you doing to me? Holy shit, I'm coming. Don't stop. Fuck my ass. Come with me."

Was he babbling? Melissa giggled—and suddenly had absolutely no control over the orgasm that erupted to mingle with his.

She could feel his heart pounding hard against her back. She closed her eyes and said a little prayer—hopeful that he wouldn't die on her and thankful that he was part of her life, if even for a brief time.

Much later, Melissa combed her hair and straightened her skirt. Max had left, apparently a very happy and satisfied man. She grinned. He'd actually left her a very happy and satisfied woman.

"You," Harry huffed, "look quite pleased with yourself."

"Shouldn't I be? You got what you wanted. If we have to do more takes, I'm willing."

"That probably won't be needed. Didn't look like you had

to fake too many orgasms."

Melissa shook her head. "Hardly. Max has phenomenal staying powers. I certainly don't have to worry about premature ejaculations with him."

"It's a benefit of older age."

"Really?"

Harry nodded. "Of course, the body still has to hold up. So where did you learn that trick to get him off?"

"What do you mean?" She knew full well what he meant.

"That finger in the ass. Max just about came unglued. I didn't teach you that yet."

Melissa walked around the camera he'd been working on and patted his chest. "Maybe you're not my only teacher."

She caught a glimpse of disappointment on his face, but he quickly smoothed it. She laughed anyway, then sobered. "I am reviewing old Center tapes. Or don't you remember?"

"Oh." He scowled.

"Later," she said, slanting a finger across his lips. She turned on her heel and exited without looking back. It was Friday afternoon. How was she going to make it through the weekend until three o'clock Monday?

Flashes of red streaked across the black canvas. Out of breath from the rapid brushstrokes she'd been making, Melissa stood back to view her work. The jagged red strokes reminded her of lightning bolts. She cleaned the brush and checked her paints until she found what she was looking for.

She smiled and began to brush long streaks of yellow across the canvas. Some intersected with the red strokes, mixing into shades of orange, while others did not. Exhausted from the painting process, exhausted from reaching deep within herself, exhausted from not knowing what she was doing, Melissa set her brushes down. She removed the protective smock, left the studio, and entered her bedroom.

She threw herself on the bed. When had she become such an emotional wreck? Now even her painting didn't make sense.

She closed her eyes, and her aunt appeared before them. Yes, falling into the huge abyss had begun with her aunt. Finding the pictures of her aunt having sex had started her down this odd path. Would she ever redeem herself? How?

Once again, she saw her aunt's contorted face—not from the photos in her possession, but from the tape. Melissa shivered remembering Aunt Phoebe's face with Harry screwing her from behind, and her inaudible words—*Fuck me, don't let me die. Fuck me.*

Melissa jerked to a sitting position. What fury had been unleashed in her aunt? What fury was being unleashed in her?

And was it merely coincidence that Harry had been involved with her aunt and now with her? Her shoulders slumped. Harry didn't know his Phoebe was her aunt. She'd tried to tell him once, but he'd shushed her. She'd never tried a second time.

She pulled out the photos of her aunt from the nightstand and reexamined them closely. Maybe she'd missed something. She didn't recognize any of the other partners. There was one picture of Aunt Phoebe with another woman. The woman's face wasn't visible. Melissa pursed her lips. Could it be Claire? Possibly. Why not?

The more she thought about it, the more plausible it seemed that her aunt and Claire would've worked together. Claire didn't work in front of the camera now, but that hardly meant she hadn't earlier on. The same was true with Harry.

So what?

There was no answer to that question.

She walked back into the studio where she'd stored the two boxes she'd brought back to her place after her aunt's funeral. It had seemed odd that her aunt had left the boxes neatly tied with her name on them.

Because there were no other heirs, the responsibility for dispensing with Aunt Phoebe's personal property had fallen on her. In keeping with her aunt's eccentricities, her financial assets had been evenly distributed between an endowment for the Center, cancer foundations, and her niece. Melissa shrugged her shoulders. It wasn't as if she didn't have money; she just wouldn't have access to it until she turned thirty. It was the same with the inheritance from her parents. Her family valued independence, determination, and hard work. Thankfully, her parents had also had the good sense to carry life insurance.

So she found herself demonstrating sex acts on camera instead of lying on a beach living off her inheritance. She probably wouldn't enjoy the beach. The jury was still out on her current work.

When she'd first opened the boxes after Aunt Phoebe's death, she'd been horrified by the photos of her aunt having sex and put them quickly away without digging further into the boxes. But she'd never been able to shake those images from her memory—and now they'd fueled her curiosity and desire so strongly that she worked in her aunt's stead.

Melissa lifted a box flap and steadied herself. Was that what had happened? Was she filling in for her aunt? She had Aunt Phoebe's job. She had her former lover—well, sort of. But her aunt couldn't have predicted any of this. Could she?

When had Aunt Phoebe planned to give her the boxes? Had she intended to do it before her death? Or did they constitute her special legacy for her niece?

Ignoring her trembling fingers, Melissa lifted the contents of the first box with a fresh eye. She set everything out carefully on her bed. There were postcards from faraway places, theater bills, several faded garter belts, books—none of which had immediate import—Center stationary, and several handwritten poems.

Melissa picked up the poetry. She hadn't paid any attention to it earlier. Her brow furrowed. It was her aunt's handwriting, but who had written the poems?

She set the crusty pages aside and continued rummaging. There was an old hat and a couple scarves. Why had her aunt wanted her to have these hand-me-downs? She might as well have given her a wastebasket.

Carefully, she pulled the string of the second box. She wasn't certain she'd delved far into this one before. The top layers were like the first box. Some reminders of an eccentric, but that was about it.

Determined to get to the bottom of the box, she dumped its contents on the bed. More pictures of her aunt at work fluttered across the bed. Melissa only paid them a cursory look. They neither repulsed her nor drew her.

She smiled when she recognized hand printed letters and others written in a careful child's script. She covered her heart with her hand. Her aunt had treasured the letters she'd written as child. Later, she might take time to reread them.

Melissa set aside an overflowing box of feathers. Another small box contained seashells, and another, pebbles. The contents of this box defied logic as much as the first one had. She sat on the bed and began the laborious task of separating entangled chains of various pieces of jewelry.

She was no expert on jewelry, so she couldn't tell if she was holding costume jewelry or if maybe some was more precious. She had an artist friend who made jewelry. Amber could tell her if any of the pieces had any monetary value.

She held up a circular gold pendant to the light. It was heavy. It warmed her fingers. She placed it at her breastplate and smiled. This was a piece she remembered even as a little girl. She recalled wrapping her fingers around it when she sat in her aunt's lap. And her aunt, to her mother's dismay, had let her play with it.

Tracing the figure etched on the pendant, Melissa nodded with recognition. Her aunt had never explained the symbol to her. She now knew it for what it was—*Yoni,* an ancient Zen symbol, though probably crafted in the twentieth century. Maybe she had come to her new vocation naturally after all—as a child, she'd gotten quite a bit of pleasure from rubbing an image of the female vulva.

She brought the pendant to her lips, then clasped its chain around her neck. She nodded at her reflection in the mirror. The pendant looked right; it felt right. Why had it taken so long for her to find it? Now that she had, she would add it with pride to her rather limited jewelry collection.

Chapter Six

Sunday morning sunshine bounced off of Inez's tight, dark curls.

"Hi," Melissa said, grinning. "Are you going to sleep the day away?"

Inez stretched and yawned and punched a pillow before sliding up against it. "Hi, yourself," she said, dragging a finger across Melissa's cheek. "Do you have something else you prefer?"

"You, for starters," Melissa said, pecking Inez's nose. "I already have coffee brewing. You want to wait until after coffee?"

"Um. That sounds good. Why don't you bring the coffee while I go to the bathroom?"

Melissa hummed a tune from her childhood days as she poured coffee. She grabbed a couple doughnuts and carried the tray back to the bedroom.

She wasn't at all disappointed when she entered her bedroom to find Inez adorned the way she liked her best, wearing nothing but a warm smile. "I brought along some doughnuts."

"Great, but if I hang around with you much longer you're going to make me fat. Why don't these calories affect you as much as they do me?"

Melissa shrugged and bit into a raspberry jelly donut. Jelly oozed across her upper lip, and she swiped at it with her tongue.

Inez giggled. "You do that so well."

"I'm glad you enjoy watching me eat."

"Oh, you're a joy to watch, all right." Inez chewed on a glazed doughnut. She made a display of swallowing and then asked, "So what's going on between you and Harry?"

Startled, Melissa nearly spilled her coffee. "What do you mean?" she gasped.

"He's quite possessive about you. He was from the beginning, but it's intensifying."

"I don't know what you mean." Melissa hoped she wasn't blushing.

"Uh huh," Inez responded, lifting an eyebrow. "I'll let that pass for now, but I do understand when Harry issues an order."

Melissa froze. "What in the world?"

Inez nodded. "Harry told me not to touch your booty."

"My what? My booty?"

"Where have you been hiding, girl?" Inez laughed. "Your booty. Your butt. Your ass."

"Oh." Melissa butt cheeks clenched. "Oh, my God."

Inez gave her a knowing nod.

Melissa found her voice. "You're telling me that Harry told you not to touch my butt, that it's okay for us to be together as long as you don't try to claim my ass?"

"Exactly. Apparently, he's staked a claim on that particular part of your anatomy."

"Well," Melissa huffed, "he hasn't said anything to me."

"Maybe he doesn't feel he has to."

Melissa stilled.

"Something's going on between the two of you." Inez paused. "I can see you're not talking. Be careful, girl. Harry's not a college guy. He'll be demanding. Harry gets what he wants. And if I'm not mistaken, he's coming after you."

"You must be mistaken," Melissa snapped. "Nothing's going on." Now she knew she was blushing.

"It's okay." Inez reached over and briefly cupped a breast. "Just be careful. Harry's in a league of his own. Of course, if you don't care about Harry and what he wants, I could grab a vibrator and pop your cherry ass."

"No!" Melissa jerked away and pulled up the sheet to cover her legs.

Inez laughed. "Enough said." She licked her fingers. "So do you want me to eat you as long as I stay away from your butt, or"—she gave Melissa a hard look—"have we lost the mood?"

Melissa smiled thinly. "I think we've lost the mood. If that's okay with you."

"Sure." Inez threw her legs over the side of the bed and reached for her clothes. "I've got plenty to do to get ready for my move."

"You're not hurt?" Melissa asked, softly.

Inez shook her head. "Of course not. We'll hook up again when we're both in the mood."

Melissa watched Inez dress silently and hunkered down in the bed, hoping she wasn't losing a friend.

Inez pulled a t-shirt over her head and fluffed her curls out. She smiled softly. "Don't worry about us. I'll be here for you in whatever way you want, as long as you want." She frowned. "Just don't let him hurt you."

Nodding, Melissa closed her eyes and her ears to block out Inez's departure.

She was alone.

What was she to do about Harry? Inez wouldn't have made up such a story. So why was it so important to Harry that she save her butt for him? What did he expect of her—of them? He seldom talked to her. And they never talked about what was happening between them—in the screening room and on the set. And now he'd brought Inez into his game.

She didn't like this one bit. Her fingers curled into fists.

Her fingers relaxed. Warmth spread through her loins. He wanted her. He really wanted her.

Did she want him? *Really* want him?

Melissa drummed her fingers on the screening room table. He was late. She'd paused the tape she'd been reviewing. She'd orchestrated this rendezvous carefully. Up to this point, Harry had decided when and how he would take her. This time she was deciding when and how she'd take him.

But he was late. The bastard.

She heard the click of the door and then the rush of air. She hit the play button and the screen came to life.

He came to stand by her chair and she heard him groan softly. She didn't hesitate. She moved to kneel on the floor and pull his zipper down in the same motion. She shoved his pants down and eagerly reached into his briefs and freed his hard cock. It slapped against her cheek.

Melissa smiled and wet its soft, bulbous head. She peeked at the screen out of the corner of her eye and saw her aunt bobbing up and down on a younger Harry.

She expected Harry was watching also. She fondled his balls and licked the length of his shaft. His groans fueled her desire. She encircled him with her mouth and took him in as slowly as she could possibly manage—which was difficult because she wanted him so badly, but she didn't want to finish quickly.

She played as long as she could and then gave up to her own passion. She clutched a butt cheek in each hand and began to slide up and down his cock in earnest. He rose to his toes and moved with her. She smiled at his groans as he skittered across that fine line between joy and pain.

She sensed his readiness. She slammed down the full length of him until her lips grazed his loins. With a tight sucking motion, she backed off and retraced her steps—over and over until he was spurting down her throat. He grabbed her shoulders to steady himself. She smiled as he pumped into her. He was hers. *Make no mistake about it.* He was hers.

His breathing turned ragged. She giggled while licking him clean. She rose to her feet. This was her moment. "We've got to talk . . ."

His mouth covered hers with a bruising kiss. He never broke the kiss while he grabbed his pants and covered himself. She never noticed when the screen went blank. He pulled away from her and she struggled for breath.

And then he was gone. The door closed softly behind him. She slumped into a chair and studied the flickering screen. What had she accomplished? Other than swallowing a man for her first time. She chuckled softly. There had been a moment when she thought she might literally swallow all of Harry. "Damn," she muttered. If that was half as good for him as it had been for her, it was damn good.

He'd want more of that, she was certain. Without question, she needed more of that.

She rewound the tape. She was beginning to feel like a tape—to be played and rewound and played again. And she definitely wanted more than that.

Hot water pelted his back in skinny spikes. Harry flexed his stiff shoulders back and forth. The spray stabbed at his knotted muscles with little effect.

He gave up, slid the shower door open, and reached for a towel. While drying off, he studied his reflection in the mirror. He grimaced. Since when were his eyes developing crow's feet? Another *distinguished* sign? "Shit," he muttered. Who had come up with the idea that getting older went hand in hand with becoming more distinguished?

At least he wasn't too vain. Damn if he was going to color

his gray hairs or worry about some damn crow's feet. He had enough to worry about. And she probably didn't stand more than five feet four inches.

He flexed his shoulders. Knots! She had him tied up so tight he might never get loose again.

And she seemed completely oblivious to what she was doing to him. Did she think she was only keeping the edge off him by playing their little screening booth game? Did she really believe that would suffice to keep him at bay?

He wanted more. He had to have more. He shook his head. He wouldn't allow himself to want more. Once down that road had been enough. They were safe at the Center. "When did you start worrying about safety?" he groused at the mirror.

He stomped into the bedroom and started sorting through clothes. Safety. He glanced down at his hardening cock. The woman had him in a constant state of arousal. And they were seldom even in the same room.

They probably hadn't had a conversation that lasted more than fifteen minutes. When they were together, he hadn't been in the mood for talking. Apparently she hadn't either, until yesterday afternoon.

He tugged his trousers up and tucked his shirt in. His fingers stilled. He sighed and glanced down toward his feet. He wished he'd been able to see her bobbing up and down. Her deftness had surprised him. Only one other lover had taken him so skillfully and so completely. She'd never hesitated. She'd taken all of him. He couldn't have stopped her if he'd wanted to.

She had natural talent. He couldn't imagine she'd been coached. She'd only done what seemed right.

So why was that so wrong?

She'd wanted to talk. Did she want an explanation for why he was there? For why the darkness brought out her uninhibited side? Surely she didn't fantasize about exchanging words of love.

He combed his hair with his fingers and headed down the hall to his coffee. The best invention known to humankind was the automatic coffeemaker.

He sniffed the coffee aroma and let it fill his soul and work on his knots. He poured a cup and let the hot steaming brew work its way down his throat.

Was she thinking of him this morning when she swallowed her morning coffee? He pulled up a stool and sat, warming his hands on the cup. How could she *not* think of him? He hoped she was. He'd hate to think he was the only one going crazy.

And under the glare of lights, he'd watched Melissa making love with just about anybody and everybody. She'd been sweet, almost poignant with Max. The guy must've thought he'd died and gone to heaven and back. It sure looked like he had. She never seemed at all turned off by his wrinkles, or by how hard she had to work to get him up and keep him up.

He drummed his fingers on the counter. He'd been surprised by how adeptly Max had taken her to the brink of so many orgasms. He'd taken her to the edge, allowed her to peek at them, then backed her off, only to approach again and again. How many times had she come? He'd lost count, and he was certain she wasn't counting. She was probably never into counting.

She could be an absolute tigress with Inez. Just once, he wanted to feel her fingernails scraping across *his* back. He could easily imagine her drawing blood. His, not Inez's.

Inez had leered at him in a triumphant way more than once while Melissa was buried between her legs. He'd have to be careful with Inez. Maybe he shouldn't have said anything to her. But he couldn't risk her playing with Melissa's ass and spoiling her for him—for the audience.

He'd explained his reasons to all of them, hadn't he? They had an opportunity to make the best instructional video on anal play yet to be made. He'd reviewed them all. He'd been involved one way or another with many of them.

This one would be different. Because Melissa was different. He'd probably never have the opportunity to film a woman losing her virginity, but he sure could tape a woman yielding her virgin ass to him.

She must be wondering about that—at least a little bit. He wanted her thinking about it. He wanted her wanting it—as much as he did.

He remembered the smirky look on Brad's face when he'd announced that he—Harry—would prepare Melissa himself. He'd implied that he'd then turn her over to Brad to fuck in front of the camera. Everyone knew he detested the idea of working on camera again. The camera often saw more than he intended to share. He wanted to hold on to his privacy—to his private feelings, to himself.

He drained his coffee and set the cup down sharply. No way would he turn her over to Brad Jefferson. He wasn't about to share her ass with anyone else. He hoped by the time he had her prepared adequately, she wouldn't want any other cock probing her butt, either.

Harry rose to his feet and placed his cup in the sink. It was time. He hadn't told her this was the morning he'd begin educating her about anal play. That hardly mattered. He doubted she was thinking about much else anyway. He smiled. That was the way it should be—both of them anticipating the response of the other. Both willing to give and to receive. Both embracing an unparalleled adventure.

Doubt niggled at his mind. Was he making more of this than he should? Wasn't that the trap he'd fallen into once before?

He headed outside toward the subway. He couldn't

believe Melissa didn't wonder about what he had in store for her next. After all, she was the one who arranged their Monday afternoon exchanges. He hadn't realized he'd find her in the screening room that first Monday afternoon.

Each Monday since, at the same time, he'd been lured to the screening room by the throaty whispers in his inner ear of the siren who prepared the space—and herself—for him.

Melissa stood outside the production room door. She wore only the red satin pajama top Harry had asked her to wear. She took a deep breath and entered the room. As she'd expected, she was the only one partially clothed.

She looked directly at Harry, who held her stare without revealing his inner thoughts. She knew this wasn't going to be a scene about masturbation.

She'd become accustomed to Harry's vibrations. This was going to be about much more. This was to be the beginning of his assault on her ass.

She tried not to grin. She was ready. At last, he was coming to her with a specific desire. They would hardly be alone, but *he* was coming to *her*. Clearly, even she could no longer doubt that he wanted her. The lust in his eyes might as well have been that of a stag seeking a mate—not just any mate: *her.*

"Have a seat on the stool, Melissa," Harry said, sitting on an identical stool beside hers.

She nodded and climbed onto the stool. She sidled sidewise so the short pajama top covered as much as possible. Harry had removed his shoes. Otherwise, he was fully dressed.

"You know what we're focused on this morning?" he asked, arching an eyebrow.

"My ass, I assume."

"Perceptive."

"Everyone else is dressed."

"Right. So this is a unique opportunity for the Center and for our viewers."

She eyed him steadily but said nothing.

Harry tilted his head to the side and spoke to the camera as well as to her. "We want our viewers to know this will be your first experience with anal play." He paused. "That is true, isn't it?"

She shrugged. "Yes."

"No one has penetrated your ass with anything—finger, tongue, cock, toy?"

She shook her head.

"Have you thought much about this?"

She nodded, trying to avoid looking directly at the camera.

"How do you feel about exploring anal play?"

She took a deep breath. "Honestly? A little nervous." Her voice quaked. She supposed that only added credibility to the tape, but she still didn't quite understand why he couldn't prepare her off-camera, then redo it on-camera. Harry seemed extremely devoted to authenticity.

"That's to be expected." His voice was gentle. "Many people are raised to think that anything to do with the anus is dirty and that anal sex is a taboo. Were you raised that way?"

"No one in my family ever talked about it. If anything, sex itself was taboo."

Harry smiled. "I'm sure many of us can relate to that. So tell our viewers where you work and what you do."

She frowned. "What I do here? I'm a research associate. Most of my work involves digging around in libraries and the Internet. Some of it takes place in front of the camera."

"And you're an artist?"

"Yes, I'm finishing my master's degree in fine arts."

"Good. It helps our viewers to know you as a person, at least a little bit—so that you're more than an attractive body."

"Ah." She nodded. So why didn't *Harry* want to know more about her than her body?

"Maybe we should get started." He reached for her hand and guided her to the small raised area set up before the fireplace. She hadn't noticed the gas fireplace was on. Harry hadn't forgotten a thing.

"Please, sit," he ordered, softly. She complied, and he knelt beside her.

"If anything we do causes you pain, I want you to say so. Anal play is not about pain; it's about pleasure. Understand?"

"Yes," she whispered, nodding her head.

"Okay, lie down please."

Melissa rolled to her stomach.

"No, lie on your back."

She rolled over to face him. "But I thought anal play meant rear entry," she said, confused.

He shook his head. "It can, but I want you on your back so I can see your face. I want to see what you're feeling." He tore his gaze from her and looked at the camera. "I'm sure our viewers do, too."

Harry picked up a bottle of lube. "Anal play requires lots of thick lube. It's a necessity."

Her eyes widened as he liberally spread lube on his fingers. "Spread your legs for me," he said. "Tilt your pelvis up some. There. Beautiful. You have a very tantalizing ass. Your dark portal stands out like an oasis, beckoning the hungry explorer."

She tried to concentrate on his words and the lusty picture he was painting for her, but she found herself focused most on his right hand. He'd placed his left hand almost nonchalantly at the apex of her loins. He ignored her pussy. His focus was fixed lower than that.

She took in a sharp breath when his finger traced a line from the bottom of her pussy to the edge of her anus. His hand traveled back and forth, as if it couldn't decide what to do next. She realized that thought was foolish. Harry had a plan. He definitely had a plan. He blew a kiss at her and then circled her anus with his middle finger. She knew there'd be more voiceover added to the tape later. Given Harry's shortness of breath, his running commentary was becoming more difficult.

"First," he said hoarsely, "I'll slip in just a little." She narrowed her eyelids, but refused to close them. "There. I can feel your tight ring—the sphincter muscle. Is this okay?"

She nodded. Where was the pain? In some of the erotic movies she'd reviewed, women made this initial entry look quite painful. Was it Harry? Surely the women weren't told to look pained. If so, why?

Concentrate, she warned herself. *Listen to Harry. He's trying to make this easy for you.*

"Relax, babe. That inner muscle will soften in a moment or two. This is where people new at anal play make the biggest mistake. Anal play isn't about force—it's about relaxation, softening and opening. Open for me, Melissa. Open for me."

She loved how her name tumbled off his lips. She did her best to remain calm. And she opened. She knew she'd opened before he announced the fact to those watching.

"Yes," he said, obviously pleased with her. "That's it. I'm coming in further."

She gave him a little smile and clenched down on his finger. Wow! His finger felt like a log. *Relax.* She saw the plea in his eyes and relaxed. And he pushed even further. He was in as far as his finger would go. She was overcome with a wave of relief, satisfaction and pure triumph.

She closed her eyes, and he waited for her. She wiggled a little against the pressure of his finger. *Delightful.* Who would've guessed? She eyed him again and saw him smiling at her. He knew what she was feeling. Working together, they'd achieved what he wanted to demonstrate on this first step of anal play. Hardly any pain, but rather a curious sense of fullness and pleasure.

Harry tucked his chin to his chest and pulled his finger nearly out. Her face must've registered dismay, for he chuckled and slid back into her.

"You," she said.

"Do you like the feel of me gliding in and out?" he asked.

"Yes."

"Good."

He stimulated her until she stood on the edge of an orgasm and then stopped. "There's more. Much more," he taunted, pulling out of her.

"Oh," she gulped.

She watched him reach for what she recognized as a butt plug. It was a long narrow pink object with a flange on one end. She watched Harry lube the plug and then place it at her entrance. She groaned as it slid easily into her. It went deeper than his finger had.

"Is that okay?"

She nodded.

"They come in many different sizes."

She nodded again. Some were so large she couldn't imagine them fitting inside her. She held her tongue.

He left the plug in her, sat back on his haunches, and smiled at her. "I'll want you to do some homework. Does that sound okay with you?"

"Yes."

"You can take these butt plugs home. Experiment with them. Explore yourself with your finger when you take a shower. You'll be surprised how quickly you can work up in size with these plugs, now that you know your anus is a pleasure spot. You'll want to play with them in a variety of ways to examine what pleases you most."

"Okay."

"I don't want anyone helping you." He glanced over at Inez.

"Okay," she said.

"Do you want to try one size larger while I'm here to assist?"

"Yes," she said, weakly.

Harry lubed a second butt plug. This one was indeed larger.

Melissa wet her lips and pulled her knees to her chest. "Relax," he counseled. "This won't be a problem."

He pushed the new plug in about an inch. She smiled wanly, realizing he was waiting for her again. Weren't men always waiting on women?

"Oh, wow!" she said as Harry pushed the plug further. It was too much. No, it was just right. She scrunched her shoulders. And he began sliding the plug in and out.

She squinted at him. Was he going to make her come this way? Her climax was rising like a hot air balloon. Goodness. She tossed her head from side to side.

Harry's arm stopped moving.

Her eyes shot wide.

He shook his head, sadly.

She twisted her head around wildly. "You can't leave me like this," she said, hoarsely. "I'm almost there."

He shrugged. "Your hands are free."

"Bastard," she spat out. She used all ten fingers to claw at her pussy and clit. And then she lurched forward. Harry shoved the plug back in her butt as far as it would reach. "Hell," she said, surrendering to a mammoth climax. *Cameras be damned.*

Chapter Seven

After showering and collecting herself, Melissa returned to her office and sat gingerly at her desk. No one had given her the rest of the day off just because she'd had a mind-blowing experience in front of the camera. Not that she'd expected they would. Video production was only one part of her job. The smallest part, if one counted time spent—though it was beginning to sap her emotional reservoir.

A part of her wished the entire anal scene had been unpleasant. Then maybe she could get up enough nerve to beg off from any more.

She shuddered as she sat down at her desk. Unpleasant? It had been too pleasurable. She could hardly wait to get home and try her butt plugs. Even her soapy finger had felt good in the brief shower she'd taken after the shoot.

But a man's cock? Her entire body clenched. Brad's cock. The pages on her desk blurred. She didn't want Brad's cock. Would he let that happen? Would Harry really turn her over to another man to fully initiate her ass?

Inez cleared her throat. Melissa jerked out of her daze. Had Inez been there all along?

"I've been trying to get your attention," Inez said, sharply. Her expression softened. "You're still back in the production room, aren't you?"

Melissa rubbed her neck and nodded.

Inez punched some buttons on her computer and came over to lean against Melissa's desk. She stared at her for the longest time. Melissa couldn't look away.

Inez pushed herself away from the desk, bent over, and brushed her lips across Melissa's.

Melissa reached out to hug her, but Inez backed away from her reach.

"I'm going to miss you," Inez said, softly.

Melissa jerked her head up. "What?"

Inez chuckled, retreating to her desk. "I was thinking maybe we should go to your place and have a goodbye fuck. But that wouldn't be right."

Leaping to her feet, Melissa closed the distance between their two desks. She balled her fists at her hips and glowered. "What do you mean? Are you leaving?"

Inez shook her head. "I love this job." Her eyebrows shot up. "Oh! I'm not going anywhere. It's *us* I'm talking about. We can remain good friends. At least I hope so. But no more bedtime for us."

"Oh." Melissa massaged her throat. She suddenly felt cold—very cold. "Why? I thought you enjoyed our time together."

"I did. Absolutely." Inez folded her arms across her abdomen. "But I watched you this morning with Harry. I'm not going to get in the way of what you two have going."

"That's nonsense. There's nothing going on between us. Certainly nothing that would rule you out."

Inez nodded fractionally. "Believe that, if it helps. Maybe you should review the video."

Melissa stood rigidly, unable to confront Inez and unable to escape her shrewd stare.

"Harry was so careful with you. You would've thought he was working with a porcelain doll. Didn't you see that on his face, hear it in his tone?"

Melissa shook her head back and forth slowly.

"Well, I did," Inez huffed. "I've never had a man treat me so tenderly. It's more like *Get on your hands and knees and I'll find a hole to fill."* A self-deprecating smile flitted across her lips.

Melissa hoped Inez knew better men than that.

"But not Harry," Inez continued, returning to her desk. "Is this okay? Does this hurt? Relax. Take your time. I was almost embarrassed by the . . . by the intimacy." Inez chuckled. "If all of that stays on the video, it should sell well, and you will have moved anal play into the world of acceptable sexual adventure."

Melissa felt her cheeks warm. "I doubt that," she said, finding her voice.

Ignoring her denial, Inez continued, "This isn't the first anal tape we've made since I started here. This wasn't like the other two I witnessed. They weren't slam-bang-thank-you-ma'am, but they weren't tender and intimate, either."

"So maybe there was some chemistry on the set," Melissa conceded. "That doesn't mean you and I have to deny ourselves what we share."

Inez shook her head wildly. "Nope. Not me. Maybe I like my job too much to stay involved with you. At some point, Harry isn't going to want to share you, and I'd rather be out of the scene before that happens."

"What if," Melissa insisted, "Harry or Claire want us to work together on the set?"

"Ah, I hadn't thought about that." Inez nodded. "That'll be fun, actually—knowing that I'm screwing the boss's woman should add an extra bit of zip to the entire encounter, don't you think?"

Melissa shrugged off Inez's question. "What if I stripped, right here—right now?"

Inez froze as Melissa deftly unfastened her blouse and tossed her bra to the side. Leaving the blouse on, she used it as a screen to play peek-a-boo with her breasts.

Inez smacked her lips. "Why are you doing this?"

Smiling seductively, Melissa ran a hand across her skirt and palmed her crotch. Her smile broadened as Inez almost came out of her chair.

Melissa twirled around and nearly lost her balance when the door to their office opened.

Claire entered. The tall blonde's puzzlement turned quickly into a brilliant smile. "So sorry to interrupt anything. Were you doing improv, or were you playing out a fantasy skit?"

Melissa reached for her bra and returned to her desk.

"Don't bother covering up on my account. It's not exactly like I haven't seen your boobs before." Claire gave Melissa a long look.

Was Claire looking down her nose at her?

"They are very perky." She cleared her throat. "That was quite a show you and Harry put on out there this morning. Shouldn't be any problem marketing that video."

"Thanks," Melissa mumbled, fastening the last button on her blouse.

Claire looked back and forth between Inez and Melissa. She shrugged her shoulders. "I did want to solicit your thoughts on possible fantasies. We want to do a series that will help couples see themselves in different settings, different scenes. Maybe fulfilling their hottest fantasy. Any ideas you might have could be helpful." Claire paused and smiled thinly. "I had thought of a couple getting it on in their work office. I was considering a man and a woman. Given what I just walked in on, I may have to rethink that scenario. So what comes to mind immediately? You can give me more ideas later."

Melissa took a deep breath before forging ahead. Brainstorming was one way out of what could have become a rather uncomfortable situation. "Let's see," she began. "Maybe a secluded beach."

"Good," Claire said, nodding. "What else?"

"Maybe the backseat of a car."

"Yuck," Inez chimed in. "Bet you haven't tried that. I've gotten more muscle strains from screwing in cars than I want to remember."

"What if the car was a limo?" Claire asked.

"Now you're talking." Inez focused her gaze on Claire. "I could be standing with my head and shoulders through the roof waving at passersby and some guy could be snacking on me."

"Nice," Claire mused.

"I've thought about making love on a grand piano," Melissa said softly.

"Really? How classy. That has possibilities."

"What about in a crowd?"

Both Claire and Melissa gave Inez questioning looks.

"It could be done." Inez pouted. "Maybe in the infield at the Kentucky Derby or at the Indianapolis Five Hundred."

"On an airplane," Melissa piped.

"Too overdone," Claire said.

"Maybe an art museum," Melissa countered.

Claire's eyes shot up. "I like that a lot. We could play with the style of painting as background. I'm sure you could help us with that. Could we rent a small gallery for half a day?"

"Sure." Melissa shrugged. "I might be able to arrange that."

"Why does the museum have to be closed?" Inez piped. "Doesn't that detract from the fantasy?"

"Screwing in front of thousands is not my fantasy," Melissa said, probably too primly.

Inez shot her a look of surprise. "What did you think you were doing this morning with Harry's finger up your ass?"

Blushing, Melissa began rearranging things on her desk.

"That's enough for now, girls. Perhaps one person's

fantasy is distasteful to another. We'll want a diverse range so our viewers can pick and choose what they desire most. Let me know if you come up with other possibilities."

Inez and Melissa watched Claire close the door before bursting out laughing. "Would you really screw in a mass of thousands?" Melissa asked.

"Of course. Haven't you ever gotten a little frothy riding the subway?"

"Frothy?"

"Frothy. Horny."

"Oh."

Inez gave her a condescending look. "When you're packed together like sardines, most anything can happen."

"Not to me."

"One of my favorites was when I was standing clutching onto a strap for dear life and a woman squeezed in front of me and grabbed the same strap. Her eyes drilled into mine from stop to stop. She never said a word, but by the time we hit the tunnel we had established some sort of bond. In the darkness, she worked her hand up my skirt and had a finger in me before I could say boo. I've never come so quickly—ever. When the lights came back on, she was licking her finger. I wanted so badly to suck on that finger, but I didn't want to be that obvious with one of New York's finest pressed up against my shoulder."

"Whew. Nothing like that ever happens to me. So did you see her again?"

"Nope. Don't know if I'd recognize her, other than maybe her penetrating eyes."

Melissa grinned at Inez thoughtfully. "We are in different leagues, aren't we?"

Inez burst out laughing. "I'm glad you finally figured that out." She hesitated. "But I still want you for a friend, and I do look forward to working with you."

"Me, too." Melissa opened the mockups she was working on for their fall catalog and found respite in her editing skills.

Late Sunday morning, Melissa stared wistfully down at the street from her living room window. Couples were walking hand in hand, swinging their arms gaily. Some were same sex couples, others weren't. It didn't matter. Every couple looked much happier than she felt.

Her life was a mess.

She was still reeling from her breakup with Inez. She sighed. That had been inevitable. At some level, she'd known that from the beginning. Inez was simply much more edgy and with-it than she was. She hugged her shoulders and smiled at a couple helping a young child struggle to walk between them. Would she ever know that feeling?

Did Harry ever think about being a father? Melissa scowled. Odd, she didn't have any difficulty imagining him playing with children and guiding them through the morass of childhood.

Harry?

She thought of him as if they had a relationship. She snorted. They didn't have a relationship. They didn't even have a sexual relationship. Not really.

Fucking him while he watched himself fucking an old lover, even if it was her aunt, hardly counted.

They rarely spoke.

And now he'd taken her ass—with his finger, at least. She shuddered. He had been tender and caring. Did Inez think she really hadn't been aware? Initially, she'd been quite tense, unusually tense. Then he'd instructed her to focus on him and on the pleasure he was giving her. She'd nearly forgotten the cameras. Intimate. Yes, there had been an air of intimacy on the set. Though how could they really be intimate with cameramen and other staff recording their every move?

Melissa stood and rotated her shoulders. She had to get out of her apartment. It was a beautiful day, and she didn't want to spend it all inside.

She grabbed her keys and some cash and headed down the stairs to street level. She walked briskly, suddenly knowing where she wanted to be.

Shortly, she turned in at the entrance to the Brooklyn Botanical Gardens and slowed her pace, pausing to watch the ducks in the Japanese water garden. This was space for relaxing—for breathing deeply, soaking in colors and breezes and scents. The riot of spring blooms was long gone, and summer was at its peak. She headed for the Shakespeare Garden and was relieved to find a shady bench empty in a secluded corner. Daisies, black-eyed Susans, and daylilies formed a casual cluster in yellow, white, and orange beside the bench. Further off, some taller mauve blooms she couldn't name were full of butterflies, and a curly-headed toddler ran up to them laughing gleefully. The child's parents stood nearby, holding hands, happy, as if they had no care in the world.

Melissa shook off a wave of loneliness. She waited till the family left and headed across the broad open meadow toward the rock garden, stopping to watch more children playing tag and hiding behind shrubs and bushes. An artist had set up his easel next to a large, tall tree that had one out-of-place, low-slung branch reaching several yards straight out, parallel to the ground. She could easily imagine relaxing under the protective boughs, but knew better than to disturb his scene or ask what he was seeing.

The hairs on the back of her neck prickled. She stopped and turned around. Nothing seemed out of place—the children were still running with abandon, lovers walked hand-in-hand stopping for brief kisses—there: a man stood on a distant knoll watching where she stood. A hat pulled low on his head served almost as a mask.

She cocked her head to the side. Harry? She jogged toward the small hill. The man turned and scurried over the rise. When she crested it, there was nothing but trees, bushes, and flowers. Not a single person was in the little glade.

Harry was really getting to her. Now she was seeing him where she knew he never would be. She laughed freely and headed back to her apartment. Harry probably never left Manhattan.

Not looking back, Harry scampered toward his car, parked a couple blocks away. That was close. What would he have said if she'd spied him? He didn't often hang out in Brooklyn—though that had been changing of late. Brooklyn seemed quaint compared to Manhattan, but it was where she lived.

What would Melissa have said if she'd caught up with him? Would she be pleased to know he'd followed her? Or would she be frightened?

He chuckled. He didn't think she'd be frightened. Maybe mad as hell, but not frightened.

What was he going to do about her? There wasn't much time left. Once he claimed her ass fully there would be no reason for them to continue working together. He was tiring of meeting her in the dark screening room, like two teenagers grabbing what they could between classes.

Apparently, the rumor was true that she and Inez were no longer a couple outside of work. Did that have anything to do with him?

And this wasn't just about him. He knew that—in spades. Melissa was a grown woman with a mind of her own, a will, and a hell of a lot of determination. She deserved so much more than him. Even if she wanted him, which wasn't entirely clear. But she wasn't running away from him.

He cursed his luck. Why did she have to look so much like

Phoebe? What was she really like? He'd never find that out if they restricted their relationship to the Center.

Apparently, she liked walks in the park. He'd enjoyed watching her alternately adore flowers and then children, or a rather ugly tree and then a dog chasing a Frisbee, or a statue and then lovers kissing. What would she have done if he'd come up behind her and nibbled on her neck, then eased her around to kiss her puffy lips?

She'd seemed so free and contented until she'd searched the hillside and spotted him. He was quite certain she hadn't recognized him from that distance. But she did have some sort of sixth sense about her that scared him more than a little.

Melissa picked up her cell phone for the sixth time and set it down beside her. She stretched her nude frame taut and wiggled her bottom, letting the butt plug tease her. She smiled. Could she become addicted to her plug? She'd jumped two sizes since Harry had worked with her.

Harry. She stared at her phone. He'd be pleased with her progress. Had the sunlight and shadows been playing tricks in the gardens? She'd swear that was Harry on the hill.

Would he be angry if she called him? She'd never done that.

Nor had he phoned her.

Which was more of a taboo—having a plug in her ass, or calling Harry?

She picked up the phone and punched in the number she'd memorized.

He answered on the fifth ring. "Hello."

His voice sounded more throaty than usual. Had he been drinking? Perhaps remembering a lost love, or a woman he'd fled earlier in the day.

"Hello, Harry."

"Oh, it's you."

It pleased her immensely that he recognized her voice and didn't seem at all surprised she'd tracked him down in his lair. He didn't sound overjoyed, but then she hadn't expected he would.

"Aren't you curious why I called?"

"I figured you'd get around to telling me."

"I just wanted you to know that I'm lying here in bed with a sizeable butt plug buried in my ass."

"Jesus. Damn it!"

She smiled at the sounds of papers rustling. "Did you spill something? Sorry if I startled you."

"Don't be. So it's a sizeable plug?"

"Uh, huh. Probably bigger than Brad's cock."

"Bastard." He hissed under his breath. "Sounds like you're managing okay."

"Oh, yeah. Though it was better when you were reassuring me. You were so sweet."

"Sweet? Me? You must've been smoking something before that shoot."

"I don't do any of that stuff," she huffed.

"I know. I'm sorry. So do you want to be reassured?"

She grinned at her mirror. "Uh huh."

"How do I do that? You already have the plug in."

"You're right. What if I go one size larger? More the size of your cock."

"Oh, baby, you do know how to get a guy's attention."

"Hold on, don't go anywhere. I'll remove this one."

"Don't worry. I'm not gonna run a marathon in the next few minutes."

"There." She sighed. "Now I'm ready for you. I mean the larger one. Are you ready to help me?"

"Yes, what do you want?"

"Well for starters, you could play with your cock for me."

"You want phone sex?" he squeaked. "Isn't that rather juvenile?"

"You've never had phone sex?"

"Never."

"Then I definitely want to be your first. Hurry, Harry. I'm feeling empty. I need you filling my ass."

"Jesus."

She smiled at the distinct sound of a metallic zipper.

"Okay," he said.

"Are you hard?"

"You didn't think I would be? I could split boards with him, I'm so hard. What do you want next? You seem to be orchestrating this show."

"I've got you at my entrance. Close your hand into a tight fist and push your cock in just a wee bit."

"Okay."

"Now I'll push you in further. Cripes, Harry I'm not sure I can do this. You won't fit."

"Easy, girl. Take deep breaths. Relax. I'll fit. Patience. You got to have patience with me, babe."

Melissa sighed and warmed to his soothing tone. She could feel her inner ring widening. "Here we go again, Harry. Is your cock partway in your fist?"

"Yes. In your ass," he corrected.

"Right. Ah," she said, folding her knees against her chest. "I've got you, Harry. I've got all of you."

"I know it. Your rump is pressing against my loins."

"Nice image." Melissa laughed. "Shall we go for a ride, you and I?"

"Why not? We've come this far."

"Okay. Slowly at first." She took a deep breath and let it out while she slid the plug out and then eased it back in. "I'm riding your cock. Can you feel me?"

"Oh, yeah."

"Steady. I'll let you know when it's time to come."

"Fine with me," he grunted.

"I'm rubbing my clit. I wish it was your tongue."

"It is, babe. Can't you feel it?"

"Yes, of course. Your cock is sliding in and out of my ass faster and faster. Christ, you're slamming in and out of me." Her toes curled. Her lips quivered. "I'm coming, Harry," she moaned. "Come with me."

"I . . . am. Je . . . sus . . . I am."

For a full minute the only sounds she heard was his ragged breathing matched by her own. Her quaking quieted enough for her to say, "Thank you."

"It's me who ought to be thanking you."

"Maybe you should," she agreed. "Harry?"

"Huh?"

"The next time you come to Brooklyn, ring my doorbell. I promise I won't turn you away." She turned off her phone and stared at it, not believing she'd found enough guts to call Harry. Forget about the phone sex—guts to call him at home and tell him she'd recognized him.

What would he do now? She hadn't realized she'd just thrown down the gauntlet until this moment. She curled into a ball and wept. Later, she'd pull Harry out of her butt.

Cussing, Harry cleaned himself as best he could with his handkerchief. Shit. She *had* spied him on the hill. What was she making out of that? That was so fucking juvenile.

He glanced at his flaccid penis. "Damn!" he shouted to the walls. She'd played with him like a spider played with a fly.

But he'd been a willing participant. And so was the fly—in the beginning.

His wall clock struck ten. His shoulders sagged as he slumped back against the couch. Tomorrow was Monday. He had to make some sort of decision about Melissa before three o'clock tomorrow.

He squeezed his eyes shut and tried to block out the taunting image of Phoebe. He sighed and moaned softly when Melissa's teasing smile appeared.

Chapter Eight

It was after three o'clock. He was late. Melissa lay face down on the screening room table, mimicking the position of her aunt on the screen. Only in that flickering image, the bent-over form of Harry between her aunt's legs stood out. His tongue teased to her aunt's delight.

Had she pushed him too hard with her phone call last night? He'd been a little late before, but never this late. How long should she wait? She swept fingers across her pussy. She'd already dispensed with her panties and had flipped her skirt up. She'd set a table for Harry. Now where was the son of a bitch?

At that moment, the door opened and closed silently, and she felt the rush of cool air. She relaxed. She wanted to purr, but didn't.

Her lover stood between her parted legs and slid a hand up each thigh. Melissa moaned her welcome. Fingers fondled her labia. Melissa frowned and tensed. Those weren't Harry's fingers. A finger pushed into her core. Inez? She wanted to scream out Inez's name but held her tongue. Inez had come for her. Had Harry sent her?

Her brain scrambled as a mouth settled over her clit and a second finger entered her pussy. Inez hurried, but Melissa wasn't about to complain. The buildup within her loins had begun even before the screening room door opened. Teeth scraped against her clit. She was beyond thought. She banged her head against the table and pummeled her lover with her heels.

She grabbed her lover's head, holding her tight, and bucked her hips in unison with Inez's tongue. Her hands flew away as if she'd touched a red-hot stove. She hadn't been clutching tight curls. She'd been holding on for dear life to soft, short strands of hair.

"Ah," she screamed as her body bucked against insistent fingers and an incredibly adept tongue.

She closed her eyes and tried to forget everything except those fingers slowing and the mouth sipping her juices.

She stilled. She threw an arm across her eyes. The fingers left her vacant.

Would her phantom lover leave her to her despair?

She heard a slight movement, and the dim light of a table lamp came on. Reluctantly, she uncovered her eyes to see Claire's victorious smile. Her lips still glistened with Melissa's juices.

"Why?" Melissa muttered.

Shrugging, Claire pulled down Melissa's skirt, covering her as if modesty were an issue. "You were available. You won't be much longer. I needed to taste you—to see if you tasted like your aunt."

"My aunt!" Melissa jerked to a sitting position.

"Yes, your aunt." Claire pointed to the screen. "You look so much like her. Harry has to be a dunce if he hasn't put this together yet. But then I wasn't certain until . . ."

Forgetting entirely what had so recently transpired between them, Melissa hung on every word. What did Claire know? Could she help her understand her aunt? Maybe even Harry. Maybe even herself. "Until what? What convinced you I was Phoebe's niece?"

"You not only have similar bone and facial structure, and the same dark rich hair color—plus sharing some of the same quirky habits—but it was this, my dear." Claire reached for the pendant on Melissa's gold chain. Melissa's eyes rounded and she grabbed Claire's hand.

"Don't be alarmed," Claire said. "I'm not about to take it. But it's an extremely unusual piece of jewelry. There were only a half a dozen like it ever made."

Melissa watched Claire cautiously as the woman stepped back and left her holding the pendant that had become so precious to her. "How do you know this?"

Claire reached down her own blouse and pulled out an identical gold chain and pendant. Melissa lurched forward with open mouth. She held it between her shaking fingers, and then sat up straighter. "Why do you have this? How? What?"

Claire's chuckle was light, as if she was entirely accustomed to feasting on a woman and then engaging in a bizarre conversation. "Your aunt and I were roommates in college."

"Really?" Melissa slid off the table and sat in a chair. Claire pulled out a chair and sat facing her.

Claire nodded her head.

"But the pendant?"

"Ah, the pendant. We were part of a sorority—well, not a recognized sorority. Let's just say a select group of adventurous young women."

"Adventurous?"

"This was the late sixties, early seventies, Melissa. *The Group, The Harrad Experiment, The Joy of Sex* were the rage. And we devoted much of our time to conducting our own experiential sex experiments."

"Oh."

"Now you're getting the picture. I knew your aunt, every way possible, long before she ever met Harry. The pendant and its image of a woman's vulva symbolized our commitment to a sexual quest."

"And the Center?"

"We'd heard about this fledgling experiment during our

last year at college. Phoebe wanted to come down to the city and help out. I joined her a year or so later after another venture failed to pan out. I've never left. As you know, your aunt retired about six years ago."

"Why?"

Claire shrugged. "She got in over her head."

"Harry?"

"You should go on quiz shows." Claire scowled. "Of course it was Harry. Harry wanted more than she was willing to give, probably more than she was capable of giving. I thought the solution to the problem was for us to fire Harry, but Phoebe wouldn't hear of that. Harry had brought a sensitivity to this business that none of the rest of us could match. He's very inventive and creative. He sees possibilities that others do not."

"Like my so-called naïveté."

"Exactly. And I know that the anal tape he's producing with you will be our best contribution on that topic ever. Even better than when he worked with your aunt. And Harry was a fantastic performer. He never held anything back, yet he could stop and start without apparently throwing off his rhythm. Amazing!"

"But he doesn't work on camera now."

Claire smiled brightly. "That's what he says. He hasn't since your aunt left."

As if on cue, the screening room door opened and Harry stepped through it. Melissa didn't know who was more startled—him, or her. Claire didn't seem bothered at all.

"Am I interrupting?" Harry asked gruffly, nearing the table.

"Not at all," Claire said, sweetly. "We're just having a girl's chat. Aren't we, Melissa?"

Melissa nodded, avoiding Harry's eyes and trying to ignore the dampness between her legs. *Some chat!*

"Is there anything either one of us can do to help you, Harry?" Claire asked, her eyes mocking.

"No," Harry stammered, "I'm looking for a specific tape. I'll be out of the way soon."

"Good. I don't think Melissa and I are nearly finished yet."

Harry nodded, grabbed a tape from the shelf and stalked out.

At least he was quick on his feet. Melissa emptied her lungs of pent-up air once the door closed behind Harry. How would she ever make this up to him? Could she?

"Now then," Claire continued, "where were we before we were unfortunately interrupted?" She chuckled. "My, my, I do wonder what our Harry would have done if he'd arrived a few minutes earlier."

Melissa's vision clouded. *Our Harry.* "You and Harry," she squeaked.

Claire shook her head vigorously. "Never. I love Harry a lot—like a brother, I suppose. But he only had eyes for Phoebe, and that was fine with me. You're the first woman since your aunt that seems to have broken through to his interior."

"Oh, I see."

"I doubt that, but no matter."

"Why . . ." Melissa stuttered, gesturing to the spot on the table where she'd so recently lain. "Why me?"

"I thought I told you. You were available, and I wanted to taste you."

"And that was enough?"

"Are you telling me you didn't like it?" Claire arched a knowing eyebrow.

Melissa shook her head. "But that doesn't matter."

"It should. Isn't that what sex is about? Enjoyment. Pleasure. Adventure. Wanting something that may be a tiny bit out of reach. Taking advantage of opportunities."

"I don't know. But I didn't invite you."

"You knew I wasn't Harry. You could've stopped us both at that point. But you didn't."

Melissa shook her head.

"You were thrilled with the unexpected, with the fantasy of being taken without granting permission. Weren't you?"

"But I thought you were Inez."

"Really?" Claire tilted her head to the side. "My fingers are much longer than hers, and I have long fingernails. And you had to know it wasn't her when you gripped my head, vise-like, out of fear I might leave before you came."

Silence hung between them until Melissa nodded her agreement.

Claire chuckled and stood. "So no harm done. You came like a dammed-up waterfall."

"I don't usually gush like that." Melissa blushed then scrunched her mouth. She had to know. "So how did I taste?"

Smiling broadly, Claire said, "Exactly like your aunt. I've had plenty of women, as you may have guessed, but I've never had two that tasted exactly alike—until now."

Melissa knew she must be turning crimson.

"Oh," Claire said, stifling a yawn, "in case you're wondering—this was a one-time event. I enjoyed you tremendously, but you're looking for more than robust sex. You and Harry both suffer from the same disease."

"What disease?"

"The desire for intimacy. Something I don't need or want."

Melissa watched the tall blonde rise to her feet, sashay toward the door, and let herself out. Once the door was shut, Melissa rested her head on the table. Her world was spinning.

A part of her wished she could be more like Claire, but that wasn't possible. Engaging in sex for educational purposes was one thing. Engaging in sex fueled by passion was enjoyable. But Claire was right—she needed intimacy in order to be completely fulfilled.

Was Claire right about Harry? Melissa groaned. Harry had never struck her as being particularly interested in intimacy.

But Claire had known him for a much longer time. She rolled her eyes. Claire and Aunt Phoebe had been roommates and obviously lovers. Well, at least they'd freely engaged in sex. And had, apparently with others, pushed the envelope of the sexual revolution.

What would she have done if she'd been alive then? And wasn't she still pushing that envelope—at least for herself—and apparently helping others do the same? Still, for her, something was missing.

She craved more than hot sex. Her pussy clenched. Yes, she'd enjoyed Claire. Immensely. And yes, she'd suspected she wasn't Inez almost from the beginning, but she hadn't wanted to admit that, even to herself. What was happening to her body had been too delicious to halt.

Yet she did want a relationship to go along with hot sex. Was that asking for too much?

What had Harry thought when he entered the screening room to find her chatting with Claire—and why had he been so damn late?

Standing in front of his fireplace, Harry swished Irish whiskey back and forth in the tumbler he held in his fist. He'd come directly home after seeing the debacle in the screening room. He never left work early. He had today.

"Chatting," he muttered, before swallowing more of the burning liquid. The room had reeked of sex. How dumb did they think he was? He'd seen Melissa's panties lying on the floor in the corner when he'd blindly retrieved a tape.

He swiped perspiration from his forehead. How had things gotten so out of hand? And why did any of it matter to him?

He set the glass on the mantle. It did matter. That Claire had Melissa didn't matter that much. Hell, everyone else in the Center had her one way or the other.

But it couldn't continue. He'd see to that. His shoulders slumped. Claire was no long-term threat—Melissa was hardly her type. And Inez had apparently curtailed her interest in any relationship outside of work.

But then there were the guys. When would one of them make a play for Melissa? Everyone knew now that the non-fraternization policy was no longer in effect. He could hardly go back and reinstate it. He didn't want to.

He thought back through which actors he'd had Melissa work with. There had been Brad and Inez. He hadn't put her and Warren together. Not yet. He smirked. "Too bad, Warren. You lose." Christ, he must be more than a little tipsy if he was talking to himself. That left Brad, who was probably already painfully hard, looking forward to the morning's shoot. Melissa had made it clear she was ready for a cock in her ass, and he'd scheduled Brad and her for the next morning.

Harry stalked into the kitchen and grabbed the phone.

Melissa tried to cry herself to sleep, but it wasn't working. Every time she closed her eyes, she saw Harry's distraught face when he'd entered the screening room. She winced. She hadn't realized until he and Claire had left that Harry had to have nearly stepped on her panties to get the tape he carried out of the room.

He knew. He wasn't a blind man. And the room probably smelled of her juices.

What would he do now? What should *she* do? It wasn't like they had a relationship she'd violated. An apology didn't seem in order. That would make much more out of what they had than was true, and she wasn't about to subject herself to more emotional abuse.

Claire had done no more to her in the dark than Harry had. She squeezed her eyes tighter. That wasn't entirely honest—Claire had been fun and very revealing. Harry had been more closed—and had threatened her heart.

And now she was supposed to go in tomorrow morning and give her ass to Brad. She didn't detest the man, but he did very little to turn her on.

Sighing heavily, Melissa pushed herself to a sitting position and reached for the bedside phone.

The next morning, Harry looked up from a conversation he was having with a cameraman and saw Melissa standing at the threshold of the production room getting her bearings. He didn't believe in angels, but seeing her clad only in a sheer yellow pajama top nearly made him a believer. He'd sent word to her in make up to be sure not to wear what she'd worn the week before. Viewers needed to know this was a second sequence and that some time had transpired for her to make the necessary preparations.

She jutted out her chin in that simple gesture of innocence and defiance he'd grown to admire, then stepped into the room.

Harry tightened the sash of his robe and walked over to greet her. "Brad called in sick," he informed her in a soft tone, trying not to attract the attention of the other workers in the room.

"I heard," she replied. She thinned her lips. "But the show must go on. Right?"

"Exactly. We're burning money by the hour with the camera crew. I'll be filling in for Brad." He watched her puzzle over that and was quite certain she was aware he wasn't asking permission.

"I thought you didn't work in front of the camera anymore."

"I don't," he snapped. "But I'm changing my mind. If that's okay with you."

She shrugged her shoulders. "Why not? You're the boss. One cock should be as good as another."

He grabbed her shoulders firmly and glared into her eyes, then loosened his grip and grinned. "You're not very good with the femme fatale act. Thank goodness." He glanced around the room and spoke in hushed tones. "You want me. You know you do. What was the other night about if you don't?"

The corner of his mouth turned up when she turned red at her roots. "You're sexy as hell when you blush."

She granted him a small smile of admission. "I didn't want to appear too easy, or too pleased."

"That's what I thought." His grin widened. "I lied."

He gave her plenty of time to chew on that one. He hoped she'd resume breathing soon. "I called Brad last night and told him I'd pay him twice his rate if he stayed away today."

Melissa's eyes rounded and sparkled, and then she giggled like a teenager. "Brad must be doing quite fine. I called him last night, too, and told him I'd pay him three times his rate if he'd call in sick this morning."

It was his turn to be surprised. "Good," he said, at last. His cock rapidly came to attention. "We'd better get started. Time is money."

He guided her to one of the two stools and motioned to the crew that they were ready. As soon as the cameras began recording, he turned to Melissa and said, "Let's bring our viewers up to date in real time. It's been a week since we did the first part of this tape."

She gave him a slightly embarrassed nod. "That's right," she said softly.

"And the viewers will recall that I gave you homework to do." He paused, delighted in the way the lights bounced off her misty eyes. She was ready. He had no doubt about that. "So did you complete your assignments?"

"Yes."

"You stretched yourself in the shower?"

She nodded. "At least twice a day."

"And you experimented with the butt plugs?"

"Yes. That was particularly fun."

"Ah." She was teasing him. This was good. Soon she'd forget entirely about the cameras and anyone in the room but him and her. "You were able to increase the size of plug, I assume."

"Absolutely." She grinned. "I should be able to manage anything you have in mind."

Harry coughed, clearing his throat. He might edit some of her comments later, but not now. "So would you rate this preparatory phase as mostly painful or mostly pleasurable?"

Melissa crossed and uncrossed her legs. He'd definitely have to do some editing. He didn't particularly want her flashing the audience. He didn't want them to think she was trying to seduce them—though she probably had no idea what a show she was putting on. The lust displayed on Inez and Claire's faces made it quite clear what she'd revealed.

"Much more pleasurable. The key is using plenty of lube and going slow."

"Good. Those are good reminders. So are you ready to continue learning about anal play?"

She nodded. He took her by the hand and led her to the makeshift bed while the crew removed the stools.

Melissa lowered herself to her knees and asked, "Do you want me on my back or stomach?"

"We'll start with you on your stomach." He reached for some body oil. "Remember, as you said, it's important to do these things slowly. I'm going to begin by giving you a brief massage. Hopefully, enough to loosen some muscles and relax you a bit more. Is that okay?"

She nodded, removed her pajama top and lay down with her cheek on her hands.

He could tell she was watching him out of the corner of her eye. He smiled and dribbled oil down her back. She flinched but said nothing. He smoothed the oil out across her warm skin. His breathing faltered. Who was he trying to relax?

He worked in small concentric circles across her back and down her thighs and legs. He paid no more attention to her rump than to any place else.

"How are you feeling?" he asked, leaning over to catch her eye.

"Wonderful," she sighed. "Do we have to stop?"

He grinned and moved to pool more oil at the base of her spine. He now paid undivided attention to her buttocks. He smoothed them, squeezed them, and kneaded them. He watched her carefully; she was as relaxed as she'd likely ever be.

He knelt between her spread legs and kissed first one cheek and then the other. She tensed and squirmed a bit, then quickly settled. He dipped his tongue into the crevice of her buttocks.

She squealed. "Goodness."

He smiled and used both hands to separate her butt cheeks. He slid his tongue lower, nearing her anus. She tensed beneath him. He traced its circumference with his tongue.

Melissa jerked and settled. "What . . ." She groaned. "Oh, I saw you doing this with . . ."

He pushed his tongue into her, and she stopped talking—thank goodness. He didn't need comparisons—not now. He probed as gently as he could. She seemed to relax. She was certainly opening for him, and that would make the next step much easier, but he wasn't ready to move on—not yet.

He smiled as she voluntarily rose to her knees—wanting more, requesting more. She pushed back against his tongue and groaned. He backed out to rim her edges and she pushed back further, demanding. She wanted his tongue in her, and he didn't disappoint. He bobbed his head, fucking her with his tongue until she squealed and then collapsed to the mattress.

He remained on his knees. His stiff cock poked through the folds of his robe, but he waited with patience.

Groggy from lust and embarrassment, Melissa opened her eyes. The first image she saw was a fuzzy Harry kneeling beside her. The man could move about quickly and with great stealth.

Stealth. What had just happened to her? She'd come, and neither one of them had touched her pussy or her clit. At least she didn't think they had. His tongue in her ass. How delightful. Who would've thought? She couldn't image a love act more intimate.

Intimate. Her eyes widened. Cripes, the cameras were still going, and people were standing around waiting for her. She rose to her hands and knees and looked at Harry. "I'm ready, if you are." She glanced down at his cock peeking out of his robe and smirked. "You look ready."

"I am," he assured her. "And so are you. Your asshole is gaping already. It's about the most beautiful sight I've ever seen—certainly the most seductive."

"Right. Since when have you become a man of rosy words? Do you want me like this or on my back?"

"On your back. I don't want to miss a bit of your expression." She nodded and complied with his request. She knew he didn't want the viewers to miss any of her expression, either. She shuddered and watched Harry repositioning between her legs. She blinked and made the cameras disappear. Yes, that did it. Now it was just her and Harry. She reached out to him.

He squeezed her fingers. "Let's tuck this pillow under you."

She lifted her buttocks off the mattress, then settled back against the cushion.

"Nice," he murmured. "Exquisite, really. You have two portals opening for attention."

She shook her head. "Don't take too long, Harry. I'm not sure how long I can last."

"Okay," he nodded. "We won't divert from our initial plan." He reached for the lube.

"May I?" she asked.

"Sure." He smiled almost shyly when he handed her the lube.

She sat up and leaned forward to lather his cock with thick lube, then settled back against the pillows. Harry applied more lube to her anus and winked at her. Christ, the man could wink at her while he was preparing to claim her ass.

He placed his cock at her entrance and locked his gaze on hers.

She didn't waver. She didn't flinch as he pushed inward. She knew when he met with resistance. He stopped and waited. He smiled at her. She smiled back.

"You ready?" he asked.

She nodded.

He inched in further.

She clenched. "Cripes, you're bigger than anything I've tried."

Harry stopped immediately. Concern etched his face. "Relax. Let yourself soften. It's just me. Flesh-and-blood me."

She did feel herself relax under his coaxing. "Hard flesh,"

she managed to quip.

"True," he said. "I'm not apologizing for that."

She shook her head. "Never apologize for that. I think I'm ready for more of you."

"Okay. Here's a little more. I'm over halfway."

"Halfway." She groaned. She hoisted her hips upward, and he sank all the way in. "There," she said, more than a little proud of herself and amused at the shock on his face. "I think you're in. Now what?"

"Where have you been all my life?"

She watched his words reverberate from him to her and back. He blushed profusely. She didn't know if he'd spoken loudly enough for the microphones to pick him up, but he looked like he feared they had.

"Hey, coach," she said, sticking her tongue out at him. "Aren't you supposed to fuck me now?"

"Jesus, woman." He licked his lips and said softly, "Here we go."

She hardly noticed him backing out, but she sure noticed him filling her again. Thank goodness they'd used plenty of lube. She lifted her legs for fear he would split her in two. And then a new sensation filled her—uncannily it was new, yet familiar.

Harry was using his cock to search for the core of her existence. She opened more and more to him. She watched him bite his lower lip, trying to hold back.

No way! She pounded her heels against his rump. She watched his eyes turn to the size of quarters. Her power in the moment was overwhelming. She laughed as his hips began to churn. She couldn't keep up with him.

He exploded within her. "Good God! What are you doing to me?"

She quaked beneath him. She gathered him into her arms and hugged him tight. Her climax, although powerful, didn't come close to being as poignant as it was to hold Harry in her arms. She dared not look, but she was certain his tears were covering her breast.

Through her own erotic fog, she heard Claire shooing everyone out of the room. They'd turned off the cameras. She and Harry were alone.

Harry's breathing continued ragged for some minutes. She stroked his shoulders and planted happy kisses on his head. He would come back to her—that she knew. Then what would he have to say for himself?

Was this the beginning or the end?

Melissa waited for the rest of her life.

At last with a shake of his head, Harry propped himself up on his elbows and stared at her. Disbelief still marred his face. He blinked.

"Welcome back," she whispered.

He shook his head. "You are one hell of a woman," he stammered.

"I hope that's a compliment."

"It is."

"So where do we go from here?" They both knew she wasn't talking about a video.

Harry smiled and covered her smile with his. She parted her lips and eagerly accepted his tongue. He backed away. "You have the most kissable lips."

"Sure." She pouted.

"You do. They're puffy, as if wanting to be kissed every moment."

"I'm glad you like them. Yours are pretty good, too. You didn't answer my question. What now?"

"What about lunch?"

"What?"

"Lunch. You know, go out to a restaurant—do you like Chinese?"

"I'd love it. That's it! You're ready to go out and get to know me"—she cocked her head to the side—"to have an actual relationship with me?"

"Sounds like."

"What an admission." She narrowed her eyes at him. "Then what?"

He shrugged. "We might come back to work, or we might go to your place or mine and get to know each other even better."

"Oh."

"If that's okay with you?"

"No more faceless dark rooms."

He shook his head.

"I will miss that." She snickered.

"Me, too."

He kissed her again.

She broke the kiss and scowled at him. "Harry, if we're going to pursue this unusual relationship of ours, the first thing you may need to do is pull out of my ass."

"Oh," he said, grimacing. "I forgot. I hope that hasn't been too uncomfortable for you."

"Not a bit. Easy. Goodness," she said, grabbing a tissue to wipe herself, "you made a full deposit."

He shook his head rather sheepishly. "I guess it was fairly obvious I didn't leave anything behind."

She chuckled. "Oh, I'd say you left everything behind. You may want to do some extra editing on that video." She rose to her feet and grabbed her pajama top. Not bothering to put it on, she shot him a look over her shoulder and was pleased to see his admiring gaze. "I'm going to take a shower. I'll be ready in less than twenty minutes. I like my Chinese hot."

Harry waved and nodded. "Why doesn't that surprise me? I'll be waiting."

Chapter Nine

Melissa awoke early Saturday morning. She yawned and smiled at the very masculine body lying beside her. She tucked her legs over the edge of her bed, careful not to disturb Harry. She grabbed his shirt, shrugged it on and made her way toward her kitchen.

Humming softly, Melissa started the morning coffee.

She buttoned a couple buttons of Harry's shirt to ward off the early morning chill. Life was good. She pinched herself. Could her life really be this good? Could it last?

Don't worry about lasting, girl. For once in your life, enjoy the moment.

What a series of moments. Like many new lovers, she imagined, she and Harry had hardly been separated these last four days. She'd been to his place and he to hers. She let her gaze roam her kitchen as she poured a steaming cup of coffee. Soon she'd have to cook for him. She was a fairly good cook, but she didn't have much experience cooking for two.

They'd gone to restaurants and they'd ordered in. Food took secondary importance when what they most enjoyed nibbling on was each other.

Melissa carried her coffee into her makeshift studio. Harry wouldn't stir for some time. She was too keyed up to sleep much. Harry seemed to manage in that department quite well.

She placed a clean canvas on the easel and chuckled. Harry managed quite well in a number of departments. She wiggled her bottom and eyed her brushes and paints.

"Ah," she muttered when a particular color caught her eye. She opened the paint, dipped her brush and spread it across the canvas. She stood back and studied it. The light yellow shade was similar to the pajama top she'd worn briefly Tuesday morning. She smiled. It fit her mood quite nicely.

She swirled the paint freely with broad strokes until the entire canvas had a yellow tint. Next, she selected a pastel orange. Her hand moved fluidly, leaving behind curving lines and large ovals. She added pink—again with flowing lines with no plan or sense of direction. She didn't often paint this freely; she loved the feeling. She heard Harry at the doorway clearing his throat. She peeked over her shoulder at him and smiled warmly. He held a cup of coffee in his hand and lifted it in salute.

"Are you one of those artists who requires absolute privacy when she works?"

"Not at all. Come in. Good morning. I'm just playing with paint combos to see what happens." She redirected her attention to the canvas and splashed a pale violet on it. The result caused her to smile. Was she creating a painter's palette?

Harry came to stand behind her and wrapped his arms around her waist. The hardness under his robe grazed her rump, and she turned her head to kiss him. He cupped her breasts and gave them a good-morning squeeze.

"They've missed you," she murmured.

He chuckled in her ear. "They were missing when I woke up. Someone had taken them away." He nibbled on her ear, and she turned to mush. "Thanks for making the coffee. And I am pleased you're an artist who likes company. I don't think I could stand being away from you for long. The bed was cold and empty without you."

Melissa put her brush down, quickly cleaned it, and turned in his arms. "Are you saying we should return to bed?"

"I'm saying you are sexy as hell standing there in my shirt.

I may never wash it again."

"Yuck." She giggled. "It does provide enough warmth." She unfastened the only two buttons she'd bothered to fasten. "And it doesn't cover too much up."

He shook his head and lowered his lips to cover a rapidly growing nipple. She held onto his shoulders to steady herself. She gasped when he lifted her off her feet, cradled her in his arms, and headed for the door. "What are you doing?"

"Going back to bed," he said, while still trying to lick a breast.

"Our coffee?"

"Later."

"Oh, all right," she teased, reaching into his robe for his cock. "Sometimes this guy doesn't have a lot of patience."

"Like right now," he huffed, lengthening his strides and turning so she wouldn't bang into the bedroom doorjamb.

He dropped her on the bed, tossed his robe aside, skimmed his cock, and grinned mischievously. He climbed onto the bed, knelt beside her, and again used his tongue to lave her breast.

She arched into him and cradled his cock in her palm. "So are you my hefty caveman this morning?"

He peeked at her. "I'm whatever you want me to be." He slid a hand down her belly until he covered her mound.

She bucked against his pressure. "I want you to be my lover."

He gave her a broad smile, separated her thighs and moved to kneel between them. "I think I'm up for that."

"You look more than up," she quipped, eyeing his meandering shaft. "He looks lost."

Harry leaned over and pressed a finger against her mouth.

Keeping her gaze on his, she sucked on his finger, wetting it all over.

He removed it and lowered it to her pussy. "From one

mouth to another," he said, softly. Grinning, he pushed his finger inside her.

She closed her eyes, moaned softly, then quickly opened them. His eyes twinkled. A second finger followed. She gasped and reached for his cock. He was out of reach. "Go ahead," she said. "I'm ready. He needs to find his home. We've got the entire weekend for slow." She tilted her hips slightly.

He nodded, brushing the back of his hand against her wetness. "You're more than ready. You could hardly be more lubricated. And you're right," he said, encircling his cock, "he's developing quite a relationship with your pussy and needs to tell her good morning."

Melissa smiled. "That's lovely, Harry. Now, a little less talk. Let's let the lovers mate." She squirmed to accent her words.

"You are so damn tempting," he said, tucking his shaft into her folds. He entered slowly, as if not to disturb.

Once he was finally in and settled, she whispered into his ear. "Good morning. Pussy wants to know if Mr. Cock has something to give her this early in the morning."

"You're not going to let him tarry a bit, are you?" He kissed her and then settled back on his knees.

She shook her head and pulled on her nipples. His cock leaped inside her.

"So be it," he grunted. He shoved his hands under her rump and lifted her off the mattress, then began pumping into her as if there was no weekend at all. There was only this moment.

"So powerful," she said, not stretching the truth. The way he held her, she couldn't do a lot with her lower body, but she still had her hands free and her mouth.

His eyes were wide open. Even though fixed on hers, they didn't seem to be seeing anything. "Come to me, Harry. Slam me harder." Her words must have detonated something inside him, for Harry roared and plunged into her, lifting her body off the mattress and shoving her another six inches toward the headboard.

"That's it," she squealed. "Use all of your strength. Don't hold anything back." She gulped for air. "I've never felt you deeper."

Harry turned beet-red. His breathing, if she could call it that, had turned ragged. His face contorted.

"Come for me, Harry. I'm waiting." She reached down to her clitoris and slid her fingers along its protective covering. "Peek down at my clit. She's no longer in hiding; she's standing up urging you on, seeking her pleasure."

She saw him glance down at their joining, and he immediately began to convulse. She started to giggle, then erupted in full-blown laughter. He was spilling into her, she was laughing, and she came around him.

He shook and continued thrusting long after he must have been finished, but she made no effort to stop him. She'd never known a man who lost control like Harry could when he came. Was it just him? Maybe she had something to do with that.

She reclined back onto the pillows and waited for him. His eyes opened, and he blew air through tightly held lips. Then his features softened. He pulled out of her and crawled up next to her. She hugged him and he hugged her. How could this get any better? And they still had the entire weekend before facing fellow coworkers.

Harry nibbled on her ear and traced the length of her jaw line with his tongue. He kissed her gently. She luxuriated in the joining of their lips and deepened the kiss.

He pulled away with a sparkle in his eye. "Sometime I may have to fuck you with tape over your mouth just to find out how long I can last with you."

She laughed and shook her head. "You know you like it when I tell you how powerful and big you are, or how completely you're filling me." She batted her eyelashes at him. "And I adore it when you lose control inside me." She reached between them and squeezed his limp penis. "And even if you don't, your cock does. By the way, Ms. Pussy really appreciated what Mr. Cock gave her this morning. He's welcome back in anytime."

"Later," Harry said, struggling to sit up. "Let's go get something to eat. If I'm going to keep up with you, I have to take care of myself."

"Sorry I'm so taxing," Melissa said, sliding out of bed.

"Don't get me wrong," Harry said, walking toward the bathroom. "I'm not complaining."

Melissa didn't try to hide a smile. "I hoped you weren't."

Sunday afternoon, Melissa swung their clasped hands back and forth as they strolled through the Brooklyn Botanical Gardens. While this had been one of her favorite places for years, walking side by side with a lover made it even better. Periodically, they stopped and stole kisses. It wasn't a huge thing. But it felt so much better stealing kisses than standing around watching other couples kiss.

Harry guided her to a bench, where they sat and watched walkers, tourists, and flower aficionados go by. No one paid any heed to them. They were alone in a crowd of people. She laughed, remembering Inez's fantasy. She shook her head.

"What's so funny?" Harry asked, putting an arm around her, tugging her close.

"Nothing. My mind just wandered." She turned and smiled at him. "It is so much more fun being here with you than coming here alone."

He nodded. "This is nice place. I could get used to it.

Funny, there are some pleasurable attractions outside of Manhattan."

She elbowed him in the ribs. "The sun doesn't rise and fall in Manhattan."

"Really? Some people think so."

"So much for some people. This is a special place."

He held up his hands in surrender. "I agree, but then we do have Central Park."

She nodded, looking down at their clasped hands. "I love Central Park, too. But . . .but I don't like it when people put down Brooklyn. This place is so alive, so diverse—it pulsates. And it doesn't deserve snobbish rebukes."

"Wow!" Harry said, taking his arm from around her. "Are you calling me a snob?" He scowled. "I doubt anyone has ever accused me of being a snob—many things, but not a snob."

"I didn't mean it that way." Melissa paused. "Are we having our first fight? Not you. But there are plenty of snobs out there, you know. Sometimes they make me feel inferior, and other times I get so infuriated."

"Like now." He covered her hands with his. "You're right, there are a lot of snobs. I'm sorry they make you feel inferior, but you are so sexy when you get infuriated. And this may be our first fight." He gave her a crooked grin. "Just so it's not our last, because making up can be lots of fun."

She let him kiss her before she said, "That does have some promise." She pecked at his lips and leaned back from him. "So was that you I was chasing up the hill last Sunday?"

She gave him credit for not getting up and stalking away, but he didn't have to laugh so hard.

"Let me see," he said, thoughtfully. "I seem to remember by last Sunday evening you were convinced you'd seen me earlier that day. So it was here, you say?"

She nodded. "On that rise. Why won't you tell me?"

He ran a finger down her nose. She wanted to bite it off.

"Why is it so important for you to know?"

"Maybe I don't want to think I'm going crazy," she huffed, "imagining guys following me who weren't even there."

He lifted her chin and brushed his lips across hers. "Is this our second fight? We'll have a lot of making up to do."

She tried not to tear up. She tried as hard as she could. She failed miserably.

Harry sighed. "Maybe I don't want you to think I was so infatuated with you that I'd follow you."

She smiled and swiped at her eyes. "I knew you weren't stalking me. You didn't scare me. I only wanted to invite you to join me for coffee at the plaza."

"I'm glad. I never want to scare you. Only coffee?"

"So. Why did you follow me?" She held her breath. "Please, don't lie to me."

He shook his head. "I'll try not to. Okay, you win. I made several trips to your beloved Brooklyn in the last couple weeks, but that was the only one you noticed."

"Several? But why?"

"Shh." He placed a finger across her lips. "You have a tendency to talk a lot when you're nervous—or when you're fully aroused. Maybe we should conduct a study on the relationship between anxiety and arousal."

"Harry!"

"Right. I wanted to learn more about you. You intrigued me. I didn't seek you out that first Monday in the screening room. I came in looking for a tape and found you screening one. What happened between us that day just happened."

"I'm glad it did," Melissa said, interlacing her fingers with his. "But that wasn't enough?"

"Hardly. And I watched you with Inez and with Brad, and then with Max."

"Were you jealous?"

"Not then. But I couldn't get enough of watching you. You

are so expressive, particularly when excited. And I was certain it was real, not put on. I wanted to know more about that."

"So you had your research hat on when you thought about me?"

"You've got to be kidding." Harry laughed. "Unless you can imagine me hanging my hat on my cock."

She shook her head and tried not to follow that line of thought too far.

"No, you have a mystery about you that I've seldom encountered. Sometimes in our line of work, we can become too jaded about sex. Oh, it can remain quite pleasurable, but there's a quality that goes missing. Maybe it's spontaneity. Maybe it's merely innocence."

"Maybe it's intimacy?" she said softly.

"Maybe." He eyed her cautiously. "You may be right."

"You ready to walk some more?"

"Sure." Harry helped her to her feet and kept an arm around her waist as they continued walking through the gardens.

They hadn't gone far before Melissa asked, "So what did you learn about me by following me?"

Harry pulled her hip tighter against his. "Not much. Not nearly enough. Let's see. You like flowers. You seem to like to watch people—either here in the gardens or from a bench near your apartment, or from your upstairs window."

She stopped their progress to stare at him. "You mean you watched me at my window and I didn't see you?"

He shrugged. "I can be fairly deceptive when I want to be."

"I guess." She started walking and he matched her stride. "Tell me more."

"You seem to like routines. I found that fascinating, since I've seen you be so spontaneous, almost inviting adventure."

"Maybe a person can be adventurous and still have

routines."

"Apparently."

"What routines?"

"You really don't want to let this go, do you?"

"Why should I? You were the one following me. What routines?"

"You're generally up by six thirty. You're in bed by eleven o'clock, at the latest. Some nights the bedroom light comes on at nine thirty or so. I couldn't tell if you were reading or playing with your butt plugs and vibrators."

She giggled. "Sometimes I'd read a book with a plug in my butt. I didn't want to miss preparation opportunities, but I couldn't focus on the damn plug all the time, either."

"Whatever you did worked exceptionally well."

She squeezed his fingers. "I'm glad you think so. So where were you? Listing my routines?"

He shrugged. "That's about it. You generally went to bed alone. Even Inez seems out of the picture."

He waited for her to nod.

"Doesn't look like there's a guy in your life."

She tipped her chin up at him and smiled. "There is now."

"Oh, I'd suggest when you want to parade around nude after dark, you should pull the drapes as well as the shades. The shades offer a stunning silhouette I appreciated very much, but I'm not certain you'd want others to share the same view."

Melissa halted and furrowed her brow. "Did you see anyone else watching my window?"

"Never. If I had, they wouldn't be watching any more. But nope, I never did."

"Damn. I thought the shades prevented anyone from seeing in."

He shrugged. "It wasn't like watching you in the flesh, but it was damn erotic. You remember when you were a kid and played with a flashlight and made bunny ears appear on a wall or a white surface?"

"Sure. You did that, too?"

"Uh huh. Only I outgrew that. I must say your silhouette was a hell of a lot more intoxicating than any bunny ears I ever saw."

"Great!"

This time Harry pulled her to a halt. "Come on, Melissa. Let's get back to the privacy of your apartment. I don't want to do anything dumb and take you behind the bushes. Knowing you as little as I do, I'm not sure you wouldn't begin screaming to passersby about your approaching orgasms."

She didn't hesitate. She stood on her toes and kissed him. "Does just thinking about me standing in front of the window turn you on?"

He ground his crotch into hers.

"I guess it does! We'd better hurry. I wouldn't want to embarrass you in front of all these folks."

She headed for the exit. "Too bad they lock the gates at night. Wouldn't it be fun to make love on that knoll you were standing on last Sunday?"

He didn't bother to answer.

"Or maybe," she continued, "we could find a golf course and make love on a green. Doesn't that sound like an adventure?"

"Are you trying to talk me into coming in my pants? Save the golf course idea for Claire. She may consider it for her fantasy tape. Now," he said, lengthening his stride, "if you don't mind, please keep your mouth shut until we get inside your apartment."

"Okay," she peeped, covering her mouth quickly when he glowered down at her.

Melissa sat comfortably on the stool next to Harry. Even this was easier. They'd been talking to the camera for several minutes already, and she'd engaged smoothly with his banter. She had no idea how much of their interplay would eventually make it through the final edits, but she was actually looking forward to seeing it.

She smoothed out her long flowing pink gown. The focus was on Harry more than on her this time, for they would demonstrate how to pleasure a man anally. He'd been very strict throughout the week for her not to tease his anus. He wanted to save that for the tape.

"So you see, or at least you will see," Harry said, wrapping up part of his introduction, "anal play is for men as well as for women." He paused and turned to her. "So, Melissa, let's make it clear to the viewers that we've not tried any of this before."

She tilted her head to the side. "You're not suggesting you have a virgin ass?"

"Of course not." Harry laughed easily. "I mean you and I haven't rehearsed what we're about to do."

"That's correct."

"Have you engaged in anal play with other men?"

She blushed slightly. "Just once, and very briefly at that."

"That's fine." He gave her a look of encouragement. "I trust you'll be gentle with me."

"Of course I will. I trusted you, didn't I?"

"Yes." Harry looked directly at the camera. "We can't emphasize enough the importance of trust when experimenting with any form of sex, and certainly with anal sex." Harry looked over at Claire. "We may want to move this section up front when we're editing."

Claire nodded her approval.

"I guess I only have a couple more words, especially for the guys, before we move to demonstrate. First, don't hesitate to tell your partner if something hurts or feels wrong. Many ancient cultures and some today believe routine massaging of the prostate gland is good for the male's health. Some believe anal penetration is also good for a woman's health. But that doesn't mean you have to lie there and grit your teeth while your partner is improving your health."

Melissa covered a giggle.

"You think that's funny?"

She shook her head.

"Good," he teased. "I was beginning to rethink trust."

"I don't want to hurt you," she said softly.

"I know you don't." He reached over and squeezed her hand. "I know you won't."

"Last thing, guys." Harry's face took on a stern countenance. "For any macho guy who may be watching who is only interested in jamming your cock in a woman's asshole, you might want to try this first. Then you may have earned the right to ask. Slow and easy."

He scowled at Claire. "We'll probably have to excise some of that. Maybe I can do it in a voiceover later." He looked apologetically at Melissa. "It's just that some of what passes for anal sex on some of the instructional tapes we get our hands on must be made by numbskulls who never had anything up their ass but stupidity."

"Hey, Harry," Melissa said, "you're not one of those guys. And I'm not like that either. Maybe we should stop talking and do some doing."

He nodded, took her hand to help her off the stool, and led her to the bed that had been arranged for them. He shucked his robe, but she left her gown on. It was quite transparent, and she'd been told it would add to the eroticism of the scene.

Harry lay on his back and smiled at her. She knew exactly what he was doing. He was blocking out the cameras and the others in the room. He nodded at her, and she knelt between his legs. She idly stroked his cock with no intention other than being in contact with him.

"Feels great," he whispered. "Here's the lube," he said aloud. She took it from him and spread it over her index finger. She watched him carefully when she brought her finger to bear on his anus. He clenched, then relaxed. She spread lube around the dark opening, retrieved more lube, and repeated her first maneuver.

He nodded, signaling she'd applied enough lube.

She smiled at him. "Here we go," she murmured, easing her finger into his anus. She hadn't gone far before meeting with resistance. She stopped.

He gave her a reassuring smile. "Now," he said softly. "I'm opening for you, girl. Come on in."

She pushed her finger forward and gasped at how easily it went as far as she could reach. She didn't need any more instruction. She probed and explored, keying her movements to Harry's moans. "That's it?" she asked, smiling.

"Oh, yeah. You found the prostate. Be very gentle at first. Stroke it like you were stroking your clit. That's right, easy." She watched Harry open his mouth, but no words came forth.

He blinked. She stroked his cock.

"No," he muttered, "not yet. Withdraw, please."

"But . . ."

"Melissa."

She nodded and slowly removed her finger. She'd thought she was expected to bring him off.

He turned his head toward a camera. "Now, guys, I don't know how closely you were watching, but you just saw a guy have an orgasm without ejaculating." He smiled wanly. "And you thought only women were capable of multiple orgasms."

He looked back at her and winked. "Now you can bring me off. Why don't we demonstrate a variation with a vibrator? Grab the blue one."

She reached for the vibrator he pointed at. "You can't take something this big."

"Can't you?"

"Yes, but . . ."

"So can I. And if I couldn't, I hope I wouldn't expect you to take my cock in your ass. Now, get on with it, girl. This will be fun. You'll see. Plenty of lube."

"Okay." She shook her head, lathered the vibrator with lube and placed more at his anal entrance. "Ready?"

"Yep. This time don't ignore my cock."

She nodded and slipped the vibrator into him. Harry held up his palm after he'd taken about two inches. "It gets fatter as we go," he said. "Give me time to open. But you might want to do whatever comes naturally."

She grinned broadly and leaned over to take his cock in her mouth. This was something she knew how to do. She loved the feel of his cock scraping the roof of her mouth and the back of her throat.

"Don't get carried away with that," Harry warned. "Not yet, anyway. Okay, try the vibrator."

Without dropping him from her mouth, she watched him carefully and pressed the vibrator forward. There was resistance, but much less than before.

"Okay," he said at last. Harry wet his lips. "Turn it on. Slow." She had to leave his cock momentarily to see what she was doing. She heard the familiar hum and watched Harry's smile split his face.

"Christ," he said. "I forgot how good this is. Have your way with my cock, lady. Enjoy. I sure as hell am."

She settled her mouth over him and just as quickly jerked her head upward. "Wow, I can feel you vibrating in my throat."

Harry laughed. "I didn't want to tell you in advance. I wanted to see that look of amazement on your face. You never disappoint." He took a deep breath and let it out slowly. "Now go for it."

And she did. She traveled up and down the length of his shaft, marveling at the new sensations vibrating from his butt through his cock to her mouth. She experimented with the vibrator, twisting it carefully, ever mindful of Harry's cues. She pulled it partway out and eased it back in. Harry nodded his approval.

"A little faster," Harry urged.

She quickened the pace of her hand and her mouth, matching them stroke for stroke.

"Holy shit, woman. I'm coming."

She tried not to chuckle. He didn't have to announce that fact—she'd felt him building for some moments. His sperm was spurting, coating her throat. She watched him with care. He motioned her to stop, and she did. She dropped him from her mouth and wiped her lips with the back of her hand.

"Turn the vibrator off and take it out very slowly. That's it, babe. Come on up here and give me a hug."

She settled easily into his arms.

Harry cocked his head to the side and said to the crew, "She's a real trooper, isn't she?"

Melissa felt herself blushing to the roots of her hair when those gathered in the room began to applaud. She tucked her head against Harry's chest and waited for their audience to file out. Once they were gone, she'd tell him a thing or two about embarrassing her in front of them.

She never had the chance. By the time they were alone, Harry was snoring softly. She smiled. It surprised her that giving anal stimulation was as satisfying as receiving it. Maybe now that the taping was finished, she and Harry could incorporate it into their more regular lovemaking. Damn if she'd ever call their lovemaking *routine.*

Later that afternoon, Harry caught himself humming a tune while looking over Claire's memo about possible fantasy topics. He pulled himself up short. He never hummed. Not even at home.

He leaned back in his swivel chair. He smiled. Melissa had so eagerly embraced her morning assignment. His ass still tingled from her thorough exploration. He was looking forward to reviewing that scene. They certainly had enough material to choose from. He glanced back at the list of possible fantasies in the memo.

He shook his head. Melissa's golf course/park idea was on the list. She'd jump out of her skin before having sex in a public place. Wouldn't she?

She was turning out to be quite unpredictable. He'd keep the uncut version of any tape he made with her. At least when she grew tired of him, he'd have his tapes. He chuckled. Not many guys could boast of having tapes of themselves making love with their former lovers. Most guys were probably quite happy not having them. Most probably tried to blot out the memories of love gone sour. He shrugged. He wasn't most guys.

He looked up as the door opened after an obligatory knock. "Don't look so crestfallen," Claire said. "It's only me."

"Come in," he responded. "I was just looking over your fantasy memo."

"It's a wonder your eyes can focus at all after this morning's backdoor session."

He held her steady gaze but chose not to rise to her bait.

"So what plans do you have for her?"

"Plans?" He scowled. "Isn't it rather early to think about plans? We've only been seeing each other for a week."

Claire chuckled loudly and sat down in a chair across from his desk. She hoisted a leg over a knee. "I guess I know where your head is. That's not what I meant. What is your plan for Melissa here at the Center now that the two of you are such a hot item?"

"Oh."

"Right. Doesn't look like you've given that much thought. Or maybe you're trying to dodge the effects of getting involved with one of our staff."

He gave Claire a hard stare.

She held up her hands. "I didn't say it was wrong. But it may have some implications that we'd better come to grips with before we have wounds festering."

"Such as?" Harry steepled his fingers and waited. He was fairly certain he knew what she was getting at, but he'd learned the hard way to exercise considerable patience and extreme caution. She would take as much as he was willing to give and then some.

"For example. Are you going stand by and watch Brad or Warren fuck your woman?"

He snarled. His nostrils flared. "Hell, no!"

Claire smirked. "I thought as much. Does she know about this change in her duties?"

He shook his head.

"What do we do with Brad? You teamed him up with Melissa. There's not a lot of work to go around. Do we hire another girl?"

"No. Melissa needs this job."

"Uh huh." She glanced at her long fingernails. "Maybe Brad doesn't."

"Damn," he snapped. "You can be a bitch when you want to be."

Claire narrowed her eyes. "Flattery won't get you far with me, Harry. And you know it."

"Okay. Okay." He ran his fingers through his hair. This was going to be more complicated than he'd expected. "Can we train Brad to do some of the other tasks around here?"

"Can you imagine Brad Jefferson interviewing people, cataloguing fan mail, or generating creative ideas for future tapes?"

Harry shook his head. "Brad doesn't have a creative bone in his body. He's nice enough, but he has a hard time listening when I'm telling him where I want him to put his cock. He won't make a very good interviewer. Maybe we could hire another girl part-time."

"That's an option." Claire sighed. "Who knows how long we'll need her?"

"And what do you mean by that?"

"I was thinking along the lines you first thought I asked about. If you and Melissa turn serious on us, it's doubtful that either one of you will want to work in front of the cameras again."

He shrugged. "You may be right about that. But serious, if it were to happen, can be a long ways off."

"Perhaps. And then of course if one of you tires of the other, then will one of you leave, or will we be back where we started, with you off camera and Melissa taking on all comers?"

"I suppose you're right," he grumbled. "But that likely won't happen soon either. I think we should advertise for a part-time position."

"Okay. Just let me clarify one thing with you. You don't mind Melissa working with the women."

He shrugged. "She can if she wants to. We can't afford to keep her on payroll if she doesn't work with production."

Claire smiled. "Plus she's one of the very best performers we've had come through these doors in years."

Harry suppressed his pride as best he could. "So you've noticed."

"I'm not blind. She's curious, inventive, spontaneous, and

willing. What more could we ask for?"

Intimacy. "Nothing."

"Then we'll work around your current situation with her until that clarifies in some way or another." Claire paused and eyed him curiously. "I do wish you well with her, Harry. Maybe this is the one you've been looking for."

His eyes glazed over.

Claire stood. "Be careful. I don't want to see Melissa hurt, but neither do I want to see you hurt."

"Since when have you become so compassionate? Next thing I know you'll want to set up a three-way with us."

"That's not even funny." Claire plopped back down in the chair. "But that reminds me. I've been going over our viewer and subscriber surveys, as I'm sure you have."

"Certainly."

"They want more edgy stuff, Harry. This anal tape is going to be a neat contribution. I think you're really onto something by setting up little personal interview questions with Melissa. Her innocence comes through very credibly. But our fans are asking questions about soft S&M—not my cup of tea—but feathers, spanking, teasing. They want help with three-ways." Her lips curved up. "The guys are interested in two women and a guy. The women seem fairly evenly split between that combination and two guys and a girl."

"I saw all of that."

"So what are we going to do about it? Let me be clear, Harry. We need you and Melissa in front of the camera to pull much of this off. At least until we can find replacements that bring some of the same qualities the two of you project.

"I wasn't convinced this was the right way to go until I saw the two of you work together. I don't care if you are lovers outside the Center or not—you work incredibly well together before the cameras. That sells. That helps our viewers. That keeps the Center in business."

"So what are you asking, Claire?"

"Can you imagine Brad, Warren and Inez in a three-way? It'd look like a porn movie made in hell."

Harry didn't hold back a smile.

"You two are classy. There's a spark, a something that takes this work beyond pure mechanical instruction and doesn't sink it into badly acted porn."

Harry nodded. "So you want us to work with a third person."

"That's right. Maybe with Inez, or our new hire if you don't want to work with Inez."

"I'll have to think about that."

"Clearly, you won't work with Brad or Warren."

"Absolutely not," he huffed. "Out of the question. I don't think Melissa would want that either."

"I suspect you're right." Claire pursed her lips. "What about Max?"

"Max?" He scowled at his desk, avoiding Claire's stare as long as he could. She'd trapped him good this time. He had too many competing interests. Melissa. Himself. And the Center. Always the Center. Without the Center, none of them would have anything remotely like what they had now. "Melissa seemed to enjoy working with Max," he said, nodding. "Max knows how to please a woman without getting in the way. That's possible. Damn." He shook his head at Claire. "I could've sat here for days and not come up with that possibility. Of course, Max might not be willing."

"You're kidding. Max would jump at being involved with the Center in any way possible. I think he has a soft spot for Melissa, and I know he respects you greatly. He'll do it, if we ask him."

"I'll think about it. What about these fantasy ideas?" A change of subject seemed more than timely.

"I'm not sure whether you're dodging or hedging."

"Does it matter? And what about you? Are you willing to go on camera? Maybe help Inez fine tune her S&M skills?"

Claire shook her head vigorously. "I don't work in front of the camera. I seldom did. Only Phoebe could convince me to do that, and then rarely. No way."

"So I can come out of retirement, but you can't."

Claire crossed her legs. "You're already out of retirement. I didn't bring you out. Melissa did, or shall we say, your possessive hots did."

He gave her a questioning look.

"You didn't think Brad wouldn't be in here telling everyone the next morning that you each called him and paid him handsomely to stay away from that initial anal shoot?"

"I should fire the bastard."

"For doing what you asked him?"

"No, for squealing on me. I told him to keep his mouth shut about it."

"Did you really think you could keep his mouth shut?"

"I probably didn't consider that long enough."

Again Claire stood. She checked her watch. "I've got a call coming in from a prospective supplier in ten minutes. We'll have to talk about the fantasies later. I think I've given you enough to chew on for now." She waved and headed out the door.

Harry shuddered when the door closed. What would Melissa think about a three-way? Shit. What did *he* think about it? He hadn't done that in years. But Claire was right about one thing. Inez, Brad, and Warren would make it look like an old-time porn film. And that wasn't what the Center was about.

Chapter Ten

Melissa rotated her neck from side to side and snuggled down into her thick white robe. She sat on Harry's couch and studied him while he sat in an easy chair reading the Sunday Times. The splattering of raindrops on his floor-to-ceiling living room windows only added to the coziness of the morning.

They'd slept in—an unusual occurrence, especially for her. She'd made coffee and scrambled some eggs with bacon. And then they'd come to his living room. She loved its airiness and high ceilings. And the view looking over Central Park could be spectacular—though this morning it remained a blurry gray. They were hidden from view as if behind a veil. That, too, contributed to her sense that all was right with her world.

She sighed. They hadn't even made love yet. She realized some women might feel insecure about that, but she felt it was a signal that she and Harry were moving on to a slightly different plateau where sex would remain vital, but was making way for an even deeper relationship.

But what about Harry? She frowned. Would she ever be certain about Harry? He seemed so open, yet there remained a hidden quality about him.

She winced. It was so easy to forget that she was hiding, too. She'd tried to tell him that Phoebe was her aunt. Twice. Each time he'd done something to stop her. She shook her head. She'd allowed herself to be diverted. It wasn't like the relationship ought to be a secret—if Harry ever asked, she wouldn't try to deny it.

She massaged her bare throat. She hadn't worn the gold pendant since that day with Claire. She couldn't remember for sure, but she thought she'd only worn it once or twice before that. Harry had never reacted to it, but then he might not have even seen it.

What would he do if he found out Phoebe was her aunt? *When* he found out. It was inevitable. Wasn't it?

Would he leave her because she *wasn't* Phoebe? Had he been attracted to her only because of the resemblances Claire had pointed out? She realized there was a family resemblance, but she'd never thought about the two of them having similar traits. She might have to pursue that topic further with Claire. She hadn't exactly been thinking clearly that afternoon. There had been Claire the lover, then Claire the revealer. And once they'd focused on the pendant, her mind had gone totally into overdrive.

Melissa inhaled sharply as she gazed at Harry, reading the paper so comfortably. It was hard to imagine a good outcome when he discovered her complete identity. But he had to. At some point, she'd have to know whether he was falling in love with her, or with the embodiment of her aunt.

She squirmed in her robe. Neither of them was ready to risk using that word, but she could feel it in his fingertips and on his lips. She trusted he could feel it through hers, also.

Maybe if she could get him talking about Phoebe, there would be a natural opening for her to explain her relationship with her aunt.

She sipped her coffee before plunging forward. "Harry," she said softly.

"Yes," he replied, setting aside his paper and smiling at her. "You look so sexy over there with your feet tucked under you. Sometimes I think you're a vision. Sometimes I wonder why I'm so lucky to have you with me."

"My, you are romantic this morning. Maybe we should put

off lovemaking more mornings."

Harry shrugged. "I'm only telling you what I'm seeing, what I'm feeling."

She nodded at him. Since he was into expressing his feelings this morning, would he talk about Phoebe? "Tell me about her."

He frowned. "About her? About whom?"

Melissa sat up straighter. At least she had his attention. "About the woman in the tapes."

"There've been many women."

She narrowed her eyes. "You know the one I mean. The one on the tapes when you came to the screening room. Claire told me you were lovers."

"She should keep her mouth shut."

"I didn't have to hear it from her. It was obvious you and she were more than performers on tape. You were lovers. That's fine. I've had a few before you. But I want to know more about her."

"Why?" he grunted.

"Because she intrigues me. The two of you working together created something special. You had a chemistry I'd like to know more about, if you're willing to talk about her."

He shrugged his shoulders and caved in to her request. "There's not a lot to say. When I first came to the Center, I was a grad student working on my dissertation. The Center library proved helpful, and I met Mr. Howard, the founder, and of course Phoebe and Claire.

"Phoebe noticed my work." His eyes took on a dreamy quality. "I couldn't believe she'd take my work seriously. She was the living image of what I thought a woman ought to be like. She was attractive, completely independent, fun loving—and she took an interest in me, for God's sake. It was like having one of the centerfold models from my teens come down from my wall to say *Hi, how are you doing? I've been waiting for you to grow up and really see me as a woman.*"

"Wow," Melissa murmured. "She was older than you."

"Oh, yeah. Some twenty years or so, but that didn't matter to me."

"But it did to her."

His jaw jutted forward. "Apparently."

"So she seduced you."

He nodded. "I would never have taken the first step. She knew that." He cocked his head to the side as if startled by his own discovery. "Our first time took place in the screening room."

"Oh, my god," Melissa muttered, remembering her first time with Harry. "Was the room dark?"

Harry chuckled lightly. "No, the lights were on."

Melissa started to breathe again.

"It was rather straightforward, actually, now that I think about it. I was working at the table when Phoebe came in and locked the door behind her. She stripped and told me she'd waited long enough. She never questioned whether I was willing. Not that she had to."

"What happened next?"

"I was paralyzed. She smiled, walked up to me, and started unbuttoning my shirt. She had my cock in her mouth before I had my shirt off. At some point, she climbed onto the table, and I followed her. Our first time was on top of the screening room table."

"Cripes. The same table that's there today?"

"Sure. What's so special about that?"

"Nothing. So you were lovers—you and Phoebe. What happened? Given the tapes I've seen, this must have gone on for some time. Why did it end?"

Harry rose to his feet. "I hope this is important. I don't particularly like dredging all of this up."

"I appreciate that, but I want to know about her. What you and she had was extremely rare. That's so clear on the tapes."

Harry leaned over, kissed her on the forehead, took her empty coffee cup, and headed for the kitchen. She waited, not trusting herself to stand. Cripes, her aunt had fucked Harry on the same table. *Damn.*

Returning, Harry handed her a fresh cup of coffee. She appreciated its warmth. He sat back down in the easy chair, sipped his coffee, and remained silent. Melissa wasn't sure it was safe to prod him anymore.

"You're right. What Phoebe and I had was rare." He let his gaze rove over her and gave her a soft grin. "And what you and I have is rare, but different."

"How so?"

"This is going to sound crazy . . ."

"Try me."

"Phoebe and I never had sex outside the Center."

"What?" Melissa steadied her coffee cup to keep from spilling any on her robe.

"Phoebe was an incredible person, but she was also pure oddity. She and Claire prided themselves on being forerunners of the so-called sexual revolution. Phoebe wasn't into courting, romance, marriage, kids—none of that for our avant-garde Phoebe."

"Do I detect some bitterness?"

"What do you think? I was infatuated with the woman-goddess. We'd go out to eat on occasion, but only to talk business. She wasn't into talking about her childhood or family, or about romantic dreams, or about us. She was dynamite in bed. We probably had sex in every nook and cranny of the Center. She'd go out of her way to conjure up a new spot or play out a new role for me."

He paused. "I was never certain whether that's all she was doing—playing with me. Oh, she delighted in me. I do know that. I don't believe she was with other guys, other than on the set, after that first encounter in the screening room. But I wanted more than that. Every time I tried to talk about us, she'd change the subject."

"So you broke it off with Phoebe."

He scrunched his lips. "I caused the breakup. I wanted her to marry me. And in a post-orgasmic moment, when her guard was down, I asked her."

Melissa covered her mouth. *What timing.* "So what did she say?"

"Nothing at first. She glowered at me and grabbed her clothes. She didn't even bother putting them on before she stormed out of my office.

"The next thing I knew, she was packing her office into boxes. She'd accepted some sort of position with her undergraduate college in Vermont."

"Whoa. That had to hurt."

"Like hell. She left it up to Claire to explain to me that Phoebe couldn't begin to do what I wanted of her. That while Phoebe had apparently developed her own obsession with me, she knew it wouldn't work outside the Center. One of us had to go. She didn't want to be around me, being reminded of what she couldn't have. She and Claire decided I was more important for the future of the Center—that it was best for Phoebe to move on. So she did."

"That sounds rather callous."

Harry shrugged. "The taste it left in my mouth wasn't peaches and cream."

"So she dropped out of your life?"

"Yep. Never a note or anything." His eyes turned deeply sad. "I only heard recently that she died from breast cancer a couple years ago."

Melissa squeezed back tears. "Oh, I'm so sorry, Harry. She put you through hell."

"Don't feel sorry for me, Melissa. Not every guy gets the opportunity to make love with his centerfold dream woman.

Though she always balked at those words. We never made love. We had sex—hot sex, but sex."

"Sounds like Claire." Melissa's hand flew to her mouth and her eyes widened.

Harry chuckled and shook his head. "You think I don't know she had you in the screening room that afternoon?"

"It won't happen again," Melissa squeaked.

"I know that, too. You're hardly Claire's type—at least for the long haul."

"So," Melissa said quietly, feeling her cheeks warm. "Am I your type, Harry?"

Harry smiled and got to his feet. He reached out his hand for her. "Stand up, woman, and let me show you."

She stood, and he gathered her in his arms. His strong hands cupped her rump, her breasts crushed against his chest, and their lips met in a midair tango. She smiled against his. Yes, she must be his type. He sure was *her* type.

Holding hands, he guided her to the tall window overlooking the park. Rain continued to pelt the window, but it was refreshing to lean against Harry's frame and imagine the park before them.

He nibbled on her ear and laved at her neck.

Melissa craned her neck, basking in the feel of his tongue. She experienced a sudden pang of guilt for getting him to talk about Aunt Phoebe without sharing her own story. Maybe she should've simply blurted it out.

His tongue scraped across the roof of her mouth. She no longer had a pressing need to talk about her aunt. "Mmm," she moaned, "that's lovely. I love rainy Monet mornings like this."

"Me, too. Particularly when I can share them with you." He snickered. "Though I would've expected you to prefer bright sunshiny days with pristine blue skies."

"I like those, too. But don't forget, I'm an artist. I have

many moods. I also enjoy the first snowfall, and certainly spring flowers."

"I bet you like to jump in leaf piles, too."

"How did you know?" she said, squeezing his butt.

"A lucky guess." His nose rubbed back and forth across her neck. His busy hands slipped inside her robe to cup a breast each.

She took a long breath as he played with her nipples. "So cozy," she murmured, lowering her eyelids.

Her eyes popped open when she realized he was tugging at the sash of her robe. "Harry," she scolded, "we're standing in front of a floor-to-ceiling window. Someone may see us."

"Nonsense," he whispered into her ear. "Can you see anything through the raindrops?"

She shook her head and did nothing to stop his fingers, already playing at her mound.

"Besides," Harry continued, "you know New Yorkers. They never look up. They're either too busy looking around to avoid being mugged, or down to avoid stepping in dog crap."

"You," she said, jabbing an elbow in his stomach.

"And this is exciting, isn't it, knowing that there might be even a one in a million chance of being discovered?"

Her heartbeat increased and she nodded.

He gently pulled her robe off her shoulders and tossed it aside. His robe quickly joined it.

"Lean forward for me. Place your palms on the window."

She did so, widening her stance at the same time.

"Damn," he grunted, "have I told you what a glorious pussy and ass you have?"

Melissa chuckled. "A few times, but I never tire of hearing how much you adore them."

His laughter filled her ears. Then his tongue slithered down her back until he was nipping her rear. Deftly, he spread her pussy lips and slipped a finger inside. She bore back against him. Her breathing was already labored.

"I love how you respond to everything I do," he said, wiggling his finger.

"Umm. I'm pleased you want to play me like your favorite musical instrument, Harry, but the rain is letting up. I'm ready, if you are."

His hard cock pressing against her thigh indicated his state of readiness. He pushed into her. "I think you're always ready."

"For you," she grunted, lolling her head from side to side, "maybe I am."

Again, she marveled at how full he made her feel. And there was a vulnerability to this position that made her even more sensitive to his every twitch. She had to leave both hands on the window to brace herself. She smiled at the realization that if they were at all visible to the outside world, which she doubted, they'd look like a Monet painting. She wondered if Monet had ever painted any scene like this one. Maybe *she* should.

She moaned as Harry's cock probed deeper and harder. Harry was closing in on his climax. She smiled when his arm wrapped around her hips until his fingers rubbed her swollen bud, unleashing pent-up passion. Harry wasn't about to be alone when he came.

She rose to her tiptoes. Harry pumped faster until she feared she might lose her balance. And then she heard him screaming her name.

"Melissa. I'm coming. Good God, look at what you do to me." His force lifted her feet off the floor and her head began flailing as she confronted her own orgasm. She closed her eyes and let it flow over her and through her. Her spasms and his melded. At last, Harry's hips stilled. He held her tight. She rested her forehead against the cool window, seeking stability.

Harry made no move to pull out of her; he was waiting for her. She continued gulping breaths until she had enough to survive on. When revived enough, she asked, "So tell me, Harry. Was that hot sex, or was that lovemaking?"

Harry laughed and sank his teeth into her shoulder before answering. He waggled his cock in her pussy. "Do you have to ask?"

"Maybe not, but I want an answer."

"It was both," he whispered into her ear. "It was lovemaking *and* it was hot sex. And for you?"

"Absolutely," she said, smiling at a tiny ray of sunshine peeking through a cloud. They'd better move fairly soon, or they would be more distinctive than a Monet image.

But Harry wasn't finished. He kissed her neck again. "For your information," he said, "I've never just had sex with you. Not on the set. Not in the screening room. I believe that's impossible."

Melissa slipped off him, turned in his arms, and kissed his open mouth. She didn't give a damn if the entire world was watching. "Me, too," she murmured. "Maybe we should make our way to the bedroom for a change of pace."

He nodded and smiled. "Lead the way, my lady. Lead the way."

The next day, Melissa rapped on Claire's office door and waited.

She heard Claire's distinctive, "Come in," and held her breath before twisting the doorknob.

Claire greeted her with a wide grin. "Well, if it isn't our girl with the smoldering passion. I wondered when you would get around to paying me a return visit."

Claire closed the distance between them and guided Melissa to a nearby chair. Melissa sat and watched Claire eye her like fresh prey.

"I didn't come for that," she stammered. "I have some questions. About my aunt."

Claire plopped down in a comfortable chair across from her and crossed a knee over a leg, not bothering to disguise the fact that she wore no panties. Melissa had wondered about that before. It certainly didn't shock her. Nothing much would shock her about Claire—or her aunt, for that matter. But she did wish her nipples wouldn't tighten just because she'd caught a glimpse of Claire's pussy.

Claire chuckled. "Will you ever get accustomed to me?" She shook her head. "I doubt it. Anyway," she said sharply, "I told you what happened in the library was a one-time event. I knew you weren't coming to me to eat my pussy. Though maybe I should consider relenting, since you never did get to taste me."

Melissa shook her head. "That's okay. Really."

"You can be so delightfully innocent at times. You don't know when I'm teasing and when I'm not. Your aunt thought you were a lot of fun. I can see why."

"She talked about me?"

"Of course she did. You were her only tie to the next generation, as she put it. I gathered she and your mother didn't get along well, and she didn't see you a lot in your growing up years?"

Melissa nodded. "My mother thought her sister was a freaky hippie. At the time, I never did understand why." Melissa glanced around the room at the mock-ups of old catalogues hanging on the walls and several still shots taken from the Center's tapes. "I have a better idea now why my mother was so upset with Phoebe."

"So your mother wouldn't approve of your line of work either?"

"Hardly." She snickered. "My mother was a good person,

but sex wasn't something to be talked about, and I'd be shocked if she thought it was something to be enjoyed. When I became old enough to have some glimmer of understanding about sex, I wondered how I came about. I never saw my mother and father touch each other." She saw the look of shock on Claire's face. "That doesn't mean they didn't, of course. I guess they had to, or I wouldn't be here, but my family was not very demonstrative."

"Unlike Phoebe?"

"Exactly."

"But if I remember correctly, both your parents were killed in an auto accident sometime when you were in college."

"That's right. My sophomore year. Ever since I was a teenager, I'd had some correspondence with my aunt, but it wasn't until after the accident that she and I became fairly close."

"But you still had no idea about the full range of her work?"

"No. I knew she'd worked here at the Center, and that this place carried on research, I thought something like the Kinsey Institute. I always did marvel at her flair for color and for the unusual but . . . I wasn't aware of her intensive involvement in sex education."

"But she did help you evaluate colleges."

"Yes. To my mother's dismay, I exchanged letters with Aunt Phoebe about my college plans. She was the only member of my family who had gone to college. My aunt wanted me to go to her undergraduate school, but my mother put her foot down. That didn't make any sense then, but I imagine she thought I'd turn out like my aunt."

"But you did anyway."

"Some. Aunt Phoebe encouraged my art. I'd send her pieces of my art even when I was in junior high, and she'd send back smiley faces. My mother thought art was impractical. After my parents died, Aunt Phoebe came to any showing I had at the college or in the community. She'd make sure we got together at Christmas and my birthday. Sometimes she'd come to the city, and sometimes I'd go to her place in Vermont. I guess I always felt welcomed, but also kept at a distance." Melissa shifted in her chair. "Claire, was my aunt ashamed of her life?"

Claire's mouth fell open. "Goodness. I never thought so. We didn't stay in real close touch after she left the Center, but we usually talked at least once a month. We'd get together maybe three or four times a year." She winked at Melissa. "I can assure you she didn't give up her desire for women."

"I suppose not," Melissa replied thoughtfully. "I wish she'd said something about that to me, rather than simply leaving a bunch of pictures she knew I'd find sooner or later."

"Sometimes we can be intensely passionate about our causes with strangers but reticent with those we care most about, for fear of rejection or causing discomfort."

"Yes, but I have so many questions for her."

To Melissa's surprise, Claire shuddered and hugged herself before continuing. "I suppose any of us who were close to Phoebe have a few questions for her. She became very distant even with me after the breast cancer diagnosis."

"Really?"

Claire nodded. Her mouth tightened. "She refused a radical mastectomy, which might have saved her life."

"No." Melissa chewed on her fist. "I didn't know. Why?"

"I'm not sure." Claire raised and lowered a shoulder. "Maybe vanity. Maybe fear of the unknown. Maybe a desire to live and die as she chose. In any case, she burrowed into her hole tighter than ever. She became more distant, more reclusive. She had a small circle of friends at the college who cared for her in those final days, but she didn't reach out to me."

"I'm sorry. She didn't want me around either." Melissa blinked. Her aunt had kept many secrets from her, yet she grieved her still. How might her life—all their lives—have been different if her aunt had been willing to be more open about what was happening to her?

Claire gave her a quirky smile. "We may not like it, but one thing we can be sure of, Phoebe chose to live and die how she wanted to." She nodded and pursed her lips. "That, we can celebrate. I'd like to believe I have half that woman's courage."

"I'm sure you do. Look at what you've accomplished here with the Center."

"Yes, maybe you're right. Back to your question, I can't imagine Phoebe ever being ashamed of herself or her vocation. She was an advocate for informed, freely willed sex. That was one thing she and Harry shared. They championed a vision of a sexually mature world that promoted healthy sex among consenting adults."

"Ah yes, Harry," Melissa sighed. "He does seem incredibly passionate about the cause—I couldn't believe his outburst on the tape to guys who might use anal sex to abuse women."

"That's Harry." Claire shrugged. "I certainly agree, but I also know he might not appreciate some sex practices I'm into, either. But nothing I do involves coercion, and I can assure you the same could be said for Phoebe. She had zero tolerance for abuse. Absolutely zero."

"Thanks for telling me that. I thought I knew her fairly well. Now I'm not certain I knew her at all."

"Do any of us ever fully know another person?"

"Maybe not."

Claire gave a heavy sigh. "You must remember that your aunt and I are products of our times. We embraced those times. They shaped us, and we, to a small extent, may have helped shape them. We took that old protest saying *Make love not war* literally and devoted our lives to the principles that underpinned those simple straightforward words. Actual coercion or use of force would have been antithetical to what we were about." She chuckled and smiled thinly.

"What is it?"

"Well, we might have preferred the slogan *make sex not war*, but we weren't about to quibble over such nuances."

Melissa nodded. Nuances! Wasn't that what she and Harry were about—nuances? She frowned. And wasn't that partly what the Center was about, helping couples hone their sexual skills, but through it, also helping them touch that bigger thing of intimacy and love? She wasn't about to voice any of those nuances to Claire, at least not now.

"Thanks," she said, clasping her hands in her lap. "This has been very helpful. My aunt lived a very multifaceted life."

"She was hardly a one-dimensional person. So tell me," Claire said, uncrossing her legs and flashing a hint of pussy. "Good. You didn't flinch that time. If you want to know, to me, clothes are an encumbrance that shouldn't be tolerated. A woman's vulva is as beautiful as the most precious flower and should be present and visible for view." She smiled. "I could say the same for a man's cock, but it is a bit more difficult for the man to share his prize possession discreetly. But I've sidetracked myself.

"I'm curious, Melissa. Yes, I've heard of you off-and-on over the years. Nothing I heard ever suggested that you might someday follow in your aunt's footsteps. What did bring you here? You didn't know Harry."

"No, of course not." Melissa squirmed in her seat. How could she explain the inexplicable? "Phoebe left two boxes of stuff for me. I found them after the funeral." She stopped and touched her temple. "I do remember seeing you at the funeral. You even offered your condolences. You were by yourself. You wore a short, sexy black dress."

"I've always thought I looked good in black."

"Anyway, I found some photos buried in one of the boxes. Photos of my aunt having sex with several different people. They were stamped with a copyright from the Center."

"So they led you here."

"Like a magnet. Initially, I was horrified and hid them, but I kept going back to look at them. She looked so happy."

"And you weren't."

Melissa shook her head. "But I don't think I came here seeking happiness."

"But you found it."

"Maybe." Melissa paused. "I think I've come to realize that the pictures—along with what I knew about her—showed a woman with a strong sense of purpose and lots of determination. I always admired my aunt, but I wasn't quite certain why."

"And now you are?"

"Maybe I'm getting a clearer idea."

"And of course you needed the money? The job."

"Yes. I have a trust fund that came to me after my parents and aunt died, but I don't have access to it until I turn thirty."

"Your parents still try to control you from the grave."

"Probably. My mother didn't want me to turn out like her sister."

"Yet here you are. Maybe this is your rebellion stage."

Melissa shook her head. "This is about more than rebellion. I think I'm discovering that the Center offers me an avenue, maybe several avenues, for expressing my art."

"Ah, I do forget that you have an artist's eye. That explains a lot. But you chose not to tell Harry that your aunt had worked here."

"No, I didn't want to get the job because of my aunt. And I had no idea that he and she had been involved. She never mentioned him."

"No, I don't suppose she would. But what in the world made you believe you could have sex in front of a camera? Not everyone can do that, and you pull it off exceptionally well, I might add."

"Thank you." Melissa grinned. "I don't know many people who would necessarily be pleased with that compliment, but I must admit I am. Being nude in front of strangers wasn't novel to me. I had posed nude for years for fellow artists. Having sex in front of strangers is an entirely different matter, but I guess I figured if my aunt could do it, then it wasn't terribly wrong.

"Of course I'd studied Center brochures and visited its web page before deciding to follow up on the job interview. There was an underlying passion in some of those descriptions that reminded me of my aunt."

"They should have. She probably wrote some of them."

Melissa drew herself up short. She was certain Claire's eyes had misted. "For whatever reason, I'm glad I came to the Center. And I appreciate what you've done for me—both in our conversations, and on the set."

Claire nodded. "Thanks." She chuckled softly. "Both you and Harry are quite expressive. Sometimes almost embarrassingly so. There are moments when the two of you require privacy even while you work."

Melissa stood to leave.

"By the way," Claire said. "That's one place where you and your aunt differ greatly. Phoebe was very passionate, but she wouldn't let herself go. Your passion smolders until it explodes across the screen." Claire split her lips with her tongue. "Or across a lover's tongue."

Remaining silent, Melissa held her breath.

"You look so delectable when you blush like that. When will you tell Harry about your aunt?"

Melissa winced. "I'm working on it."

"Good. He needs to know, sooner rather than later."

"I know. I'm trying." She stopped. "You won't tell him?"

"Of course not." Claire shook her head. "That's one challenge you have to figure out on your own. I may be around to help pick up the pieces, but you must tell him. He'd never forgive either one of us if I did."

Shuddering, Melissa made it to the door and let herself out.

CHAPTER ELEVEN

Rubbing her eyes and squeezing the bridge of her nose, Melissa tried to maintain her equilibrium. She glanced out her studio window. The first blush of fall colors brought a smile to her face. She'd have to take a break and invite Harry to go with her to the Gardens, or she'd miss the transition from summer to fall. Had it only been two months since he spied on her from the park hillside?

She walked back over to stand in front of her latest charcoal of a nude woman kissing a fully clothed man. There was a sense of timelessness yet urgency about the image that she liked, but something was missing.

She knew it was best to walk away from a work when she reached an impasse. If she pressed on, she'd only make a mess of it. The characters would let her know how to proceed in their time. What a week she'd had. Her apartment was a wreck. She hadn't done dishes for three days. She'd lived almost entirely on pizza. But none of that mattered. Her art had progressed—further than it had for years.

She'd begged off from Harry and from Center work because her period had arrived—which was true—and because she had to finish a certain number of sketches for her final show at the university—which was also true. Yet she'd been driven back to her art by forces she couldn't begin to name.

Coming face to face with her aunt through Harry's stories, Claire's revelations, and the highly charged pendant had triggered something deep inside her creative pool. She couldn't turn off the images. She couldn't stop sketching. She couldn't stop feeling.

In the process, she was finding herself. She knew she was. And she actually liked what she found.

She talked with Harry at least twice daily. She smiled at her drawing—at the man fully clothed. Did Harry realize he often revealed more about himself over the phone than in person?

Their forced separation, if anything, had deepened their relationship. She appreciated that he valued her need for space to rediscover her art.

Now it was thriving again. She twirled around in front of the easel and stretched from the tips of her toes to the tips of her fingers.

She glanced down at the sketch. What had been missing from the drawing was obvious. She redrew part of the sketch to show the nude woman unbuttoning the man's shirt. It would be up to the viewer to decide if the two lovers had merely undressed the woman in preparation for lovemaking, or if the man was reluctantly succumbing to the seductive allure of the woman, or if the man had commanded the woman to strip first before having his way with her.

She smiled and signed in the lower corner *Melissa.* For now, she'd leave the piece untitled. If she decided it needed a title, she knew what it would be: *Expectancy.*

It had been Renoir who'd said something to the effect that he only knew when a painting was finished when he felt he could reach out and pinch the subjects. She definitely had that feeling about *Expectancy.*

Melissa lifted the sketch off the easel and set it on the floor beside the others leaning against the wall. One entire wall of her studio was lined with sketches—some done in charcoal, others in pastel, and still more in pencil. Some were of partially clad or nude women, others of partially clad or nude men, and even more of men with women or women with women in various states of lovemaking. And she had many more partial sketches in her sketchbook.

She'd sketched nudes for years. Her mother had thrown out a small sketchpad she'd had as a teenager when she discovered the nude figures it contained. And her mother had always disapproved of her daughter seeking a degree in art.

On the other hand, her aunt had encouraged her to draw. She'd said she possessed a natural flair for art, that she should develop it and see where it would take her.

Melissa pursed her lips. Probably even her aunt had never foreseen that her niece's art would take her to where she was now.

Inhaling deeply, Melissa hugged herself. Had she finally found the meaning and purpose that had proven so elusive?

Her doorbell sputtered. She went to the door, not sure whether she should chastise Harry for interrupting her or throw her arms around him and make mad love to him on the entryway floor.

She opened the door and jerked back in surprise.

"May I come in? I hope I'm not interrupting anything important. I have to talk with you before tomorrow."

She'd never seen Inez so distraught. "Of course. Come in." She hugged Inez and led her to the couch. "Do you want something to drink?"

"No." Inez twisted her fingers in her lap. Melissa remained standing, not quite sure what to do next.

"Harry talked to me Friday."

"Oh." Melissa nodded and sat beside Inez, placing her hand between hers.

Inez nodded. "He's told you what he wants?"

"Yes. He wants the three of us to work together. I believe the shoot is scheduled for tomorrow morning, or is it the afternoon? I've been so wrapped up in my work I forgot."

Inez looked at her in disbelief. "You forgot! I can't do a three-way with the two of you."

"Why not?" Melissa frowned. "Are you telling me you've never been involved in a three-way?"

Inez gave her a lopsided grin. "Of course I'm not saying that. It's just . . . It's just that the two of you are a couple—and I don't want to get in the way."

"I hardly think you'll be in the way. We've all seen the customer surveys. There is a desire out there for help with three-way sex. That's what we're all committed to—helping people live sexually healthy, adventurous lives. Right?"

"Of course, but . . ."

"No buts about it. You and I have worked together since I got involved with Harry outside of work. That seemed fine with you."

"Of course it was. That's part of my job."

"Good. And so is this. I agree with Harry and Claire. The three of us have the best opportunity for displaying the kind of threesome that keeps with the quality the Center desires to produce."

"But Harry's your man."

Melissa squeezed Inez's fingers tighter. "I'm not positive about that, but at least for the time being, our commitment to our work, to our art, is what matters most. So are you going to be okay with that?" She'd never seen Inez look quite so vulnerable.

Inez swiped at her eyes. "Okay, I guess. Maybe you and Harry are more into this Center vision thing than I am. If I had a man, I'm not sure I'd want to share him with you—especially on camera."

"That's funny," Melissa blurted. "I have absolutely no qualms sharing Harry with you on camera." She smiled. "But if you go after him off camera, I'll scratch your eyes out."

Inez laughed and threw her arms around her. "You've really come into yourself these last several weeks. You're not the same person who sat across from me testing vibrators."

Melissa brushed her lips across Inez's and leaped to her feet. "Come on, I have some things to show you. And maybe you can help me out."

Inez followed Melissa into her studio." Have you had this much energy all week? Wow! Look at this. You did all of these?"

Melissa nodded.

"They're beautiful. Erotic. Tasteful. They are so *you.* My goodness. I knew you were talented but . . ." Inez bent down to inspect some of the sketches more closely. "I love this one with the two women coupled in sixty-nine. They look so totally engrossed with each other—with loving—that nothing could divert them from the path they're on."

"I'm glad you like it. It's us, you know." She cocked her head at Inez's quizzical look. "Well, not exactly. I wasn't trying to draw us as we actually look. It was more important to capture the feeling coursing between the two women that you just so aptly expressed. I could never have done that drawing if I hadn't come to know and love you first."

"Wow! I still can't believe this." Inez stood up and peered at more of the sketches.

Melissa picked up the sketch of the two women and handed it to Inez. "It's yours. I want you to have it."

Inez shook her head.

"Please."

"But you could sell this for real money," she said, placing her fingers carefully around the sketch. "Mine. An original piece of art. I've never owned an original piece of art."

Melissa chuckled. "I don't know if you'll want to display it, but I do want you to have it."

Inez held the sketch at arm's length. "You're right, it might be more of a conversation piece in my living room than I want, but it'll be perfect in my bedroom. Hopefully, anyone who gets to my bedroom will be inspired by this."

"Now then, I have a favor to ask of you."

"Shoot."

"Will you pose for me? I can work from memory. I can work from photos. But working with a live model is always best."

"Will I?" Inez arched an eyebrow. "It will be an honor. Maybe you'll make me famous. What do you want me to do?"

"Don't count on that. For now, I'd like to do maybe a bunch of quick working sketches. We may have you come back to do more at another session, but I can't wait to get started."

"You are really into this."

"It's been an amazing week. Okay. Let's see. Obviously, I'll want to do some nudes, but let's start with you partially clothed. Suggestive. Artsy. Let me look at you. That short black skirt is definitely going to work. Why don't you slip off your panties? We're not going to need them. Good. The spaghetti strap top works, but get rid of the bra. Excellent!"

Melissa stood back. She walked to the window and opened the curtains to increase the late afternoon sunlight and shadows. "Beautiful." She stepped in front of Inez, brought her long curly hair down the front of one shoulder, and left the other shoulder bare. "Let's pull this one strap down your arm and free a breast. Oh, perfect," she purred, tapping the dark nipple until it stood taut.

"Cripes," Inez complained, "you're turning me on."

Melissa eyed her from the other side of the easel and began quickly sketching. She winked at Inez. "We do want this to be as authentic as possible."

"You and Harry," Inez grumbled. "No wonder the two of you are such a good match."

Within minutes, Melissa had what she wanted. It would take much longer to finish the sketch, but she wasn't into finished products now.

She set up a clean sheet and grinned at Inez. "Okay, turn

around. Imagine that you're enticing a lover with your gorgeous butt. Bend over slightly. Grab a butt cheek with each hand and separate them a little. Too much. That'll look too pornographic. We're looking for subtle." Melissa chuckled. "Though there isn't much about your ass that's subtle. Let's hike this skirt up a little higher. There. My, you are turned on." She slid a finger along the length of Inez's exposed pussy and licked her finger. "Nice." She grinned and returned to her easel.

"Are you trying to get me to have sex with you?" Inez squeaked.

"Of course not."

"Could've fooled me."

Melissa smiled. Inez's trembling fingers were clasping her buttocks just right. "Not 'til tomorrow morning."

Her arm moved fluidly, and the image of Inez's provocative butt began to appear on the paper. "I am looking forward to that. Maybe I'll skip breakfast. There. You want to peek at this? There's lots left to do, but you can see what I'm striving for."

Quickly, Inez came to stand next to Melissa and peered at the emerging sketch. "Jesus. It's already seductive as hell. Cripes, it's seducing me, and it *is* me."

"I'm glad you like my work." She pressed a finger against Inez's lips and then followed with her lips. This time Inez wasn't satisfied with playing the passive model. Electricity jolted from one set of lips to the other. It was a bruising kiss. Melissa pulled away and blinked.

Inez's lips were heavy and pouting. "Don't move," Melissa said, "stand right there." Hurriedly, she grabbed a fresh sheet and began sketching those puffy lips and the lust-filled eyes. This had to be the last sketch for the day, or she wouldn't be able to control her own passion.

"It's fascinating to watch you work from this side of the

easel," Inez volunteered as Melissa played with shades of light and dark. "It's like watching something come to life. You're so bold to take a blank sheet of paper and expect to produce anything worth looking at."

"Thanks." She put her charcoal down and faced Inez. "A lot of the result depends on the model. You were super. I hope you'll pose for me again."

Inez nodded her head and raised an eyebrow.

She hugged Inez close. "I've put you through a lot. Do you need to come?"

Inez shook her head. Again, her eyes misted. "I think I already have. Didn't this affect you at all?"

"Of course it did." Melissa giggled. "I'm as wet as you are."

Inez gave her a shy smile. "We could bring ourselves off."

Melissa shook her head. "If you want to do yourself, I'll be happy to play the voyeur." She grabbed Inez by both hands and stood at arm's length. "I could probably even help you by telling you what I see, but I want to save the edge I'm on until tomorrow morning."

"That's good for me, too." Inez nodded. "I may not sleep tonight. I'm really jacked up for tomorrow."

Melissa smiled conspiratorially. "I was hoping that might happen. For my first three-way, I don't want a reluctant lover."

Harry fidgeted at his desk, scanning the brief script he'd drafted for the three of them. He despised working with scripts, but with three people involved, it seemed prudent. Still, it would only serve as a guide.

He hadn't seen Melissa for nearly a week. They'd talked regularly, but no phone sex. Neither one of them had even suggested it.

Now that he thought about it, he didn't know if that was

good or bad.

Was she already taking him for granted? Was she preparing him for the fall?

"Keep your head on your shoulders," he grumbled. Their conversations had been lengthy and ranged from frivolous to serious matters. He'd learned Melissa not only was an art major, she also had minored in communications, which was another explanation for why she was so at ease in front of a camera. It had taken him much longer to get comfortable with the camera and to discover how best to ignore it when necessary.

Why hadn't he found out about her experience in media and communications during her job interview? It hadn't come up. So what else hadn't come up?

Why the hell was he so antsy this morning? It was going to be great to see Melissa again and get on with their lives. She'd sounded so thrilled with her art, with what she'd produced. He was looking forward to seeing it. Not that he was an art critic. But if it was important to Melissa, then it was important to him.

He glanced again at the script. He had made a couple changes after Melissa phoned him last night. He'd let Melissa handle the initial set up. That should make Inez a bit more comfortable.

He scrunched his mouth. Inez. Oh, well. He sighed. He hadn't planned on actually screwing her. He'd set up a scenario where he'd be screwing Melissa and Melissa would be eating Inez. Another was for Inez to give him head while Melissa nibbled on her pussy. But Melissa had said no way.

She wasn't going to be satisfied with this three-way arrangement unless he actually fucked Inez. Her words. She didn't care if he was on top or Inez was on top, but his cock would be in Inez's pussy or Melissa wouldn't go through with it.

He had to admire Melissa's loyalty and commitment. She'd

made her case. For the tape to come off as genuine, everyone had to be comfortable. Inez couldn't be allowed to feel like she was merely an add-on, or like she was in danger of coming between him and Melissa. He chuckled. Well, she'd be between them, but apparently, only in ways they'd all agreed to.

He'd left the revised scenarios on their desks when he'd arrived early at the office. He hadn't heard any objections, so he assumed they were still a go.

Melissa smiled into the camera after completing her initial introductory remarks. She sat on a stool between Inez and Harry. They each wore soft green robes. Inez seemed only a little nervous. She had confided when she arrived that she was hot as hell. Harry seemed a bit reserved. They hadn't met until they arrived on the set. He'd hugged her pleasantly enough, but he'd already had his game face on.

So far, she was having a blast. She'd forgotten how much she enjoyed holding a mike. She'd already laid out why they were doing this particular tape. She'd been appropriately coy and teasing, hopefully putting viewers at ease and letting them know what to expect.

The three of them would go through a series of possible three-way positions. Their objective wasn't to demonstrate multiple orgasms, but to show ways that three persons could share a level of intimacy that perhaps two persons could not.

It was time to get a little more personal. "So, Inez," she asked, looking at her friend. "This is not your first three-way, correct? We don't want to mislead our viewers."

"Of course," Inez responded weakly. "I'm fairly experienced with three-ways."

"But you've not been in a three-way with either of us," she said, glancing at Harry.

"That's right."

"And tell our viewers where you work, Inez."

Inez smiled easily. Thankfully, she was getting into this. "Right here. Like you. I'm a research associate."

"Uh huh. So on the average week, how much time would you say you spend in front of the camera producing instructional tapes?"

Inez pursed her lips. "A half a day a week, maybe. Some weeks a little more. Some weeks not at all."

"So this isn't how you primarily earn your paycheck?"

Inez laughed. "Hardly. I'm sort of an amateur computer geek. I do research and make sure our technological capacity is at least minimally acceptable. And at this point, that's what it is, minimally acceptable."

Laughing, Melissa glanced at Claire. "Yeah, I know that'll probably have to go. So, Harry," she turned to look at him, "what about you? I assume this will not be your first three-way."

"It's been a while, but you're right. And what about you, Melissa?"

"I was getting there." She made a show of pouting at him. She knew it was their banter that might help some reluctant viewers sit up and take notice. This could be fun. Really. She tilted her head to the side and spoke directly to the camera. "As you may have guessed, this will be my first three-way. I'm eager to get started. Why don't you come along and join us?"

She stood up, and the three of them walked toward the bed. The cameras were turned off until they had a chance to arrange themselves on the bed. This tape was definitely going to be a series of starts and stops.

"Okay," she said to the camera while lying on her back. "I think we're about ready to begin. I'm not going to provide you with a running commentary. You can see what is going on. Now I'm going to forget you're watching and enjoy this. I'll be back to talk with you later. Bye."

She smiled at the camera and extended her arms to Inez, who knelt on one side, and Harry, who knelt on the other. They each kissed a corner of her mouth and then tilted their heads so all three sets of lips touched. Their tongues teased until Inez laughed and moved lower to cover a breast with her mouth. Harry followed suit.

Melissa arched her back. What a thrill to have both boobs suckled at the same time! She moaned and chewed on her lower lip. What had she said about multiple orgasms? Her hips began undulating. She could feel Harry laughing against her breast, but more importantly, she could feel two hands sliding across her belly. They pressed her hips against the mattress. One hand worked the bottom half of her vulva and the other the top half. She choked back a scream when two fingers entered her at once.

Her body quaked. She'd never last if she let them take her this slowly. She eyed Harry wildly and reached for his shaft.

He chuckled, left her pussy to Inez, and scooted up the bed until she could take him in her mouth. By the time she had him seated deep in her throat, Inez was devouring her pussy. *She* must've been the one to skip breakfast. Inez hoisted Melissa's legs over her shoulders as if they were toothpicks and dove as far as she could into her core.

Melissa thrashed about, trying not to dislodge Harry. She'd only traveled his full length a few times before he pulled away from her and sat back on his haunches. She grabbed his finger, sucked on it instead, and watched Inez's black curls bounce as she continued to plunge in and out of her. Melissa closed her eyes. She wanted to cry. Instead, she came. "Goodness," she muttered to no one in particular.

They let her lie there. She blinked her eyes several times and then she turned to the camera and said what popped into her mind, "Like any form of sex, I guess in a three-way you have to be willing to be surprised.

"What's next, guys?" she said with a half-smile. They went through a couple more scenarios without getting particularly carried away. She tried to stay focused. She was looking forward to the finale.

Once they were in position, the cameras started to hum again. She turned to face the camera. "As you can see, we've changed positions again. I doubt many three-way encounters will involve as many position changes as we're trying to demonstrate on this tape. But these are variations of some of my favorite positions." She straddled Harry's chest, facing Inez, who straddled his abs. She reached out to kiss Inez briefly. She could see a trace of anxiety in Inez's eyes. Then she pressed gently downward on Inez's shoulders.

She nodded as Inez eased herself across Harry's loins and raised herself above his waiting cock. Melissa bent down and positioned him at Inez's entrance. She watched with approval as Inez inched her way down his shaft.

"Wow," Inez murmured. "Nice, huh?" Inez settled against Harry's hips. She squirmed, seating him inside the way she wanted him.

"Good," Melissa whispered, kissing Harry's belly and then Inez's clit before scooting back so Harry had easy access to her pussy.

His finger and tongue separating her outer folds told her she was in the right place. She reached down and traced the outline of his cock buried in Inez. "Now," she mumbled.

Inez began rising and lowering over his shaft.

"Excellent view," Melissa said.

"Hush," Harry said, giving up his purchase for a moment.

His tongue rooting at her pussy and his thumb sinking into her ass drove whatever breath she'd been holding from her lungs. Inez was wailing, riding feely and pulling on her own nipples.

Melissa managed to think enough to graze Inez's clit between two fingers. And then there was only blurring of movement and sound. Inez's shrieks. Harry's bellowing. And her own screams.

She had no idea how long they lay there afterwards—like a sculpture. Harry's belly rose and fell evenly under her cheek. Juices flowing from Inez were still visible. And her entire pussy and anus throbbed so much that she couldn't discern which was which.

Vaguely, she realized the cameras were still going. She peeked at Claire, whose eyes were wide with excitement. Had Claire just removed her hand from under her skirt? She certainly looked like a woman who'd had a climax.

Why were the cameras still running? Because Claire hadn't caught up with her own senses? Or because they were waiting for her to say something?

She raised her fingers in a tiny wave toward the camera. "Fabulous," she managed to say. "Hope you enjoyed this half as much as I did. Bye." She shut her eyelids and rested.

At last the camera crew left.

Melissa rose to her hands and knees. Inez lifted herself off Harry. They all stood on wobbly legs and hugged. Then without saying a word, they each left the production room.

Moments later Melissa stood in one of the Center showers trying to comprehend what had just transpired. The ending of the session had been so incredibly powerful. And the prolonged silence after. It was as if they had been departing the inner sanctum of the holy of holies.

She hugged herself tight. Maybe they had.

Chapter Twelve

Later that evening, Harry sat with Melissa on her couch, sipping wine and munching on a variety of cheeses and crackers. She'd just shown him the sketches she'd been working on. He still couldn't get over his surprise—some of the sketches were as seductive as she was at the moment, licking sticky cheese from her fingers.

"Don't you wish?" she teased, catching him eyeing her.

He squeezed her thigh. "I must be an open book."

"Sometimes. Other times you can be quite impervious."

"Sounds like you make quite an effort to decipher what I'm thinking."

"I try."

He nodded, raked his nails down the inside of her bare thigh, and relished her sharp intake of breath. Thankfully, her short skirt had ridden quite high already. He removed his hand and reached for his glass. He didn't miss her momentary dismay. "That three-way session was spectacular this morning," he said, after swirling some wine in his mouth and swallowing.

She nodded. "Glorious. Absolutely astounding. Far beyond my expectations."

He warmed his fingers again on her inner thigh.

She widened her legs a little and crunched down on a cracker. "But I do look forward to having you without sharing,"

"You were good." He caught the twinkle in her eyes. "Not only the sex. You were great with the audience. Very effective:

informative, yet provocative. Do you know how many people are going to cream their pants when they see you wave your fingers and give that little *bye* of yours?"

"I hadn't planned on doing that."

"I didn't assume you had. We need to give you more air time on-camera." He tapped his fingers against her thigh. "You might want to consider that little finger roll and *bye* as your signature."

"Really?" Melissa sighed, giving him a dreamy look. "Sort of like how I sign my sketches and paintings—Melissa."

"Exactly."

"Do you ever wonder how many people actually watch our tapes?"

"Sure. We have some sense from sales, and we have anecdotal information from surveys and questionnaires."

"It's awesome to think that what we do at the Center may help some couples stay together or breathe new life into relationships."

Harry shrugged. "You're a new convert."

She glared at him.

He smiled. "I admit I still believe all of that, too. If I didn't, I couldn't do what I do. But sometimes I wonder if we're only presenting a soft porn option to some folks."

"If it works," she said, interlacing her fingers with his and drawing them up her thigh. "Do you ever wonder how many people you've helped over the years?"

"Sometimes."

"Or," she murmured, moving their hands so his palm could feel the heat radiating through her panties, "how many people are out there screwing while they watch us?"

He laughed. "Are you becoming an exhibitionist now?"

"If I enjoy what I'm doing, does that make me an exhibitionist?"

"If so, then I guess I'm one, too." He leaned over, slanted

his lips across hers, and cupped her mound. Her hand remained firmly on top of his.

"Harry," she said, breaking away from his mouth, "do you ever wonder how many guys and women are out their masturbating while they watch us?"

Harry's laugh was rich. "You're full of questions, aren't you? I don't spend a lot of time wondering about it. Of course it happens. Does that bother you?"

She tucked their hands inside her panties. "Not at all. If someone—man or woman—finds pleasure from watching me, that's great." She smirked and started unbuckling his belt with her free hand. "I'd prefer if they bring each other off, but I can certainly imagine couples making great strides just from becoming comfortable pleasuring themselves in the presence of the other." She encircled his cock and pulled on it. "That's a beginning, don't you think?"

"Oh yeah. Most definitely. A fantastic beginning." He leaned back against the couch, and she shifted to kneel beside him, keeping his hand close to her pussy. He eyed her as she arched upward just enough to guide his finger into her heat. He laughed. "Is this what you want for our first time alone for a week?"

"Why not?" Her lips curved into a delightful pout. "I love to watch you come. And we have all night, don't we?"

"Of course. Foolish me to assume we might need some sleep." He pushed his trousers and briefs to the floor and kicked them to the side. He glanced at her panties. There was no way she was going to get them off with his finger still in her. He smiled—there was a way. With one hand, he ripped them off.

Her eyes rounded and then she smiled broadly. "My, my. My man is strong tonight." She spread her knees further, and he slid a second finger into her. She leaned over and licked his cock, then took him into her mouth and ran her tongue around his shaft. She slid up and down, and he placed his free hand on her neck.

Melissa shook her head and pulled off him. "Uh-uh. Not that way. I want to see him come."

She placed both hands on his cock, one at the base and the other on top of that one, then began to glide them gently up and down the length of his shaft. "Humor me," she said. "It's a visual thrill to watch you ejaculate."

"Damn," he muttered. "How did I get involved with a visual artist?"

"I can stop"—her hands stilled—"if that's a complaint."

"No. I'm not complaining. He wants to give you a show." He began working his fingers in and out of her in earnest. He knew that was the surest way to get Melissa to stop talking. Her hands picked up the pace. His toes curled; he tried to forestall the inevitable.

She eyed him suspiciously. "Are you trying to hold back? Look at him. He's turning purple. He's mushrooming. Good God, I wish I could draw this. There. There's that little pearly drop. He's so close."

Harry pressed back against the cushion and tucked his chin to his chest. She had him, and she knew it.

"There he goes," she squealed. His hips bucked and his mouth fell open. It was hard to focus on her hand movements. "Good grief, you're coming all over the place. Look at him spurt torrents. It has been a long week."

She laughed as she milked him. He groaned, but she showed no mercy. He could think of only one way to stop her. He curled his fingers up inside her. She screeched, released his cock, and pressed her palms on his chest, struggling to keep her balance. She rose and fell three times as he stroked her G-spot. Then she pulled his hand away from her body and nestled against him. Together they shook and quaked. He couldn't discern how much of their shaking had to do with orgasms and how much was simply due to laughter.

They were back together. He didn't give a damn how she wanted to do it. They were back together again. She could jerk him off all night if she wanted to, but he did hope to convince her to try some alternatives before the next sunrise.

The next morning, Melissa smiled lazily at Harry, who lay dozing, facing her, their bodies intertwined. She nipped at his pectorals, waggled her butt, and squeezed her vagina muscles against his still semihard cock.

He groaned and cracked an eye open.

"I love waking up with you in the morning and making love like this. Your skin is so warm. You engulf me with heat."

He flexed his hips gently. "I'd say I'm the one engulfed in heat." He combed his fingers through her hair. "I enjoy making love to you half awake, too. Though you do seem to wake up awfully early."

"A tiny price to pay for this," she said, tracing the line of his neck and then his jaw with her tongue. She pressed her moist lips against his. "Hi, good morning again."

He smiled back and kissed her briefly. "Hi and another good morning to you, too."

She propped herself up on an elbow and eyed him thoughtfully. Would her giddiness get her in trouble?

"What's so funny?" He squinted at her.

"Nothing," she said. "How long have we been together now?"

"Somehow I think you know the answer to that question," he said, tapping the tip of her nose. Then he sobered. "Two months, give or take. Are you bored already?"

"Hardly." She tilted her head and arched an eyebrow. "Will you freak out if I tell you I think I'm falling in love with you?"

His eyes rounded and then a grin swept across his lips.

Her heart pounded.

"Thinking about it and doing it may be two different things."

So he wasn't going to come clean, but then he hadn't pushed her aside and dashed for the door, either. She pouted at him. "I've never fallen in love before, so maybe I have to think about it first."

Harry pressed a finger against her lips, and she nibbled it and sucked it into her mouth. "No, you won't freak me out. I may be quite experienced with women, but I'm not very experienced with love. I do know I love being with you." His eyes sparkled. "That you may be thinking about falling in love makes my heart race."

She chuckled and interlaced their fingers over his heart. "That's good enough for me," she said, planting kisses on their knuckles. "I just wanted to warn you about what might be happening."

"I'm duly warned. Thank you." He slid his free hand down her back and caressed her rump. "We may both be on that slippery slope, but let's take our time. It can be a very hard fall if things don't work out well."

She saw the brief streak of pain in his eyes. *My aunt.* Sometimes she completely forgot about Phoebe. She nodded. "I'm in no rush. So how old are you, Harry?"

Harry startled, blinked, and then laughed. He squeezed her butt cheeks. "It takes everything I have to just keep up with your mind jumping about at times. Where did that question come from? And isn't it a little late?"

She shrugged. "I'm only curious. You know I'm twenty-five." She waited.

His fingers slid up her back until they were again combing her hair. "Thirty-seven," he said, sighing. "I know that's pretty old for you. I wish I were younger, but I'm not."

"Thirty-seven is perfect," she said warmly. "Absolutely perfect." They were closer in age than he'd been with her aunt. Somehow, that mattered. "Can I ask you a hypothetical question?"

"Can I stop you?"

"Don't be so smug." She kissed him on the lips and rolled him onto his back. She placed her palms on his chest and raised herself to a sitting position. He reached for her breasts, but she caught his hands in hers and held them. "Purely hypothetically. If this falling that we think we may both be involved in goes somewhere, really goes somewhere . . ."

He flexed his cock inside her vagina. "We are already somewhere, babe."

"Stop it," she complained. "I'm trying to get a question asked here."

"Sorry," he said, not looking a bit remorseful.

"If this were to work between us, would you want children?" She couldn't decipher his faint grin.

"Do you want children?"

"I asked you first, but yes, I do."

"Me too," he replied, relaxing beneath her. "I have for some time. I thought it might be getting too late for me."

"But now?"

He shook his head. "Let's not get ahead of ourselves. You've helped us name a foundation to build on. Let's not try putting too much weight on it until that foundation is stronger."

She raised her hands high above her head and stretched. "I agree. You are a wise and gentle man." She watched gleefully as his hands sought her rising breasts. He teased her nipples, and she moaned in response. "Do you think we're going to be late for work?"

He nodded.

"Won't people talk?"

"Let them."

"Okay." She rose up on her knees and lowered herself down the length of his shaft. His smile warmed her heart. She rose again and fell. Yes, she was falling, all right. Falling in love. And she wasn't merely thinking about it.

It wasn't until later that night that Harry began to shake. He stood in his darkened living room looking out across the dimly lit park. He leaned his forehead against the window. Why hadn't he stopped her from talking about love when he had the chance?

He was sinking, and it was only going to get more treacherous and more difficult to extricate himself. No matter how much he might want to fall in love with Melissa, it wasn't going to happen. He was star-crossed when it came to love. Phoebe had taught him that lesson, and he didn't really want to learn it again.

Melissa wasn't Phoebe. But *he* was still *Harry*. She'd wait until he'd given her his heart—then she'd split.

Why had he allowed himself to get hooked, even this much? The Center had become a safe place the last six years or so. He got as much sex as he wanted, and there had been no expectations, either from the women he'd known at the Center or even those few he'd been with outside the Center. He'd made certain each woman knew what he did for a living. No female seeking more than some good casual sex hung around for long after that.

But Melissa had hung around. He'd never had such an intense relationship with a woman other than with Phoebe. And this relationship with Melissa was much more rounded; they actually enjoyed being with each other outside the Center.

So why couldn't it work? She didn't seem bothered by their age difference. He could get his head around that—though he'd be a fairly old father. Father—damn, he really had given up on that. He dropped his head against the window. Why shouldn't he be able to take his kids to a ballgame, or to a park, or teach them how to read? His kids. His and Melissa's kids.

His chest expanded and he gulped for air. He felt like the Tarot Fool preparing to step off the cliff. There were no safety nets when it came to loving a woman.

Harry stopped trembling and stood back, suddenly flooded with the memory of their lovemaking in front of that very window on a soggy drizzly morning. He bent forward and kissed the spot where he imagined her forehead had rested that morning.

He was nothing if not a fool.

Melissa's pulse careened from one beat to the next. Her hand flew across the sketchpad until she was satisfied with the outlines of a man and a woman engaged in rear entry sex. Would she ever be able to draw a couple making love without imagining Harry's cock, his arms, his lips?

She stepped back to assess the sketch. Her entire body felt so alive these days. Her soul had found new life. Was she in danger of soaring to another universe?

She put her pastels aside and cracked her cramped fingers. She'd taken good advantage of Harry's absence and didn't regret at all begging off from traveling with him to California. She hardly had a desire to hang around a sociology conference.

She needed to make her final selections for Wednesday's critical meeting with Claire and Harry. Harry didn't know about the meeting yet, but he would soon enough.

Claire had been pushing her for weeks to share her thoughts about possible new directions for the Center. Melissa shook her head. She couldn't entirely shake the suspicion that Claire's relationship with Phoebe colored how the woman evaluated her work. Yet Claire had seemed quite impressed with how she handled herself with a mike, and she knew Harry had told Claire about her communications background.

Melissa's skin warmed as she studied a painting of two women hugging. She'd purposefully left it so the viewer would have to decide if the two women were engaged in foreplay or whether their embrace came from post-climax afterglow. She added the picture to her selections for her Wednesday meeting.

She did have a number of ideas for the Center, and this might be her one opportunity—or at least her best opportunity—to set them forth. It had been important for her not to share those ideas with Harry in advance of the meeting. It wasn't just that Claire was the senior co-director; Melissa didn't want either of them to think she was using her personal relationship with Harry for professional gain.

She arched an eyebrow at the finished pastel of Inez clutching her butt cheeks. She'd entitled it *Promises.* "Nice," she whispered, welcoming that familiar tingle in her loins. It pleased her immensely to see her art come to life, and the fact that it still turned her on had to say something about the quality of her work.

Eyeing one of her very favorite pieces, she picked up the pastel of a woman sitting astride a man. Their satisfied smiles spoke a thousand words. She'd entitled the work *Declaration.* She set it aside, not wanting to share it at the meeting.

Neither she nor Harry had used the *love* word since that sleepy morning. That was just as well. She'd learned what she wanted to know—Harry wasn't going to freak out at the idea of falling in love.

She wrapped her arms around her abs. She had to tell him. She had to find a way to tell him about her aunt. God, she hoped he wasn't confusing her with her aunt. If he was, the only future she could foresee was devastation.

She pursed her lips. Should she be jealous of Aunt Phoebe? That hardly seemed reasonable, but since when was anything about love reasonable? She'd witnessed her aunt and Harry making love dozens of times. And they did possess a chemistry that scorched the screen.

Melissa exhaled. She'd also reviewed the tapes she herself had made with Harry. They too, exposed a chemistry on the screen that was highly charged, and yet even more mysterious. Claire was right. She and Harry did share some quality that was not as apparent in Harry's work with her aunt. It was a quality that had no name. Or maybe she wasn't quite ready to give it a name.

She laughed. So was Harry part of her aunt's legacy for her? That was a sobering thought, but there was no way that was possible. Harry must have been in his mid-twenties when he first got involved with her aunt. That would make Melissa maybe only twelve or thirteen years old. No way was even her rather off-the-wall aunt scouting out a romantic partner for her niece at that point.

Melissa began putting away her materials. She rotated her neck, releasing tension. Claire had said she was so much like her aunt, yet very different. Claire had described Melissa as a woman with smoldering passion who, unlike Phoebe, was unafraid of unlocking that passion and sharing it deeply.

Melissa cherished those words as she made her way to her bedroom and prepared for bed. She crawled under the covers and hugged a pillow tight, wishing it was Harry.

She let the many sketches and paintings she'd done in the last several weeks dance across her memory. She thought of her work on the set at the Center and her surprise at being so at ease with it all. She recalled her initial lovemaking with Inez, and the dark encounters in the screening room with

Harry, and she even allowed herself to revisit the one encounter with Claire. She retraced the lovemaking she and Harry shared and its intensity.

That she was a passionate being came as no surprise. She'd always been passionate, but she hadn't been fully aware of the depth and range of that passion. She covered her mound with her palm and let her hand rest there, absorbing her heat.

She needed nothing more than that. It was enough to know she still smoldered.

Chapter Thirteen

Trying to control a case of nerves, Melissa sat in the Center screening room and checked her watch. Almost time.

She'd readied her PowerPoint presentation. It had taken several hours to photograph the sketches and drawings she wanted to present in her collection and then download them into the computer. But she was ready. She'd saved her artwork for last. Hopefully, she wouldn't blow the meeting before then.

It did seem a little strange to be sitting in a fully lit screening room waiting for Harry to arrive. And of course, Claire would be joining them. Melissa winced. She wouldn't have to wonder who was approaching her in the dark this time.

She smiled and nodded when Harry and Claire entered and took seats on either side of her. "I hope it's all right meeting here," she began, "but I thought a PowerPoint presentation would be simplest. I will also leave you with hard copies of the written material."

"You really are hi-tech," Claire said, watching the screen come to life after Melissa punched several buttons on her laptop.

Melissa smiled at Claire. "Right on cue, Claire. Although Inez is more hi-tech than I am, that is where I want to begin, but first I do want to thank you for pushing me to put some ideas down on paper. I think, as you both know, the Center and its work have become very important to me during these past months. It's as if I live it and breathe it.

"I hope you're not miffed that I didn't share these ideas

with you first," she said to Harry.

"You're doing this the right way. You're your own woman. I'm glad you didn't involve me until now."

Melissa chuckled. "You both have been very involved with what I have to suggest, but I did want to do this a little more formally."

"That must explain the navy power suit you're wearing," Claire quipped. "Quite sharp, actually. You dress up very well."

Ignoring that comment, Melissa said, "Why don't we begin, then? The current web page is really little more than a billboard." She looked quickly at Claire. "I hope that doesn't sound offensive."

"Don't worry about me, girl. I asked for your input. I'm scared to death by technology. If you have ideas that can help us do a better job with our mission, I want to hear about them. I'll never question your commitment to the Center's vision."

"Thank you. I appreciate that very much." She wished she could acknowledge her aunt's efforts at shaping the Center and its mission, but she couldn't yet. In fairly short order, using the PowerPoint displays as her guide, she laid out her major ideas for possible changes and additional avenues the Center might consider taking.

"So what do you think?" she asked with a catch in her voice.

"Wow," Claire began. "You're certainly wanting us to catch up to the twenty-first century. Some of your suggestions will cost money. Others require more of a shift in direction. I definitely like the idea of making the web page interactive." She peered down her nose. "It's not like I've never been on the kinds of interactive web pages you're talking about. But I wouldn't have a clue how to make that happen or even how to tell someone what I really want. I guess I'm a woman of the past century in some ways."

"I don't believe that for a moment. And I don't have all the high tech skills either, but I do know what would be useful. Inez is the one with the robust technical skills."

"Good," Harry interjected. "So we can make the web page interactive, make downloadable videos available, and get a sharp online catalogue that can be updated as often as we want with existing staff."

"Most of the work, if not all," Melissa replied, "could be done in house. We might need to support Inez to keep her up to date. Of course, our efforts at enhancing our technological presence would take us away from other things."

"Right. That's something we'll need to work through, because we"—he looked over at Claire—"do want you on camera more. Not necessarily demonstrating every technique, but providing commentary. You connect very well with our viewers, and we need constancy there. What do you think, Claire?"

"Absolutely, if Melissa is willing. At least introducing productions to viewers and doing the voiceovers." Claire cleared her throat. "And as much as possible on screen performing. I've even received feedback from some of our benefactors about your signature wave of the fingers and the single word *Bye*. They find that very sexy. Very seductive, apparently."

Melissa nodded. "I enjoy all my work here, but there is the matter of finite time. What about the talk radio concept?"

"Bold," Claire offered. "Quite ambitious for the Center. An educational radio or even TV show about sex and sexual relations does seem like a natural avenue for the Center to explore if we want to expand in the future."

"I don't see us doing that," Harry said, "without significant financial backing from a benefactor."

"That's my role," Claire responded. "I suggest we play with the concept more, enough so I can run it by a few people I have in mind. I'd guess I could get funding for a year or so. Hopefully, by then we'd have a stronger advertising base. I like it. And I must say I'm intrigued with your notion of—what did you call it—e-publishing?"

"Yes, that's it." Melissa held her breath, amazed the idea appealed to Claire at all.

"I don't know if we're at the place to do it," Claire continued, "but I like the idea of supporting a few writers who can get across our ideas and principles through fiction. I've never read anything more boring than some of the so-called sex manuals." She scowled. "I think I told you some of the novels of the sixties and seventies inspired both . . ." She stopped mid-sentence, her eyes rounding.

Melissa stopped breathing and her knuckles whitened as she gripped the table tight.

"They inspired both my personal and professional life," Claire added, nodding softly.

"I do see that as a long-term goal," Melissa said, finally inhaling steadily.

"Good," Harry interjected. "We can't take too much on at once, but basically I believe what you're thinking about makes sense. We've done and are doing some good work here. But we can make it better. And we all can have a role in that. Is there anything else?"

"Yes, there is." Melissa brushed a lock of hair from her forehead. "I have one more suggestion. I guess to be honest, I probably should say this is a piece I want for myself." She couldn't ignore the goose bumps forming on her wrists. "The concepts I've laid out will require a lot of time as well as financial backing. I'm prepared to devote my foreseeable future to the Center to promote those concepts, but I am an artist, and I don't want to give up my art entirely, even for the Center."

She pushed her chair back and stepped to the light switch to turn off the lights. Only the lamp from her projector provided light. "I believe we're all quite comfortable in the dark," she quipped, returning to her chair. She gulped. Had she really said that? Thankfully, both Harry and Claire were chuckling. "I'd like a small section in the Center catalog to display my art. Harry has seen some of my work, but I know you haven't, Claire. So here is a sample. I've put together a dozen photos of pastels and charcoals. Of course, if the Center is willing to help market my art, it would take a commission on anything sold."

"Of course," Claire responded. "So show us. You have me on pins and needles."

Melissa proceeded to click through her art samples.

Claire's oohs and ahhs made the final result a fairly certain conclusion.

After she presented the last slide, Melissa flipped the lights back on.

Claire stared at her with an odd look. "I'm awed," she said. "I know you're talented in other ways. I never knew you were this talented. Why didn't someone tell me?

"She is good, isn't she?" Harry said, apparently not picking up on Claire's distress.

"They are so erotic, so tasteful, so artful," Claire said, still looking quite strained. "Yes, absolutely. Take as much space as you want in the catalogue. I'm told that every time we add a sheet, we add four pages. How's that sound?"

"Splendid." Melissa caught her breath. "That sounds great. I'll be ever so grateful. You don't know how hard it is for an unknown artist to find an avenue for his or her work."

"Why not display some pieces here at the Center?" Claire asked. "Maybe we could have a showing. Or maybe the Center could sponsor a showing through the help of our benefactors. Maybe they need a classier place to be presented than here. But we can make it work. My God, girl, you're gifted." Claire's eyes misted. "I'm . . . I'm so proud of you."

Melissa peeked at Harry, who gave her a puzzled look.

"What do you think?"

"They're great," he said, arching an eyebrow at her. "I hadn't seen all of them."

"No," Melissa glanced at her laptop and then back at him. "I've been quite busy while you were away."

He smiled easily. Whatever he'd been puzzling over seemed to have been resolved. She was really worried about Claire, though. The woman was on edge.

"I particularly liked," Harry said, "the pastel profile of the man and woman making love in front of the window. Those were raindrops on the window, right?"

"Yes," she said, demurely. "I hoped you might like that one."

"I loved them all," Claire broke in. "I'm still creaming my panties. But it was the last one that will stick with me. So subtle, and yet so suggestive. And I'm not a subtle person. But the young woman with one hand cradling a bare breast and the other hidden under her skirt clearly fondling herself. My goodness." Claire gawked at her. "Where did you come up with that idea? It reminds me . . ." She shook her head. "It reminds me of someone long ago." Again, she looked at Melissa as if she were seeing an apparition.

Melissa murmured, "Thanks."

"You are a remarkable addition to the Center, Melissa. To our lives, really." Claire shook her head and stood. "Now, I really have to get back upstairs. Drop off your hard copy when you're ready."

Melissa watched Claire walk to the door.

Claire turned. "That last picture. I assume you still have it."

"Of course."

"I want to buy it."

"I'll give it to you."

"No, I'll buy it, but I don't want any other prints made from it. It is one of a kind."

"That's fine." Dumfounded, Melissa watched the tall blonde exit and the door shut behind her.

"Wow!" Harry said at last. "What was that all about? I've seldom seen Claire so emotional. Well done," he said, taking her fingers to his lips and kissing them. He stood. "You look different in your power suit. This entire presentation offered a different side of you than I'd seen before."

"Were you disappointed?" she asked, eyeing him closely.

"Not at all. Your self-control may have surprised me some. Your zeal came through loud and clear. You'll be good for the Center, I expect for a very long time, if you're willing."

She nodded and watched him leave. Once the door clicked shut, she stared at her laptop. She wasn't entirely sure what had transpired during the last hour. But her concept had struck a positive chord. And her art certainly had been not only acceptable, but honored.

So what was nagging at her? Claire had been overwhelmed by the presentation, particularly the art. Harry had been very supportive and seemingly pleased for her. Was she worrying about problems that weren't there? He'd seem supportive, but a little distant. Had her professionalism threatened him in some way? They shared such a strong commitment to the Center—her expanding role, if it were to actually happen, shouldn't threaten him.

Had he been aware that Claire nearly slipped—possibly twice? *Damn. Damn. Damn.* She had to tell him soon. She had no idea what had caused Claire to react so temperamentally, but she couldn't be certain it wouldn't happen again.

Having worked on her presentation nearly nonstop for days, Melissa went directly home and collapsed. She didn't awaken until the next morning. If Harry had called, the phone had not awakened her. There were no messages.

She gobbled a piece of toast and gulped her coffee. She

didn't want to be late for work.

When she arrived at her office, a manila envelope with her name on it sat on her desk. Inez was out of the office. Maybe she'd left her some instructions.

She pulled out its contents. Tilting her head to the side, she gawked at the document. She sat down hard on her chair and scanned the simple first page.

It was a contract—an offer from the Center for a full-time position. She was being promoted to associate director, with a very nice raise. Would she ever breathe again? The contract would be good for a year from the day she signed it, and it could be renewed annually. The last page of the document had Claire and Harry's signature as well as that of the chair of the board of directors, a woman she'd never met.

Melissa closed her eyes and fumbled for a pen. She'd better sign this before someone changed their mind, or before she woke up from her dream.

A half an hour later Harry glanced at his door and hollered, "Yeah." He smiled to himself. He didn't have to wonder who was knocking on his door this early in the morning.

"You look breathless," he said, standing to gather Melissa in his arms. "I wondered how long it would take you to get here."

She rubbed her nose against his shoulder.

He knew she was trying hard not to cry.

"I dropped the contract off with Claire."

"Signed?"

"Of course." She looked at him quizzically. "You didn't think I wouldn't, did you?"

He shook his head. She hadn't bothered to ask him what he thought before she signed it and returned it to Claire. "No. I was certain you'd accept the offer. Congratulations, Melissa.

You'll be great for the Center. The place needs new blood at the management level. Your enthusiasm and creativity will help all of us."

She leaned away from him and then stepped back. "How come I don't detect the kind of unbridled enthusiasm on your part that I might have expected?"

"How do I know what you expect?" he said, too harshly. He regretted his words as soon as he saw the pain in her eyes. "I'm sorry," he said quickly. "This isn't just about you."

"Tell me." She sat down in a nearby chair. "I think you'd better explain yourself."

Shit. He'd done it now. Women didn't talk to him that way unless they were really pissed. Melissa definitely looked all woman when her temper flared. It was about to flash into a four-alarm fire if he didn't do something soon. "It's Claire." He slumped down in his chair and looked at Melissa from across his desk. It was like an abyss. "She's always coveted the purse strings of the Center. Apparently, she took over fundraising from Mr. Howard not long after she and Phoebe came here. She cultivates and nurtures the contacts with the foundations and the so-called benefactors. She writes the grants and so on."

"And you wanted to do that?"

He shook his head. "Not at all. I can't hobnob with folks. I'm not good at sucking up." He stared at her twinkling eyes—how quickly her moods changed. "I don't suck up well with benefactors."

"I'm glad you clarified that little factoid. Yes, I do believe I understand. So Claire controls the purse strings and therefore significant changes in Center directions."

He shrugged his shoulders.

"And any significant hires, like creating a new position called associate director."

"She asked my opinion." He frowned, but Melissa waited

for him to fill in the blanks. "Frankly, I thought she was being precipitous. I've been asking for money for more basic research for years. We've talked about doing more of our own in-house filming. But there's never been enough money. Claire is a procrastinator. She drags her feet.

"I'm sorry. I don't mean to be childish, but then you come along and sweep her off her feet. And you did do great. And you have some very innovative ideas. But . . ."

"But?" Melissa cocked her head at him. Her eyes might have been made of steel.

"As she probably told you, she made a few phone calls last night to a few people with deep pockets and voila—in a matter of hours, the Center has a new management position and is embarked on some new adventures."

"Not bad, but hasty in your judgment?"

"Something like that. It's not personal."

Melissa smiled thinly. "Of course not. In case you're wondering, I'm not about to rip up that contract. I hope we can work together."

"Don't get your back up, Melissa. It's a fantastic opportunity for you and for the Center and I am thrilled for all of us. And yes, I'm a little miffed with the process."

"But not the outcome?"

He shook his head. "We'll all benefit. My role doesn't change much, if at all. I still have research, and I have overall responsibility for film production and hiring of staff in that part of the operation. If anything, having you here may free me up to do more of my research, if I ever can figure out how to fund it."

Chuckling, Melissa said, "Maybe I'll be able to help make the case for the research as part of the Center's foundation. It has been and should be. I should've said more about that in my presentation, but I saw that as your bailiwick."

"Don't worry about it. And you're right; you may be able

to help present the case. That's always been my weakest suit. So do you hobnob well with the rich and famous?"

"I don't know. I've never tried." He watched her chin jut forward. "But if I have to, I'll learn how. If that's what I have to do."

"As you always do," he murmured.

"So what about us, Harry? Does my promotion, my expanded role at the Center impact us?"

He steepled his fingers. "Of course it does. Our working relationship will be different. You'll be much more responsible to Claire than to me."

"You know that's not what I meant. Us, Harry. You and me?"

His shoulder slumped. "I know what you mean. I hope not. I guess we'll see what happens."

"I don't want the Center to get in the way."

"But you don't want us to get in the way of the Center, either?"

"That's right. I've missed you, Harry."

He rose to his feet, and she came into his arms again. He bent down and slanted his lips across hers. It was a hungry kiss. He sensed her desire and was keenly aware of his own. Her tongue teased his lips until he opened his mouth and their tongues entwined.

What would she do if he started unbuttoning her blouse? Would she make love with him in his office? Or did her new promotion change that, too? He opened his eyes. Hers were still closed. He could kiss her the entire day. He didn't think she'd welcome him deepening that kiss and taking their embrace to the next level. Things had changed overnight.

Strange. He pressed her tight, not wanting to let her go. One lover hadn't wanted to have sex with him away from the Center. He expected Melissa would only have sex at the Center now if they were working on set.

She broke away. "Sorry," she said, wetting her lips and straightening her clothes. "I have to be going." She winked at him. "Do you want to come to my place tonight or have me come to yours? I'll cook."

"My place. Are you sure? We should go out and celebrate your promotion."

She shook her head. "Maybe this weekend. Tonight I don't want to share you with anyone. Not even a restaurant crowd."

He breathed a little easier. This was still his old Melissa. "I don't want to have to share you either." He kissed her forehead and patted her butt as she turned to leave.

He gave a huge sigh once she'd closed the door behind her. Damn, he felt like he'd just walked across a bed of burning coals. He'd been singed, but he'd survived. This would work. It had to. But it hadn't before.

And Melissa was not Phoebe. But he wasn't sure this Melissa was the one he'd interviewed several months earlier.

CHAPTER FOURTEEN

Bedraggled, Melissa shut her office door and leaned back against it for support. She closed her eyes and sighed. So far, the morning had been an emotional roller coaster. The high she'd had from signing the contract had been blunted some by Harry's response. While his comments weren't supposed to be personal, it was difficult not take them personally.

Now there was one more individual to deal with about her newly acquired status. Reluctantly, she opened her eyes.

Inez gave her a curious look and then leaped to her feet and dashed to the door to hug her. Melissa wrapped her arms around her friend and clutched her tight. "You know?" she whispered.

Kissing her cheek, Inez nodded. "Claire just left. I'm so happy for you. You're going places, girl."

Without letting Inez go, Melissa leaned back far enough to get a good look at her. "You're not jealous. Not hurt?"

Inez frowned. "Why should I be? I like what I do. I don't want to be part of management." Inez smiled. "You've got the talent, the degrees, and the ambition. I'm pulling for you." Inez reached out and touched her cheek. "So is it okay for me to kiss management?"

Tipping her head back, Melissa laughed easily, then slanted her lips across Inez's. She breathed in the woman's scent and lowered her hands to clutch her butt. She deepened their kiss by probing with her tongue. Inez's moans expanded her heart.

She inhaled deeply without breaking their kiss. Inez

wrapped a leg around her rear. They rocked back and forth, rubbing and grinding crotches.

Inez shuddered. "My God," she moaned, resting her head on Melissa's shoulder. "I guess I got my answer."

Melissa patted her buttocks and stepped away. She breathed deeply and nodded. "That was the best kiss I've had all morning."

"Uh, oh." Inez scowled. "So Harry's not thrilled with your promotion."

"It's nothing personal."

"Right. I don't care how much anyone says otherwise, everything about this place is personal."

"You think so?"

Inez nodded and wrapped her arms around herself. "That's something I've learned from you." She retreated to her desk without further explanation.

Melissa sat at her desk and tried to concentrate on something—on anything. She gazed over at Inez, who she expected was also pretending to work. She cleared her throat. "You want to tell me what you meant by that last comment?"

She watched Inez shrug and glance away as if she wanted to be somewhere else. She sighed deeply before speaking. "I listen to you as you talk to people through the camera, Melissa. I watch you. Hell, I feel you. You've taught me something about intimacy. I thought I should distance myself from sex—somehow treat it as just sex—and save myself for my true love. Whoever the hell that is. But you're intimate with everyone—even the viewer. And you still have a special place in your heart for your lover."

Melissa felt herself crumpling. She wished Inez was right, but she wasn't so sure about that. She stiffened. But it did take two people to turn intimacy into love. She couldn't make Harry hang in with her if he wanted out. She wouldn't want him that way, even if she could make him.

"Are you listening to me?" Inez asked. "I'm over here baring my soul and you look like you've checked out."

"I'm sorry." Melissa shook her head, focusing on her friend. "I hear you. You triggered another thought. Sorry. I do appreciate what you're saying. And I believe it. Sometimes I fall short of my own expectations."

"Welcome to the human race. So with you moving up to management, will we still be working together—on set?"

Melissa grinned. "You better believe it. Plus you and I will be able to put our heads together and come up with some of our own ideas for scenes and scenarios."

"Nice." Inez shot her a come-hither smile.

"Now," Melissa tried to look stern, "let's get back to work, or I'm going to have to find an old camera and set it up so we can pretend we're working."

Inez smirked with longing. "I could deal with that."

Melissa shook her head. "Enough for now."

Inez nodded and turned to her computer.

Melissa sighed softly. Why couldn't her relationship with Harry be as easygoing as her relationship with Inez? Because they were mucking around in something called love and commitment—something beyond even intimacy. And then there was her ever-present aunt.

She had to tell Harry. Tonight? She shook her head. No, they were already on shaky ground. Not tonight.

Hours later, Melissa lay curled against Harry's backside plagued by many more questions than answers. It had nearly been a lovely evening. Nearly.

She'd concocted an elegant soup, and Harry had put together a fine salad. Soup, salad, and chardonnay made for a mellow dinner and a slow-paced evening.

They hadn't dwelt on her promotion, nor had they ignored it. Harry seemed easier with it than earlier in the day. Even their lovemaking had been mellow. She'd felt treasured. She grazed her lips across Harry's back.

His soft snores calmed her. Yet something had been missing, or perhaps something had been there that hadn't been before. She pulled the sheet up over them. It was as if there had been an invisible barrier between them.

She squirmed her crotch against his rear. She caught her breath. Her clit was still seeking, demanding. She needed more. Should she wake Harry? Would he even want to satisfy her?

Her hand strayed toward her crotch. She jerked it back. She wasn't going to bring herself off that way with a man in her bed. She moaned and gently rubbed her pubic area against his butt until friction inevitably ignited the spark and she lay back and basked in her own warm glow.

Harry felt the cool air when Melissa moved away from his ass and cracked an eye open. His hand encircled his straining cock, but he did nothing more to seek relief.

Apparently, he hadn't satisfied her enough. Wasn't that the way the entire day had gone? He couldn't quite say the right thing, nor do the right thing. Since when had he become so inept?

He didn't like that feeling, not at all. So who would break off first? Him or her? He'd thought—he'd hoped—that Claire might be right, that with Melissa he'd found the right woman. Maybe there was no right woman. Maybe that was the joke on him, on all of them.

Three days later, Harry watched Max's mouth turn into a glorious smile. The explanation for the older fellow's grin was only inches from Harry's face. Melissa was sliding up and down the man's shaft trying to get him hard in her mouth—

apparently with some success.

Harry watched her boobs bounce next to his nose. He flicked his tongue out at a taut nipple. Even that didn't divert her attention. Flexing his hips, Harry delighted in Melissa's heavy moan. He'd reminded her that he was buried deep in her vagina and that this three-way was about more than getting Max off with her mouth.

She dropped Max and gave him a questioning look.

Was that a trace of anxiety in this new calm and collected Melissa? Good. Fear would be better. "Are you ready?"

She nodded.

"And you, Max. Are you ready?"

Max nodded with a slight grin and grabbed his fairly hard cock. "As ready as I'll ever be."

"Let's get on with it." He saw the pain in Melissa's eyes. He sighed. "You've got the biggest cock in your vagina. You shouldn't have much trouble taking Max in your ass."

She nodded. "Let's do it," she said to Max, giving him an encouraging smile. She took him in her mouth again briefly, and then Max shifted until he knelt behind Melissa.

Harry knew the moment Max's cock pressed at Melissa's anus. Her eyes widened. She locked her gaze on his. *Ah.* This was his old Melissa, drawing strength from him for what needed to be done.

He nodded at Max, and Max pushed further in. "Goodness," Melissa muttered. "So full. Wait!"

Max stopped immediately.

Harry knew the last thing Max would ever want to do was hurt Melissa.

"Okay, Max, more," she said. "Oh my God," she whimpered as Max grunted and pushed steadily forward.

Harry could feel the length of Max through Melissa's tight sleeve. "He's in, girl. How are you doing?"

Melissa blinked. "I'm not sure. I've never been this full.

Ever."

"Remember to relax," he said, combing his fingers through her dark tresses. He felt her lungs expanding and emptying against his chest.

"That's a nice thought," she said. "Now what?"

"Now we'll take you for a ride and see what happens. Max, why don't you begin?" He wasn't certain how long Max would hold up or last.

"Okay," Max replied.

Harry felt Max slide cautiously partway out of Melissa and then fill her again. Melissa's mouth slackened. After a half dozen strokes, Max halted to catch his breath.

Blowing a kiss at Melissa, Harry asked, "You still okay?"

Melissa nodded. "Dreamy, but okay."

"Good. We should probably demonstrate that the guy on the bottom isn't just a bystander."

Melissa nodded.

"Max, sit tight for a moment."

"I'm not about to go anywhere," Max grunted.

Harry began thrusting his hips slowly, driving in and out of her. The tight fit had an immediate effect on him. He shuttered his eyes and stopped.

When he opened them, Melissa was beaming at him. "That looked pretty good for you, too." She licked perspiration from his neck. The hardest part of working on the set was the heat from the lights. They were all dripping profusely.

"So can you both do me at the same time?" she asked innocently.

He nodded. "We'll alternate strokes. Go ahead, Max. When you're ready, you set the pace. I'll keep up with you."

Max nodded and shifted a bit. When Max had pressed as far as he could into Melissa's anal canal, Harry pulled part way out of her vagina. When Max backed partway out, Harry flexed to fill her.

"Oh hell," Melissa whimpered. "I'm humming . . . and quaking all over the place. Please keep going." She shut her eyes.

Harry knew she was retreating inward.

Max picked up the pace. Harry watched Max carefully. The man turned red, and his breathing shortened. He was either nearly ready to come or about to have a heart attack.

Melissa eyes popped opened. "There's no escape," she wailed. "Come on, Max. Don't hold back. Fill my ass."

"Jesus, lady," Max gasped, jerking behind her. "I can't help it. You're getting your wish."

Melissa thrashed like a rag doll. Harry lost any semblance of control and plowed into her over and over until he emptied himself.

Moments later Harry pried his eyes open. Melissa heaved against his chest. Max lay draped over her back, breathing evenly, thank goodness. Harry was certain Melissa had come, probably more than once, but he hadn't heard her. It would have taken a foghorn to penetrate his own senses once he began to climax. That was some extreme sex.

He watched her eyes open and a tiny smile flit across her lips. She mouthed one word: *Thanks.* She looked toward the camera. He saw her mouth two words—*wow, bye*—then lift her fingers in a slight wave. Then she nestled her head against his chest and was soon dozing.

The lights were turned off and the camera crew departed.

Melissa groaned when Max pulled out of her. He quietly left the room.

Harry let out two lungs full of air. He really loved this Melissa. The adventurous, willing Melissa. He trusted she'd find her voice again.

At three o'clock that afternoon, Harry watched Melissa in the production room sitting on a stool and talking into a mike.

She was wrapping up commentary for the three-way tape.

He'd thought his presence on camera wasn't required. Neither Melissa nor Claire had disagreed with him. He admired Melissa's sense for style and taste. She wore a long blue dress buttoned down the front. Quite prim and proper. Hardly the same woman who the viewer would just have watched in various three-way encounters with a man and another woman, and then with two guys. On anyone else, the outfit might not have looked sexy at all. On her—well, she'd look sexy wearing anything, especially in front of a camera.

He listened in on her final comments.

"So you see, folks, in that last scene, I sort of lost my voice." She blushed, projecting an air of innocence.

Had he fallen for a consummate actress?

"I still don't know that I have words to fully describe my emotions in that moment. I doubt I was even aware of all of them myself." She squirmed on her butt a little. "Maybe I'll reexperience some of them in my subconscious.

"So I leave a parting thought with the ladies. If you want to experience the feel of two cocks but can't see yourself ever wanting a second man in your bed, remember your vibrator. A penis in one orifice and a vibrator in the other will work quite fine."

She threw Harry a quick smile. She was right about that. It had helped prepare her for Max.

"And, ladies, if you don't have a man in your life and maybe don't want one, but you still want to experience some of the feel of the three-way with two cocks," she paused and smiled, "use two vibrators. I don't think I have to tell you where to put them. And I can vouch that while it's not exactly the same, it also works quite fine.

"Remember, ladies, a dog may be a man's best friend, but a vibrator . . ." She let the word vibrator roll off her lips and then waved her fingers. "Bye."

Claire and Inez applauded wildly. Both women hugged her and kissed her, a bit more soundly than he thought was necessary.

But Harry smiled when it became obvious that Melissa was looking around them seeking him out.

He stepped toward her, and she broke away and ran to him. He lifted her in his arms and swung her around. She laughed and squealed.

"You should be in Hollywood."

"Never," she said between giggles. "I don't need any stage larger than the one right here."

He set her feet on the floor, and she tucked an arm through his and led him toward the door.

"That was astounding this morning. I do think we deserve to make an early departure today." She looked up at him, waiting for his response.

He wasn't about to disappoint her. "I don't think I could concentrate on anything else anyway. Sounds fine."

"Why don't we go to my place? We can either go to that Italian bistro down the street or order in."

"Sounds good."

She whacked her hip against his. "I'm not sure I'm going to be ready for a cock later, but I might find a tongue quite soothing in a couple places that are still smoldering from this morning. And"—she stuck her tongue out at him—"I might like to taste anything else you might have to give me—a liqueur of sorts. Maybe I'll call it Harry's parfait amour."

He tucked an arm around her waist and bumped his hip hard against hers. How long would it take her to come down from her adrenaline high? "Damn, who made you so irrepressible?"

"I hope that's not an objection."

"It's not," he said, shaking his head, "but if it sounds like one, feel free to overrule it."

"I will," she said, happily, "I will."

A week later, Melissa smiled at her sketchpad. She was working on a pencil sketch of a full-breasted nude reclining on a couch. It was somewhat reminiscent of *Olympia,* done by one of her favorite Impressionist artists, Manet.

Her female had fuller, perkier breasts. The Olympia model had perhaps been a prostitute, and Manet's portrait of her had created quite a scandal. Melissa's model, Virginia, was a fellow art student. Olympia had been clad only with slippers, a bracelet, and a necklace. The feet of Melissa's model were not visible, prompting the viewer to wonder who might be standing there viewing her. Virginia wore a gold chain. One of Olympia's hands hid her mound from view. Virginia's hands discreetly flexed her panties aside. The viewer could see the outcropping of curls forming the gateway to her vagina.

Melissa's breathing quickened. Any man or woman standing at the end of the couch Virginia was lying on would have a clear view of the treasure she boldly yet tentatively offered. Olympia projected the air of an experienced seducer. Virginia cast a spell of questioning virtuosity.

Melissa bit down on her tongue and darkened Virginia's mound a bit more. She stood back and nodded. The mound was clearly visible, but it was not the immediate focus. The observer's eyes would be first drawn to Virginia's face, which tilted toward the viewer with subtle invitation. And then watching eyes would travel over the large breasts and settle at last on her pussy, framed by her arms on two sides and by the wisp of her panties held in tension by her fingers.

"Enough," Melissa mumbled. She yawned. She needed to get her rest for tomorrow.

Tomorrow could be huge. She and Harry had reestablished a fairly even keel on which to navigate their relationship, but it was good to have a night or two apart from each other. She might be ready for some sort of commitment, but she wasn't ready for them to set up house together.

She wandered into her bedroom and started getting ready for bed. She'd tell him tomorrow night. Her life might be clearer after that. She no longer harbored any thought that he might be confusing her with his Phoebe, but that didn't mean he'd be thrilled to find out his former lover was her aunt.

She fully expected Harry to storm off in a childish huff. He'd proven quite capable of that. But she also believed he could eventually get his head around her being Phoebe's niece. At least she hoped he could. She couldn't go on any longer with her aunt hovering over them.

She climbed into bed and hugged a pillow to her breasts. First, there was the little matter of helping with the fantasy scene Claire had been working on for months. They'd agreed on a scenario that melded one of Claire's ideas with one of her own.

Claire had wanted her to arrange for a room in some sort of art museum or studio. Paintings in the background would serve as symbols for the fantasy. She didn't know if she had connections that could make that happen, but she'd suggested an alternative—one that had appealed to her even as a girl.

Often when she studied a painting, she'd transpose herself into the scene. She'd suggested they bring to life another of her favorite paintings by Manet: *Le Dejeuner-sur-L'Herbe.* The painting showed two couples on a picnic. The men were fully dressed. One woman was nude, the other nearly so.

Whenever she saw that picture, she'd always wondered why, and what happened next. And now she was going to find out.

She kissed her pillow. She'd talked Harry into playing the painter. He would have two roles, really—both the painter, and her partner in the picture. Inez and Max had agreed to help out by playing the other couple.

She'd been thrilled when Max agreed. He'd said he would do anything for her. Max had turned out to be a closet romantic, and he was becoming a regular at the Center. He thrived on knowing he could still contribute to something he believed in. Her butt clenched—he could contribute, all right.

Tomorrow they'd drive to the Catskills, where Claire, through her contacts, had access to an estate overlooking the Hudson. She prayed it wouldn't rain. Impressionists were known for doing much of their painting outside. Besides, this was supposed to be a picnic.

She hoped she could sleep. The fantasy should be lots of fun. Claire had sunk a great deal of time, money, and energy into setting it up. Once Melissa had heard the scene was set for the fantasy shoot, she'd decided not to tell Harry about her aunt until tomorrow night. She wouldn't be completely shocked if Harry disappeared for a day or two. And she didn't want all of Claire's efforts and Center resources to go to waste because of a personal spat between her and Harry.

So with some luck—probably lots of luck—in another twenty-four hours, she and Harry might move to a new plateau.

She closed her eyes and prayed for sleep and much, much more.

Chapter Fifteen

Feeling incredibly expansive, Melissa stepped out of the limo. She grabbed Inez by the hand, and together they dashed down the long estate lawn to where they could look down at the Hudson.

"Can you believe this?" Melissa sang out. "Limos!" She twirled around to gawk at the huge mansion on the crest above them. "This place has to be worth millions. We're being treated like royalty."

"I've been on some outside shoots," Inez said, grinning from ear to ear, "but nothing like this. Claire must've really latched on to someone with a bankroll this time. It's an incredibly warm day, and the trees are brilliant! She must have an *in* with God."

"She can be quite convincing when she wants to be."

"Yeah, for her age, she can be one sexy lady."

Melissa hugged Inez. "Believe me, once today is done and you've had Max, you won't be making any more snide remarks about age."

"Maybe."

"I guarantee it. I guess we should get back up the hill. The guys weren't that far behind us. It looks like we have two dressing tents set up. And look," she said, pointing to a partially secluded area to their right. "Claire is setting out blankets and picnic baskets. She's already bringing Manet's work to life. This is so perfect."

"Are you sure Max is going to be okay with me as his partner instead of you?"

"Sure he will. You two have met. You've talked to him."

"A little. He does seem nice enough. But are you sure I'm not going to have to do all the work?"

Melissa howled. "Ask me that after the shoot." She tugged Inez's hand and guided her toward Claire.

"This is a tremendous spot, Claire."

"I'm glad you like it," Claire replied, straightening one of the blankets. "I tried to select a spot that resembled the painting you showed me. You girls need to go change. The tent on the right is yours. I've laid out period costumes and jewelry for each of you."

"But," Inez said, "I thought in the picture one woman was nude and the other wore a flimsy white gown."

"That's true." Claire grinned at Inez. "But Melissa and I thought it'd be much more erotic for our contemporary viewer if the two men tantalizingly disrobe their women. We don't simply want to do a slam-bang-thank-you-ma'am film, do we, Inez?" Claire tucked a finger under Inez's chin and lifted it. "Don't be nervous. Max is going to enjoy you, and you'll enjoy him. Now run along," she added, tapping Inez lightly on the bottom.

Melissa and Inez changed out of their work clothes and into the period pieces. They hadn't been provided with undergarments. Apparently, those weren't needed.

"I still can't believe that woman," Inez said with a shake of her head.

"What woman?"

"Claire. Who else? When she raised my chin, I thought she was going to kiss me. And then she tells me not to be nervous about Max. How did she know I was nervous?"

"Don't underestimate Claire. She can be surprisingly perceptive. I'm glad we don't have to routinely do as many buttons as women used to contend with." Melissa fastened the last of the tiny buttons up her front and looked over to see Inez struggling with another long column of buttons.

Once finished, they both stood and admired each other. "Very fetching, Mademoiselle." Melissa grinned, picking up the single piece of jewelry on her chair. She recognized it immediately as Claire's pendant that matched her Aunt Phoebe's. She was honored that Claire would entrust her with it, even for a brief time. "Can you help me with this chain?"

"It's beautiful," Inez said, looking at the gold circular pendant.

"It is, isn't it? I believe it belongs to Claire. I expect that diamond choker you're wearing is hers, too. I doubt the Center has real jewelry in its prop room."

Inez stroked the diamonds resting on a strand of black velvet. "You think these are real?"

"Absolutely. Enjoy. Come on, we'd better get going, or they'll send someone after us."

They stepped out of the tent. "There. You see? The guys are already in place. Hurry." She dropped the pendant inside her dress to keep it from swinging. They didn't exactly run, but Melissa loved the feel of springy grass between her bare toes.

She drew up short at the edge of the two large picnic blankets. Max stood and took Inez by the hand and ushered her to their blanket. She couldn't make out what he was whispering in Inez's ear, but whatever he'd said brought a warm smile to her lips.

Melissa caught Claire's eye and saw the relief registered on her face. She really had been worrying about Inez. Wasn't that interesting?

Melissa dropped down across from Harry, who hadn't bothered to get up. She smoothed out her long dress and glanced shyly at him. "So how is our painter today? You look debonair. Manet couldn't have looked any better."

"So happy I meet with your approval." His dark eyed gaze

ripped through her.

Was it lust? Or was it something else? "Are you okay?"

"Don't worry about me. This is your fantasy. It's time to play it out."

"Then you take over. You're playing the role of artist and director."

"Okay, I will." He rose to his haunches. Would she really want him to take over if she knew what he was planning? "Models in Manet's time were frequently women of the night, fallen doves. Right?"

She nodded.

"They no doubt stripped for their men before offering themselves as part of the picnic feast." He pointed at her. "So strip."

Her eyebrows shot skyward. "That's not the way the script is written."

Harry smiled at her distress. "This is the revised script. I'm in charge, remember? Do as I say."

She scowled at him and glanced over at Claire. "Oh, okay," she said. "Let's do it, Inez. It won't matter much." She looked back at him. "You're sure in a foul mood today."

He folded his arms and waited for her to begin stripping. "Thought painters were supposed to be foul and moody."

She didn't respond, but she did reach for the top button of her dress.

Harry knew she was trying to stare through him. He winced. Foul mood didn't even begin to cut it.

Who had set him up this way? Melissa or Claire? Did Melissa even know? She had to know. Claire screened everything with her these days.

He hadn't been certain until they'd turned into the driveway of the estate. This was the last place he and Phoebe had made love. He shook his head and watched Melissa undoing a second button. He corrected himself. He'd forgotten. Phoebe didn't *make love.* This was the last place he and Phoebe had fucked. And on top of that, Melissa was wearing the same costume.

What the hell was going on? Whatever it was, he didn't like it one bit.

Melissa had enough buttons undone that he could reach in and fondle a boob, and he did so without asking. She eyed him suspiciously, but when he stroked it, she began to purr, as he knew she would. She'd be doing much more than purring before he was finished with her.

"Let me help you," intoned a soft male voice from behind him.

Harry glanced over at Max, who was intent on assisting Inez out of her dress instead of making her strip. *Let him play the gentleman.* He wasn't feeling very gentle at the moment. He twisted Melissa's nipple.

She flinched and glowered at him. "Are you going to make any effort to appear to be painting?"

He nodded. "I probably should. We do have to advance the fantasy for our audience. Continue with your buttons. We don't have all day." He stood and stomped to the easel and brush.

He felt like an idiot playing the role of a painter. He didn't know a thing about how to paint. That was Melissa's area of expertise. That, and a lot of others, it appeared. At the top of her skill list should appear *deception.*

Max helped Inez stand and pushed her dress to her feet. He beamed and cupped a breast in each palm as if he'd found the Holy Grail. Harry gritted his teeth and met Melissa's eyes. She had paused to wait for him. "Take the damn dress off," he practically growled. Melissa stared at him stonily, then rose to her feet and deliberately turned away from him. She peered over her shoulder and stuck her tongue out at him and at the camera. She ducked a shoulder and arm out of her dress. The dress dipped, showing much of her bare back. Since when had a partially clad back become so erotic?

He straightened his arousal and began scratching lines on the sketchpad. Melissa shrugged her other shoulder from the dress, and the dress pooled around her feet. She bent over and slowly removed one foot from the dress; her ass shimmered in the soft light. Her pussy and asshole couldn't have been clearer or more provocative. For a moment, he wished he had two cocks.

Harry cleared his throat, and Melissa straightened and leaned over again to release her other foot from the folds of the dress. Her butt swayed and taunted. Clearly, she knew what effect she was having on her audience. And she was showing him she could play whatever game he wanted to play. *We'll see about that.*

"Enough," he said sharply. "Lie back down on the blanket."

She did so, facing away from him. She propped the foot of her right leg on the knee of her left—again framing her dual treasures for him and the audience—and turned her head slightly until their eyes met. She looked like temptation personified. Sometimes looks weren't deceiving.

"Damn you," he snarled. The tableau had gotten away from him. Inez was furiously bobbing up and down Max's shaft, and Melissa was intent on wrenching the script away from him. Yet she was still playing the courtesan.

In three strides, he towered over her and kicked off his pants. He didn't bother removing his shirt. In short order, he stretched out behind her and positioned his hard cock at her pussy. "You're wet and ready. You adapt very easily to the role of the harlot, don't you?"

"I'm always ready for you," she quipped, fondling his

balls. "I am whatever you want me to be."

Cunning bitch! Without finesse, he rammed his cock into her. She gulped air trying to catch her breath but said nothing. He didn't give her a chance to settle but pumped in and out quickly.

"Why?" she murmured. "Why are you doing this? This fantasy was supposed to be so lovely."

He pinched her butt cheek until she screeched. "I thought this was the way those artsy types fucked in Paris."

She ignored him. Sounds from the next blanket intruded on his focus. He blinked and stilled. He'd forgotten about Max and Inez. They clearly didn't need any further direction. Inez was screaming her head off sitting astride Max, riding him like a crazed bull rider. Harry smiled. It was unlikely she'd ever get the old guy off that way, but she sure seemed to be enjoying her new sex toy. And the ear-splitting smile on Max's face suggested he was very much enjoying Inez's efforts, successful or not.

He glanced at Melissa. A light sheen of perspiration covered her back. He began to shift his position. "Roll over onto your back," he commanded, lifting her leg over him so he could kneel between her legs.

She cupped a hand at her throat. Her eyes were filled with fright.

He definitely had her attention. He smiled grimly and rocked back and forth, driving his shaft deeper each time. He lifted her knees and spread her thighs until she supported her legs on the balls of her feet, providing him with better leverage. Again, he began rhythmically pounding into her. She didn't speak, but he could read her lips—*Why?*

He nodded. "I'll tell you why," he hissed. "Was this your idea, or Claire's?"

Her puzzled expression confused him, but he barged ahead. "This was where I last fucked Phoebe. You're wearing her dress. When you and Inez ran down here from the tent . . ." He paused. His eyes misted over. He shook his head. "For a moment I thought you were Phoebe, come back to taunt me."

The pain on Melissa's face was palpable.

He pulled nearly all the way out and rammed back into her.

She grunted her shock, and he smiled with satisfaction.

Movement to his right caught his eye. Inez was finishing Max with his cock in her mouth and her finger in his ass. Max heaved and thrashed. Then Inez sidled up against him, and the two of them cuddled like long-lost lovers.

"So be it," he murmured, shifting his attention back to Melissa, whose eyes were wide with shock and fear. "Who do you think you are?" he grunted, plowing back into her.

She tossed her head from side to side.

"Who are you?" he bellowed, without relaxing his hips.

"I don't want to come this way," she whimpered. "Don't make me."

He laughed caustically. She was going to come, all right. He'd see to that now for sure. She was already beyond denying him that small victory. He shortened his stroke and quickened his pace. He had her.

"Good God," she wailed. Her fist flew to her mouth trying to block off her cries as an orgasm obviously coursed through her. He never paused and another swept across her.

Harry's lips curved into a sneer. His eyes settled on her pendant. He saw black. He saw Phoebe. *Her* pendant. He stilled. "Who are you?" he asked, harshly.

She gawked at him through horror-filled eyes.

He gulped for air and began pounding in and out of her again. He paused. "Phoebe's daughter. I've been fucking Phoebe's daughter all this time. Holy shit!"

She shook her head wildly. "No! That's not true."

"Christ, what a fool I've been." His hips churned anew. "Her daughter." He stopped abruptly. He ignored Melissa's sobs. He laughed hysterically. "The joke really is on me."

"No," she whimpered. "I . . . I tried to tell you." She sucked air through her nostrils. "But I'm not Phoebe's daughter. I'm her niece." Her words tumbled out of her mouth. He strained to hear. He strained to block his ears. "And I never knew you were involved with her until after I began working at the Center."

He cocked his head to the side and laughed sarcastically. "And I'm supposed to believe that? I may be stupid, but not stupid enough to be deceived twice by the same lover." Harry gave her a twisted grin. "Ah."

"What?" she said, trying to pull away.

He grabbed her by the hips. "Be still," he ordered. He sneered down at her and licked his thumb. "A special treat. Your mother loved to come like this." He began to strum her clit like he was playing a banjo.

"No, Harry," she pleaded, squeezing him with her thighs. "Please, I don't want to come again. Not like this."

He laughed. "Your mother would often say those exact words, pretending to resist, but I never stopped. She never wanted me to stop. Not really. And neither do you."

He smiled with glee when Melissa lurched forward and then backward and began to thrash beneath him. His thumb played her unmercifully.

"Oh God," she whimpered, covering her eyes with her forearm. "Fuck me, Harry. Fill me."

He waited only long enough to know for certain she was coming. Then he pulled his still full cock out of her and lurched to his feet. He grabbed his pants but didn't bother to put them on. "I'm not wasting my seed on you, bitch." She'd rolled into a ball, still shaking in the throes of orgasms. He doubted she'd even heard him.

Taking long strides, he marched toward the men's changing tent, ignoring Claire's shouts of *Bastard!* He grabbed his street clothes, not bothering to put them on either, then stalked to the limo, climbed in, and told the driver to take him back to the city.

He cast one last glance toward the picnic tableaux. *How appropriate.* Both Inez and Claire were hugging the traitorous Melissa. *Women!*

"Are you okay?" Claire repeated her question.

"No." Melissa paused, swallowing a sob. "But I will be." She tried to smile through her tears. Claire and Inez seemed nearly as upset as she was.

"What got into him?" Inez asked. "I've never seen him like that."

"He thinks I did him wrong—real wrong," she sobbed. "I did, but not as bad as he thinks." She glanced over at the cameras. "The cameras!" she shrieked.

"Don't worry about them," Claire said, running her fingers through Melissa's hair. "I cut the cameras as soon as I realized where this scene was going."

"Thanks." She glanced over at Inez. "Too bad. You and Max seemed to be doing quite fine. The tape would've made a nice memento."

Inez shrugged and gave her a weak smile. "We might have to try that part again."

"Where is Max?"

"I think he ran after Harry. But Harry was out of here like a shot."

Claire nodded. "The bastard must've startled the limo driver."

Melissa couldn't hold back a giggle. Her giggle turned into a laugh. And then she cried.

Two sets of arms held her until she couldn't cry any more. She shook her head. She looked from Inez to Claire. She brushed her lips against each woman and whispered, "Thanks." She shook her hair and began testing her muscles to see if she could stand.

"I think I'm ready," she said, getting to her knees. "I want to go back to my apartment now."

"Do you want company?" Claire asked. She shot a quick look at Inez. "I'm sure either one of us would be willing to stay with you for as long as you need."

"Thanks," Melissa replied. "I don't want to offend, but I think I want to be alone tonight. I have many decisions to make."

"Of course." Claire paused. "But do take your time."

Inez spoke up softly. "Let me know if you change your mind and want me to drop by."

"I will." Melissa stood. "Now let's figure out how we're all going to get back to the city with one limo and the film crew van. Damn Harry!"

Triple-checking the e-mail message on her laptop screen, Melissa leaned back in her studio/office and sighed heavily. It was critical for her message to convey the appropriate tone. She hated resorting to e-mail, but Harry wasn't answering his phone. She wasn't about to leave a voice message, and showing up on his doorstep was out of the question.

She reread the e-mail aloud one more time.

Harry, below are three pictures. The first is my mother and father. The second is my aunt with me at my college graduation. And the third is the woman you knew as Phoebe fucking your brains out.

Yes, pictures of her working came into my possession after her death. I had no idea the two of you were lovers until quite a while after I started working for the Center.

No, I am not at all ashamed of what she did, what you and she did, or what I have done. I do wish I had been more persistent and courageous in telling you about my relationship to your Phoebe. But . . .

In case you're curious, I have no intention whatsoever of leaving the Center and my newly discovered passion. That is my work. It was Phoebe's. It is yours. She chose to leave it. I don't know what you will choose – but I choose to stay.

If you have anything to say to me, you know how to reach me.

Melissa

She rubbed her eyes, squinting at the screen. Not too personal. Not too apologetic. Not too expectant. Yet crystal clear about her role at the Center.

She scrolled through the pictures one last time. She'd dropped them directly into the e-mail because she didn't think he'd bother to open attachments from her.

Even so, she wondered if he'd bother to look at the photos. No matter what he did about the Center or about her, she wanted him to know proof positive that he hadn't been fucking Phoebe's daughter.

Cripes, she'd never thought of the possibility he might draw that conclusion. She had to own up to her mistakes, but she couldn't take responsibility for his reaction.

She cranked her neck from side to side. Was she ready to push the send button? She'd already screened all her calls from the time she'd arrived back in her apartment. There had been no call from Harry.

Melissa grinned faintly. Inez had called. After asking how she was doing, Inez had told her again how surprised she'd been by Max's attentiveness. Melissa had already heard it all while the two of them plus Claire rode in the limo back to the city. Still, listening to Inez's amazement was better than listening to her own agony.

And Claire. What was she going to do with Claire? The

woman had been quite distraught when she'd phoned earlier in the evening. Claire worried she might be so angry at her that she'd leave the Center.

No way! Maybe she should be mad at Claire. After all, Claire was the one who set the scene so Harry might make the inevitable connection, but she certainly had not expected him to explode the way he did. Melissa moaned. Claire had done what she thought was best for the Center and what she'd hoped was best for Melissa and Harry.

Maybe she should be spitting bullets at Claire—after all, she had planned on telling Harry tonight.

Right! How could she be angry with Claire? There was absolutely no guarantee she would've found the strength to be straight with Harry. Or that she wouldn't have been just as easily diverted as she had been before. At least Harry now knew. Well, he didn't believe the truth, but he was about to see it.

She flexed her fingers and was more than a little surprised when her index finger pressed the send button without the slightest tremor.

"So, Harry," she murmured aloud, "chew on reality for a while."

"Son of a bitch," Harry groused, seeing the source of his new e-mail. He'd been putting off getting in touch with her, and now she'd taken the initiative. "Damn."

He took a double swallow of whiskey and pressed the enter button with an unsteady finger. The words were a blur as he rapidly scanned them scrolling down the page.

"Shit! Oh shit!" What had he done! She'd been telling him the truth—at least at the end. She wasn't Phoebe's daughter. She was her niece.

He pushed his chair back and studied the pictures closely.

There was a striking resemblance across Melissa, her mother and her aunt. He struggled to breathe. Phoebe had looked so proud at her niece's college graduation. He recalled Melissa saying her parents had been killed in a car accident sometime during her college years.

He filled his lungs to overflowing when he reconsidered the last picture. He couldn't disagree with Melissa's assessment. Phoebe had him pinned to a chair, facing away from him. His face was contorted with orgasmic passion, and hers displayed unabashed pleasure and triumph. How had that picture fallen into Melissa's hands?

He scrolled back up to the message. He crossed his arms over his chest. Why in hell had Phoebe left her niece pictures of the two of them working on set?

Harry leaned forward and ran his fingers roughly through his hair. None of that mattered now. He'd blown it real bad. Had he actually called her a bitch?

He studied the words carefully and grimaced. She wasn't like her aunt. It didn't look like she was going to cut and run.

They'd have to figure out some way to work together, because he wasn't about to leave the Center either. He knew their days of working on set together were finished, but they'd still have to figure out how to coexist.

It probably wasn't possible to grovel enough to expect more than that.

Chapter Sixteen

Running a brush through her damp, tangled hair, Melissa couldn't recall sleeping so late on a Saturday morning. Images of recent Saturday mornings flitted across her brain. She winced. Those memories weren't really of sleeping in, and she absolutely wasn't in the mood to wonder about Harry.

She'd checked her e-mail as soon as she'd climbed out of bed. So far, no reply. She tugged at a tangle. He might not have even seen her message. Maybe he'd pressed the delete button without reading it. Maybe he'd gone to a bar seeking solace. Maybe he was just now waking up in some other woman's bed.

"Fuck yourself, Harry Gage. You're done fucking me."

She placed the hairbrush aside and reached for the gold chain and pendant with the Zen *yoni* etching. She smiled at her reflection in the vanity mirror as she fastened it around her neck. Rubbing it gingerly between thumb and finger, she experienced a kind of familial warmth she hadn't felt in years. She might never take it off.

Her fingers stilled. Wasn't that what Claire had said about her identical pendant that afternoon in the screening room? Claire seldom went anywhere without her gold pendant, yet she had left it for her on the chair in the tent at the estate.

In hindsight, maybe she should have switched jewelry pieces with Inez. She shook her head. No, what was done was done. There was no use replaying it over and over again. She'd spent half a sleepless night doing that.

Let it go. She'd done what she needed to do. She'd sent the proof of who she was to Harry and had made clear her intentions. She lifted the pendant to her lips. Her aunt's pendant. "My pendant," she whispered, correcting herself. It was time to get on with the rest of her life.

The doorbell sputtered to life. Scowling, Melissa grabbed her white terrycloth robe and padded toward the entryway. Now that he was here, what was she going to say to Harry?

She peered through the peephole. "Oh my," she murmured, freeing the locks and opening the door.

"Good morning," Claire said softly. "I hope I'm not interrupting anything."

Claire whirled into the entryway, dropped a shopping bag, and enfolded Melissa in her arms without uttering another word.

Slightly overwhelmed, Melissa clung to Claire, refusing to give in to a sob. How could she wallow in self-pity knowing there was a world out there that still cared about her? "What are you doing here?"

Claire rubbed her nose through Melissa's still damp hair and inhaled sharply. She leaned back and smiled mischievously. "I love the smell of freshly washed hair."

Melissa parted her lips to speak just as Claire slanted a finger across her open mouth. Wide-eyed, she watched Claire duck her head, then felt Claire's soft lips press against hers. Melissa blinked back tears.

She'd hardly puckered a response before Claire said, "And tasting a woman's lips before she's applied lipstick is also a treat. So," she said, breaking away, "how are you doing?"

"Much better," Melissa replied, finding her voice. She guided Claire into her small living room.

There was a fresh softness about Claire this morning she hadn't witnessed before, but then she'd never seen her boss other than at work. Her short blond hair didn't look nearly as sophisticated or severe. She wore a blousy top with three buttons undone, displaying ample cleavage and her golden pendant. A long calico skirt fell to her ankles. Melissa had never seen her in a skirt or dress that even came below mid-thigh.

This Claire struck Melissa as being more mellow, but no less sexy. Her eyes sparkled and her lips enticed. Her nipples had been mere shadows when she first arrived. By the time she'd pulled out of their embrace at the door, they were taut.

Melissa cleared her throat, trying unsuccessfully to ignore her own pebbling response. "Would you like some coffee?"

Claire shook her head. "I've already had more than my daily allotment. You've done a super job decorating—modern, yet cozy. Are you sure you forgive me for my part in yesterday's little fiasco?"

Little! That was an understatement. But Melissa held up her open palms to forestall Claire's rambling. "It was bound to happen sometime, someway. I told you that on the phone last night." She furrowed her brow. "Why are you here, Claire?"

Appearing a little sheepish, Claire said, "I guess telling you I was in the neighborhood will hardly work, because I haven't been to Brooklyn since I was a little girl. And that was a ways back."

Melissa couldn't suppress a giggle. "So you're one of those Manhattan ethnocentrics."

"Uh-huh."

Melissa clasped her hands at her waist, resolved to wait out the ensuing silence.

"Okay." Claire inhaled and exhaled before continuing. "I want you to sketch me."

"Really? I'm honored." Melissa's pulse quickened. Her fingers ached. It would be good to work again. This might be exactly what she needed.

"You'll do it?"

"Of course. Why wouldn't I?"

"I'm talking about one or your tasteful erotic type drawings. Me in the nude."

"I didn't think you'd want to be sketched wearing a business suit."

"I am fifty-seven."

Melissa scowled. "Do I care? Maybe we can come up with something that will inspire fifty and sixty-year-olds to pose for erotic drawings. Let me change and I'll be right back."

"No," Claire said, grabbing her hand. She hesitated momentarily before adding, "I don't want to wait. Surely, you must sketch or paint from time to time wearing only a robe."

"Of course." Melissa tugged on Claire's hand. "Come on, and I'll show you my studio.

"As you can see, it's not much," she said, leading Claire into her favorite room. "A couch, easy chair, desk which is my workspace and which also substitutes as a prop sometimes. And of course lots of art supplies."

"And beautiful sketches and paintings," Claire intoned, as if they were standing in a church or a museum. "You are extremely talented. We really must set up a show for you through the Center."

"So do you have a particular medium or pose in mind?"

"No, you're the artist. I see you have a music center." She reached into her shopping bag, withdrew a CD, and handed it to Melissa. "Do you mind playing this? It's one of my favorites from the seventies. It will embolden me."

"No problem. Though I would never have guessed you needed anything to strengthen your resolve." Melissa peeked at the label. "Helen Reddy. I like her stuff."

"Thought maybe it'd be too old-fashioned for you. I'm glad you like it. She throbs with heat."

After putting on the CD, Melissa looked around the room considering various props. "I'm thinking maybe a charcoal with you in the easy chair."

"Sounds fine."

"Why don't you get out of that dress, and we'll try several different poses until we find one that fits you best?" Melissa turned away to set up her sketchpad.

By the time she was ready, Claire sat in the easy chair with her legs crossed. A dark kimono was loosely wrapped around her shoulders, hiding nothing from view but serving to provide an excellent, tasteful contrast with her rich ivory skin.

Melissa's breath lodged somewhere in her throat. "You're beautiful, Claire. Stunning."

"You're being kind, but thanks." Claire placed a palm under each of her substantial breasts and lifted them. "They sag more than I'd like."

"Hardly. They may slope a little, and I love how your nipples turn up."

"It must be the artist's eye," Claire chided. "And you're right; my nipples are sure indicators of what's happening inside me. Notice how they've extended since you commented on them."

Melissa blew air through pursed lips. Notice? How could she not notice? Furthermore, she was afraid hers were behaving as if they were in a contest with Claire's. Melissa grabbed a piece of charcoal and began sketching in broad strokes.

"Not this way," Claire hissed. "This is hardly erotic."

Melissa shook her head. It was plenty erotic for her. "Okay. Let's try several poses. Stay as you are, uncross your legs, and part them. Holy . . ." She covered her mouth, then quickly uncovered it.

Claire grinned.

"I've never seen such a . . ."

"Don't call it white, please!" Claire interjected. "It's pale blonde and always has been." She chuckled. "I do like to watch initial reactions to my pussy. It is rather unique, don't you think?"

"Rather," Melissa responded breathlessly. "Is she always so . . . open? She looks like a flower opening to greet the morning sun."

"I like that imagery." Claire held her gaze steadily. "But to answer your question, she's only this open when she's really turned on."

"Oh." Melissa blinked twice. "Maybe we should try another position."

"Okay." Claire gave her a half smile. "You tell me what works for you."

Melissa stepped around the easel and considered Claire and the chair. "Maybe we should try playing with angles. Why don't you sort of slouch down?"

"Like this?"

"No. More on a slant. Pictures are defined by angles and lines." Melissa stepped forward to help arrange Claire the way she wanted her and hesitated. She gazed into Claire's playful eyes. She took in a sharp breath and reached for Claire's elbow.

Why was this getting to her so? She'd worked with many nude models, positioning them one way and then another. Most every model had to be helped. The human language usually proved inadequate for communicating an artist's intent for a pose or a mood. "Lean your right elbow on the right arm of the chair, like this. Bring your hand up and rest your chin on it. That's correct. Now," she stood back, "place your left foot up on the opposite chair arm. Wow," she murmured as Claire's pussy folds separated even more. "Okay, let's bend this right leg at the knee and bring it to the base of the same chair arm. There. Perfect. *That* is seductive. One breast is in plain view and the other partially hidden. Your legs are spread nicely, forming the shape of an *M.*"

"I like this," Claire chirped. "You've convinced me. What

about my other arm? It's just sort of dangling here." Claire winked. "I could easily bring it around the back of my left hip and play with myself like this."

"No," Melissa said quickly, "that won't be necessary. That's too pornographic. We're after art, eroticism."

Claire grinned. "I did bring along my favorite vibrators and dildos in case we needed them. But you're the artist. I'm in your hands."

"Right," Melissa murmured, casting her eyes around the room for something—for anything that might tone down Claire's pose a bit. "Ah."

She reached into a box and pulled out a small pink fluffy feather. "Try this."

Claire reached for the feather. "I didn't know you were into kinky."

"Claire," Melissa gasped. "I'm not, and I am trying to get some work done here."

"You want me to cover up my pussy with a feather?"

"Of course not. You have a beautiful pussy. I'm only trying to provide her a little background to soften the edges of the view. Hold it like this, so the tip of the feather is tilting toward what is apparently your prize possession."

"It is," she said with pride, putting the small feather in place. "This does work. Are we ready to begin?"

Melissa nodded. If anything, the feather intensified the sensuality of the pose. She retreated to the security of her easel. She sighed and began sketching the outline of the pose Claire held perfectly.

As she worked on Claire's breasts, her breathing quickened. Who had started up the furnace? Brooklyn landlords seldom turned furnaces on until it was twenty degrees outside and six inches of snow covered the ground.

She quickly sketched in the feather and Claire's ultimate prize. She shook her head trying to keep her vision clear. She had Claire's face framed, and then she stopped. She frowned at her model. "We should talk about attitude."

Claire frowned. "What?"

"Attitude. Facial expression. What sort of mood do you want to project? Your posture is . . . nonchalant. There is a sense of self-assurance and personal comfort about you."

"Speaking of personal comfort," Claire retorted. "Why don't you take that damn robe off before you melt in front of my eyes? If you drip much more, you're going to ruin my sketch."

Melissa looked up slowly from her work to meet Claire's penetrating eyes. Her heart tripped over itself.

"It's not like I haven't seen all you have to offer plenty of times." Claire scowled. "And you even passed my personal taste test with flying colors, you may recall. Get comfortable, Melissa. Please!"

"Oh, all right." She shrugged out of her robe and welcomed the immediate change in temperature. *Comfortable* might be unachievable under Claire's appreciative gaze, but with any luck she could at least remain cool.

"I had a tight body like yours once."

"I hope I look half as good as you do when I'm your age," Melissa blurted out.

Claire laughed easily. "I'll take that as a compliment. So what about this attitude idea of yours?"

"How about sultry, dreamy?" Melissa offered. "You could have your eyes closed dreaming about a lover. Maybe the young woman my other sketch reminded you of."

"The one with the woman fondling herself under her skirt?"

"Yes."

"No."

"No?"

"No, I don't want to close my eyes. I want to watch you

work. I want to watch you turning hotter than hot. By the way, I love how your nipples gradually swell as you turn on. How about this look?"

"Goodness, that's perfect," Melissa whispered, more than a little awed by the change in mood. Claire stared steadily at her with open eyes and slightly arched eyebrows. Her lips pouted ever so little. She conveyed an impression of experience blended with confidence, two attributes Melissa suddenly longed for. "How would you describe that look?" she asked, sketching furiously, trying to capture Claire's expression before she lost its essence.

Claire didn't miss a beat. "Frankly hungry."

"Oh."

"I'm glad you're wearing Phoebe's pendant."

Melissa peeked at Claire. "Me, too. I may never take it off."

"She gave up wearing it at some point after she left the Center. She didn't have it on the last time I was with her."

"Maybe she'd already put it away for me?" She added more soft touches to the drawing.

"She did love you, Missy."

Melissa's chin shot up. "She was the only person who called me Missy."

"I wondered about that," Claire said softly, "once I figured out who you were. But you're wrong. Missy was the only name I knew you by before we met."

"Really? Well of course, that makes sense."

"Is it okay if I call you Missy?"

Melissa shrugged her shoulders. "Why not? Though I'd prefer you call me Melissa when others are around. That's my professional name."

Nodding, she watched Claire replicate her *frankly hungry* look. "Now, don't say anything to distract me. I'm going to fill in some areas here that should be enough for me to get back to later for a more detailed sketch."

Melissa chewed on her lower lip and slowed her hand to shade in Claire's hairline. She inhaled through her nose before outlining the patch of pale blonde hair sitting atop Claire's mound. She wouldn't tell Claire, but she'd decided to make a pastel of her rather than a charcoal. This would do as a sufficient working sketch, but Claire's elegant pussy deserved highlights in pastel. Charcoal would simply not do. Wouldn't Claire be surprised?

She set her charcoal down on the easel and glanced over the top of her sketchpad toward Claire. "Oh my God," she moaned, biting her tongue. Claire had changed positions. She now sat slouched in the chair squarely facing the sketchpad with her thighs parted wide. The black kimono provided an erotic frame for her body. Claire's pussy looked like a white flower with a pink interior, and her very full clitoris reigned proudly over its domain.

"I'm glad I distract you, Missy." Claire sent her a conspiratorial grin. "I thought you might need a distraction this morning." She dipped her fingers to play idly with her pale blonde curls.

Locked in place, Melissa absently wiped her mouth with the back of her hand.

"I need your tongue, Missy. Only this once," Claire cautioned. "I don't think I have to tell you where I need it."

Melissa shook her head slowly from side to side.

"Listen to the music, Missy. Let it fill you. Come and fill me with your tongue."

Melissa cocked her ear to the side. She listened. She smiled softly. The words of "I Am Woman" reverberated within her.

Melissa rounded the easel and sank to her knees before the most splendid pussy she'd ever seen. Claire grinned broadly and placed her hands on either side of Melissa's head, coaxing her. Her tongue slithered easily between the open pussy folds. She arched away slightly to look at Claire. "It's like sticking my tongue into a silver chalice of warm honey. Thank you."

"Be my guest. Imbibe to your heart's content, girl," Claire purred. "I haven't been this ready for a woman or a man in a very long time."

Melissa pouted. "I thought you were the wanton woman of the Center."

Claire laughed and briefly closed her eyes. "Don't believe everything you hear about me. My Center persona serves my purposes. As you once implied on tape, a woman's best friend can be her vibrator." Claire smiled wanly. "Sometimes that's simply not enough."

"I feel lucky."

"You got that wrong. I'm the lucky one. But a little more tongue would be nice."

Melissa nodded and snaked her tongue deep into Claire's heat. She probed this way and that, spurred by Claire's responses—her moans, her pelvis rising and falling and her thighs opening and closing. Melissa couldn't explain her sudden surge of invincibility—maybe later—but this was the beginning of the rest of her life.

She poured every positive emotion she could muster into Claire. She sipped on her engorged clit. She raised the woman's quaking buttocks and drank greedily from her flow.

Trembling, Claire sighed and gulped deep breaths.

Melissa sat back on her haunches and smiled at her. Only then did she realize she'd made no attempt to bring herself off, nor had Claire.

Claire nodded slightly, as if reading her mind.

This wasn't about sex. It was about something much bigger, much deeper. Hopefully, someday she'd have a name to give it.

Much later, Melissa and Claire stood at the door

exchanging their goodbyes. They'd talked about so much, but never about Harry. Melissa appreciated that a lot. She hoped she'd convinced Claire to come back on the set to work in front of the cameras again. The Center needed more focus on sexual needs of men and women over fifty. Who among them could do that work better than Claire?

"Thanks," Claire said rather shyly, "for everything."

"Me? Thank you."

"You are a special young woman, Missy." Claire grinned. "I think I may come out of retirement to work in front of the cameras just so you and I can be together again."

"I'd like that. A lot," Melissa murmured, hoping she wasn't blushing too much.

"And I might follow up with Inez." Claire winked. "And I must admit that Max fellow is a mystery to me—I've never worked with him directly."

"Great! You'll love him, and Inez won't turn her back on you, either."

"One more thing." Claire paused and ran the tip of her tongue across her upper lip. "The picture you did of the young woman caressing herself under a wraparound skirt doesn't remind me of your aunt, but of someone I knew before her."

"Oh."

"Uh-huh. I believe she was my *true love,* but we never found out because I never told her I needed her, nor did she tell me. That is one of the few regrets in my life—that I didn't tell her I needed to love her."

Claire pressed her lips against Melissa's open mouth and tapped her tongue. She stood back, and a puzzling glint came to her eyes. "I'm glad I had the courage to come here this morning and tell you I needed your tongue."

Silently, Claire let herself out and shut the door softly behind her. Melissa leaned back against it and crumpled to the floor. She tugged her robe around her. She sobbed and she laughed.

She'd never loved anyone in the moment more than she had when she was tonguing Claire. And what had brought that about? The seductive banter and the provocative poses? Or the simple straightforward request—*I need your tongue?*

Claire could've shown up at her door and tried to lecture her about human relationships. Melissa groaned. She probably would've listened like a rock, and Claire probably knew that from Phoebe's stories of her rather headstrong niece. No, Claire had taken a very different tack. She'd chosen to teach her with her body and with her music—visually and by ear.

Melissa blinked her eyes open. The CD was still playing in her studio—she must have set it on *repeat.* Never mind, she'd return it to Claire on Monday.

Now she had to get dressed. It was time to drag Harry out of his cave. She finally understood what she had to tell him.

Her back jerked away from the door as its buzzer began its weak wobbly refrain. "I'll get your CD, Claire," she said, flinging the door wide.

"Sorry to disappoint you," Harry said, running his fingers through his unkempt hair.

Her shoulders slumped. "You! Come on in. I've seen winos looking better than you. Want some coffee?"

"Thanks."

She didn't know if the thanks was for the apt description or for the offer of coffee.

He followed her into the kitchen. "That is," he added, "if you promise not to pour scalding coffee over me."

"I'm not into promises."

Blood drained from his face.

"Not yet, anyway." She kept her hands busy preparing the coffee. "The more I think about it, pouring hot coffee over you might not be such a bad idea." She eyed him slumped at the corner of the kitchen counter. "You deserve it, you know."

He nodded. "I do know."

She wondered how long he could hold that pained look. It would make for a fascinating sketch she might be able to use later—if there was a later. At least he was here. So now what? Did she expect him to grovel? To make desperate love? To declare undying love? She hadn't gotten this far in her own mind. *Damn Harry.* She hated it when he was one step ahead of her.

"I didn't mean to hurt you," Harry stammered, looking more ill at ease than she'd ever thought he could.

"Meaning and doing are two different things," she said. At least a little groveling would be okay.

"I went berserk."

"I noticed."

His expression was one of self-flagellation. He was squirming on a sword, and she'd hardly said a word. Maybe she *could* get into S&M. She shook her head. No, not for her. "Here," she said, handing Harry a full mug. "I've decided not to boil you in hot coffee."

"That's something."

"Be thankful."

"I am. Now what?"

"I'm not certain. Let's go to my studio. That's where I think clearest." She frowned at him. "I think I need to be thinking very clearly at the moment."

The soft music of Helen Reddy greeted them as they entered the studio. She went to the window and opened the curtains wide to let in more light.

She turned to watch Harry studying her sketch of Claire. His expression gave away nothing.

"Provocative," he said at last. "I'm sure it will be another of your fine pieces of work."

"Too early to tell, but she can be quite seductive."

Harry didn't wince but did make a show of sniffing the air. "Her scent is still quite evident."

"Claire hardly wears perfume."

"I wasn't talking about perfume."

Melissa stood in front of the easy chair where she'd so recently knelt. She gave him a half smile. "I knew you weren't. So does that bother you?"

"No. Why should it?"

"Surprise you?"

"Not really. Claire stayed here a long time. I figured something was going down."

"That was me going down. Claire provided a welcome balm." Melissa tightened the sash of her robe and tried her best to read Harry, but he was being quite hidden. "So you saw her enter the building and waited?"

He nodded, holding his gaze steady.

"You can be a very patient man at times."

"Isn't she a little old for you?"

"We're not an item, if that's what you're assuming." She brightened. "But I may have talked her out of retirement. She's a much softer woman than most of us assume. She wants to devote time and energy to more tapes for men and women over fifty."

"You're one of few people I know who has seen through her façade." Harry whistled softly. "She hasn't done any on-camera work since Phoebe left."

"You mean my aunt?"

Harry's cheek twitched. "Yeah, your aunt."

"Not my mother."

"No. Not your mother."

Melissa thinned her lips. "So does it bother you, that you've been fucking your former lover's niece?"

His head jerked to the side as if she'd slapped him. "You really want to get right to it, don't you?"

"Do you have a better time in mind?"

He shook his head and shrugged his shoulders. "It bothers me that you didn't tell me."

"I tried."

"I know you did."

"I should've tried harder."

"Yeah, that too. But you didn't. I wasn't blind; I was struck by the resemblance at first, but then I forgot. I guess I wrote it off as coincidence."

"You didn't confuse me with my aunt?" Melissa held her breath. "Not even in the dark of the screening room?"

"No. With Phoebe on the screen, it was hard to totally forget her. But I never confused the two of you. You may look somewhat like your aunt, but you're quite different from her. Though sometimes I'm pretty dense."

"You won't hear any argument about that from me."

"So will you work with Claire if she does decide to go before the camera again?"

Melissa clasped her hands at her waist and lifted her chin. "Of course, I will. I'm part of the Center staff. That's part of my work."

He tilted his head to the side and smiled grimly. "I'm part of that staff, too. So are you and I going to work together in front of the camera?"

Melissa held herself rigid. Air escaped through her pursed lips. "Probably. If you promise not to use me as your personal battering ram again."

"God damn." He groaned and took a step toward her. She backed up until her legs hit the chair. Harry stopped. "I am so sorry about that. I've never treated a woman like that. I don't know what got into me." He shook his head. "But that's a promise I'm willing to make."

"And what if you break it?" Melissa felt her innards quaking.

Why did she have to ask that question?

"Then I'll leave the Center and you'll never see me again."

"You'd leave the Center—your life's work?"

"If I break that promise. But"—he held up a palm—"I'm not about to break it. Ever."

She nodded, searching her soul, reading her body. The lyrics of "I Am Woman" filled her mind and Claire's scent filled her nostrils. She took a deep breath and squared her shoulders. "I need you to love me, Harry. Right now. Right here."

His eyes widened. She was afraid he might faint or bolt. Then he nodded. "And I need to love you."

Relief swept through her as she opened her robe and let it drop to the floor. Harry's fingers flew over buttons and zippers, but he couldn't get out of his clothes fast enough for either of them. Finally, he stood before her with his engorged penis weaving about, speaking clearly of his need. Her loins ached for fulfillment.

Harry reached for her with trembling hands. He smiled, and his eyes misted. "Sounds like Claire must've given you the *say what you need* lecture, too. She stopped by early this morning and read me the riot act before I had a chance to disappear."

Melissa stood on her tiptoes and traced his lips with her tongue. "Fortunately for me, Claire didn't give me a lecture; she gave me a demonstration."

She ducked under Harry's arms, stretched out on the couch, and held her hands out to him. "Why don't we do it this way, with you on top? The last guy who tried this position with me never did finish the job."

"You look incredibly sexy lying there wearing only your aunt's pendant. I don't think Phoebe treasured anything more than that."

"It is precious." She blinked. "I'm glad you find it sexy on me. Guess you can see it without turning into an ape-man."

"You trust me?" he asked, kneeling between her legs.

"Enough for this," she said, leaning forward to guide him to her entrance.

She smiled wanly as he slid slowly into her. She wrapped her legs around him and squirmed beneath him. She grabbed his cheeks, pulled his mouth down to hers, and drove her tongue into his mouth. He didn't move.

She lay back and frowned at his intense stare. "Do you need an instruction book?"

"You're okay with this?"

His boyish incredulity stirred her. "If I wasn't, you sure wouldn't be where you are. I need you to love me."

"We're going to work things out?"

"Only if you fill me to the brim this time." She gave him a crooked smile and pinched his jaw. "Jesus H. Christ, Harry, I don't have a crystal ball. I'm trying here—real hard—okay?"

She wiped the back of her hand across her perspiring forehead. "It may take months before I'm ready to slide much further down that slippery slope we've talked about. That escapade at the estate made it clear I'm still trying to figure out who you are and who I am. You're welcome to come along for the ride, and I'll let you know when we get to the next stop. I need you to love me now, Harry. I thought you needed me to love you now. Now is all I can guarantee."

She dug her fingernails into his back. "If that's not good enough, then you can pull out, but if you do, you'll never get back in my pussy off or on the job. So what will it be?"

She gasped when he pulled out until his cock rested at the doorway to her pussy, then smiled broadly and pushed excruciatingly slowly back in. "That's good enough for me," he grunted. "That's probably more than I deserve."

"Probably," she said, beginning to tap his butt rhythmically with her heels. "Now, like I said, I need you to fill me to the brim."

He nodded. "I'll try. I'll do my best."

"That's all I'm asking," she managed to say as he increased their tempo.

She pulled his head close so his mouth covered hers again. Her tongue and her hips matched his cock stroke for stroke until he began jerking above her. Once she felt him spasm deep inside her, she let go of the orgasm she'd been nurturing. "Yes," she cried softly, "fill me."

He remained above her, resting his weight on his hands, looking somewhat remorseful. "I'm sorry. I may need you to love me more. It may take a very long time to fill you."

She grinned and nodded her agreement. "You may be right. I may need you to love me for a long time, a very, very long time. Do you think you'll be up for that?"

Harry didn't say a word until after he'd turned them so she sat astride him. He squirmed beneath her, and his cock grew harder with each wiggle. He thrust his hips up once and she gasped. He settled and took a deep breath. "Try me," he challenged.

She sat back and tugged at her nipples. His eyes rounded. "Enjoying the show?" she asked, dropping one hand to her clit. His cock expanded inside her. "You're right. He is up. So soon," she teased. "Does he have more for me already?"

"Guess you'll have to find out for yourself."

"I believe I will," she said, rising up the length of his shaft, then freefalling until her butt bounced off him, propelling her upward again.

"What a beautiful sight," he mumbled.

"Are you going to help?" she asked without pausing. "I'm nearly there."

"Only if you need me."

"Cripes," she wailed, darting her eyes at him. "I need you to love me."

"Good," he replied, raising his hips to meet her thrust for

thrust. "I needed to hear that again. And I do need to love you."

Melissa flailed her hands high above her, arched her neck, and howled. She smiled when she heard Harry calling out to her and to the gods. He did have more for her. She was soaring at such a high altitude she ran out of air. She collapsed to Harry's chest. His strong arms steadied and cradled her until she could breathe on her own.

Through a cloudy haze she murmured, "Do you think you'll ever get me filled?"

"I sure hope not," he said, loudly enough to penetrate her grogginess.

"Me, too." She smiled and let herself drift off, confident he'd be there when she awoke.

About the Author

Adriana Kraft is the pen name for a married pair of retired professors writing erotic romance together. We like to think we've broken the mold for staid, fusty academics, and we hope lots of former profs are enjoying life as much as we are.

Having lived in many states across the Midwest, we now make our home in southern Arizona, where we enjoy hiking, golf, and travel, especially to the many Arizona Native American historical sites.

Together we have published more than fifty romance novels and novellas to outstanding reviews. We love hearing from readers at adrianakraft99@yahoo.com, and here is our website:

When It's Time to Heat Things Up https://adrianakraft.com

Find us at:

Blog https://www.adrianakraft.com/blog

Twitter https://twitter.com/AdrianaKraft

Facebook https://www.facebook.com/adriana.kraft.5

Facebook Fan Page
https://www.facebook.com/AdrianaKraftAuthor

Instagram https://www.instagram.com/kraftadriana/

BookBub https://www.bookbub.com/authors/adriana-kraft

Extasy Books Page https://www.extasybooks.com/adriana-kraft

www.ingramcontent.com/pod-product-compliance
Lightning Source LLC
LaVergne TN
LVHW050621100826
845148LV00011B/1676